SOUTHPORT

SOUTHPORT

EDWARD NORVELL

RTP

RESEARCH TRIANGLE PUBLISHING, INC.

Published by
Research Triangle Publishing, Inc.
PO Box 1130
Fuquay-Varina, NC 27526

ISBN 1-884570-68-2

Cover Design by Kathy Holbrook

Library of Congress Catalog Card Number: 97-65322

Printed in the United States of America
10 9 8 7 6 5 4 3 2

This book is printed on acid-free paper.

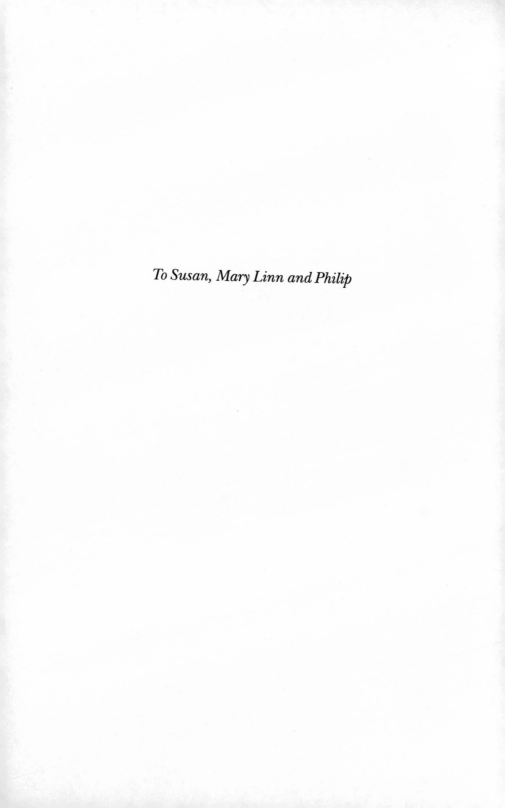

To Susan, Mary Linn and Philip

ONE

THE RUSTED BLACK PICKUP TRUCK stopped in front of Bloom's Grocery Store on the waterfront in Southport. Jumping out onto the oyster-shell pavement I took a deep breath of the salt air and thought, I am finally free. I didn't know then that running away was the easy part.

The old man who had picked me up in front of Daddy's farm in Duplin County waved good-bye and drove off. I had nothing but the clothes I wore, the things I carried in Uncle Warren's duffel bag, and three hundred dollars—all of my savings and what little Mama could give me.

It was the first Saturday in June, 1975. Staring up at the pale blue sky, I could feel the sun's warmth and the fresh ocean air on my face. Seagulls hovered over the docks at the marina. Excitement rushed through me as I looked past the waterfront to the mouth of the Cape Fear River. The river ran between Bald Head Island, with its cover of dark green trees, and Oak Island, with its black-, white-, and gray-banded lighthouse. Though it wasn't that far away in miles, Southport was a different world from Duplin County, where I grew up.

I knew I'd love it there, even on that first day. I had followed my heart and it had proven me right. My daddy always told me, don't let your heart rule your head. He was wrong. I knew deep inside that my home was near the ocean, even though I'd only seen it a few times before. It was an instinctive feeling, like a deep, ancient memory that haunted me until I finally followed it.

Turning around, I looked at the two-story, white frame building facing the waterfront. Over the door was a long, metal sign announcing Bloom's Grocery Store. It was flanked by two round Pepsi-Cola emblems. There were two big, plate-glass windows on either side of the double screen-door, and a one-story front porch. A Help Wanted sign hung in one of the windows so I walked in.

"I'm looking for work," I said to the man behind the front counter.

"Can you push a broom?" he asked. It was Mr. Bloom, a gruff old man with bushy gray eyebrows and mustache, wearing a dirty white apron over his clothes.

"Yes, sir," I replied.

"Then you're hired."

When I told Mr. Bloom I had no place to stay, he offered me a room over the store. The room was used for storage, but had a small bed in it and a bathroom down the hall.

I WORKED AT BLOOM'S for three weeks, spending my free time on the docks at the marina. I was dying to work on a boat and ride the swells and waves to the place where you can't see land anymore—where all you can see is water and sky. I had never seen that before. One Friday afternoon Bill Jackson, a charter boat captain, walked into Bloom's store and started a conversation with me.

"How would you like to go deep-sea fishing, young man?" Captain Jackson asked me in the back of the store where Mr. Bloom couldn't hear.

"I'd love to."

"Have you ever been deep-sea fishing?"

"No, but I can learn."

"You're new around here, aren't you? What's your name?"

"Todd Field, sir. I moved to Southport from Duplin County three weeks ago."

"What brought you here?"

"I wanted to live on the coast. After my high school graduation, I hitched a ride on a farmer's truck and ended up here."

"So, you're from tobacco country. Do you like Southport?"

"Yes, sir. Back home everything's flat. Too much of the same. On the coast, there are no two days alike. I like that."

"You'd like being on the ocean then. I could use a strong boy like you on my boat. Why don't you see how you like it?" he said, looking me over.

I was six feet tall, weighed 165 pounds, and was in good shape, if I must say so myself.

Mr. Bloom walked up to us with a frown on his face. "Trying to steal my boy, Jackson?"

"Just talking. First time I met Todd. Haven't seen him here before today."

"He's a farm boy—strong, hardworking. Most farm boys are good workers—they don't know any better," Bloom said, laughing. "Not like those who work the sea," he said, glaring at Captain Jackson. "Ain't that right, Todd?"

I continued to sweep the linoleum floor in the aisle between the grocery shelves. I didn't answer him.

"My offer stands," Captain Jackson said to me with a wink. "You need to get salt air in your lungs—it's better for you than this musty old place." He looked around, wiping dust off a shelf.

"Keep your hands off the merchandise and stay away from my employees. You've already stolen some of my best boys. For the life of me I don't understand what's so damn thrilling about getting up at five o'clock in the morning to take a bunch of drunks out to get seasick in the Gulf Stream."

"You're jealous, Bloom. Just because you get seasick on a boat doesn't mean everybody does. If your boy works for me, he'll have plenty of time to work for you, too."

"Yeah, I've heard that before."

Captain Jackson left the grocery store. I watched him cross the street, which gleamed white with the sun, and head to the marina. The water sparkled in the creek beyond.

AFTER WORK I WALKED to the marina where Captain Jackson kept his boat, the *Martha Jane*.

"Captain Jackson, I'd like to take you up on your offer."

"I thought you would. A big, strong boy like you won't be satisfied working in a grocery store for long. Not when you can go to sea." He was rigging lines, preparing for a charter fishing trip the next morning.

"I'm going out tomorrow morning. You think you can take it? My best boy left me last week," he said, still working with the lines. "I can't afford to have someone work for me who gets sick. If you can't take it, that'll be the last trip out with Captain Jackson, you understand?"

"Yes sir. I'll be here tomorrow morning. What time?"

"Five A.M."

"Yes, sir." A little early, I thought, but I would have gotten up at three if I thought it would get me out on a boat.

"Help me with these lines," the captain said, handing me some wire, hooks, deep runners, spoons, and a pair of needle-nose pliers.

He showed me how to attach the shiny, silver lures called spoons, to swivels and rigs. We would use them to catch Spanish and king mackerel, which were running that time of year. Then we strung mullet to the deep runners, which looked like colorful plastic streamers, and put the rigs in an ice chest. Captain Jackson prepared some trolling lures shaped like little fish for some of the more exotic fish, like tuna, wahoo, and dolphin.

I must have looked odd when he mentioned dolphin, because he quickly explained that the dolphin we'd be catching were really a type of fish, not the porpoise. He said the restaurants even called the fish "mahi-mahi" to prevent their customers from thinking they were eating Flipper. I just smiled.

We worked late cleaning up the boat after we finished with the lines. I also washed out the large, plastic coolers that would hold the fish we caught.

"Where are you staying?" Captain Jackson asked.

"Over Bloom's store. He's letting me stay there while I work for him."

"You think he'll let you stay there after you go out with me?"

"I hadn't thought about that," I said.

"If you do good tomorrow you can work for me full-time, and I'll find you a place to live. If it doesn't work out, you can go back to Bloom's. Does that sound fair?"

"Sounds fair to me," I said.

I COULDN'T SLEEP THAT NIGHT because I was so excited. I dreamed about going deep-sea fishing, then taking long sea voyages on a big, white boat. I didn't have an alarm clock, but I was up at 4:30 and on the dock by 5:00 the next morning.

The sun hadn't risen as Captain Jackson and I made last-minute preparations. I picked up several bags of ice for the coolers from the marina ice machine and loaded one with two cases of Budweiser and a couple six-packs of Pepsi and Sprite, for Captain Jackson's customers.

Four men, appearing to be in their forties or fifties, drove up at 5:30 in a silver Buick Electra 225. One of them did the introductions—Mr. Deal, Mr. Murphy, Mr. Overcash, and Mr. Sides. The sun began to lighten the sky, and the sounds of the crickets and cicadas were slowly replaced with the sounds of egrets, pelicans, and seagulls.

Our customers looked sleepy. Captain Jackson told me they were on a business trip from Cannon Mills, near Charlotte. They were very quiet at first. Everyone but Mr. Overcash stretched out in the cabin—two in the V-berth and one on the sofa—for the long ride out to the Gulf Stream.

I untied the boat and made sure everything was in order with the lines and fishing rods before I joined Captain Jackson on the bridge. The boat was a forty-two-foot, fiberglass Chris-Craft, outfitted with the finest equipment— Loran, radar, a depth finder, ship-to-shore radio, and compass. It was white, shiny, and clean. Captain Jackson was very proud of his boat and kept it in excellent shape. He named it the *Martha Jane* after his wife.

Captain Jackson showed me the channel of the Cape Fear River, told me which channel markers meant keep left and which ones meant keep right, and pointed out the markers at the mouth of the river warning of sandbars and shoals. He explained how the channel changes and that you can't always trust the markers, especially after a storm. He pointed out Bald Head Island to the left, and Oak Island and Fort Caswell to the right, as we left the river and headed out to the open sea. I was so fascinated by it all that I forgot to even think about getting seasick.

The sea was not rough—a good day for a first time out. Captain Jackson taught me how to steer the boat by the compass, keeping it to certain coordinates.

"Todd, you take the wheel while I check below," Captain Jackson said after we cleared the channel and were out in the open sea.

"Are you sure?" I asked, hesitating.

"Sure, it's easy. Just do like I said. Keep her steady, head into the waves at a forty-five degree angle, and you'll be fine."

I was lucky that the sea was as calm as it was that day. I got off course a little when a series of waves pushed the boat to one side, and I wasn't confident enough to turn into them or master them.

"You're off course." Captain Jackson said, climbing up the ladder to the bridge.

"I can't keep the boat from being pushed by those waves."

"Here, let me have it," Captain Jackson said, expertly turning the boat into the waves, riding them, and putting the boat back on the correct compass reading.

"See how I did that?"

"Yes, sir."

"You try it," he said handing the wheel back to me.

I tried and was soon able to master the waves.

Captain Jackson smiled. "You'll do great, kid. I know talent when I see it. You sure there isn't a sea captain back somewhere in your family?"

"My mom was from Beaufort, and her dad had a boat."

"I knew you had salt in your blood. No more tobacco farms for you, young man," he said, smiling. There was a sparkle in his eye.

I began to feel a little sick as the sea got rougher, but I soon forgot it as we approached the Gulf Stream, fifty miles out, and Captain Jackson and I prepared the lines for the customers.

I piloted the boat as Captain Jackson put out four lines—two on the outriggers and two on fishing rods placed in chrome cylinders on the gunwale in back. I had never seen anything like the Gulf Stream. It was like a clear blue river within the ocean—you could actually see the line where it met the rest of the ocean. The ocean was deep blue with a greenish cast to it, but the water of the Gulf Stream was a much deeper blue and much clearer. When we crossed into the wide band of crystal-clear water, the air got warmer and more humid. You could almost feel the fish and sea life teeming in the water below us. As soon as we were in the Gulf Stream, we started getting strikes on the lines.

"Here, someone take this line!" Captain Jackson yelled, as the reel spun on one of the rods in back. His customers, two of whom had just gotten up from the V-berth, stood back, watching. They were exchanging glances as if they couldn't decide who was going to take which line first.

"Somebody take it, by God, or the fish will get away," the captain said, staring at the men.

"You take it, Henry," Mr. Deal, a balding man wearing a Redskins ball cap, said to Mr. Overcash.

"You're all my customers . . . you take it. I don't want to be the first to catch a fish," Mr. Overcash, the organizer of the trip, said.

"I'll take it," Mr. Murphy said. He was younger than the others.

Then the other reel in back began to spin, and first one, then the other outrigger popped out. Soon each man was seated and holding a rod, reeling in as fast as he could. Captain Jackson went from seat to seat, making sure the men were holding the rods correctly in the holders, and helping where he could.

Mr. Overcash reeled in the first fish, a big yellowfin tuna. Captain Jackson raised the gaff at the end of a long pole and hooked the fish as it came alongside the boat. In one motion, he lifted it from the water and set it into an open ice chest. He then closed the lid and removed the hook from the forty-pound fish. The tuna thrashed around violently in the ice chest as Captain Jackson turned his attention to the next fish, a twenty-five-pound wahoo that was on Frank Deal's line. Mr. Deal was covered in sweat as he struggled to get his fish closer to the boat. Captain Jackson yanked the line up with both gloved hands, landing the fish flopping on the deck. He put his foot on the fish's head and pulled out the hook, then lifted it and threw it into the ice chest on top of the now subdued tuna.

Mr. Murphy's fish got away. It was a dolphin—a beautiful, rainbow-colored fish, about thirty inches long, that turned a dull gray when it left the water. We could see it jumping as it swam away. Mr. Sides caught a thirty-pound king mackerel.

As soon as the hooks were rebaited and thrown into the water, the fish struck. Again and again the men pulled in mackerel, tuna, wahoo, and dolphin. The men were exhausted and began to drink beer in the cabin, leaving only Captain Jackson and Mr. Overcash in the back, fishing.

Captain Jackson climbed the ladder to the bridge.

"You done good, Todd," Captain Jackson said to me, putting his arm around my shoulder. I pulled away, instinctively, and immediately asked him about the instruments on the control panel in front of me.

Captain Jackson explained the compass and the tachometer, and taught me how to use the radio and Loran unit, which showed us where we were located, by compass coordinates. He also explained the ship's depth finder, how it showed the contours of the ocean floor, and where fishing holes, artificial reefs, and wrecks that attracted fish, were located. He told me that if I learned to read it carefully it could even show schools of fish.

"Go below and fix yourself a sandwich. I'll take over up here. While you're down there, clean up a little, too."

"Yes, sir," I said and climbed down to the deck below. I mopped the deck with sea water, washing off the fish blood, and cleaned the coolers. I also gathered beer cans in a bag and cleaned up the cabin, then fixed a ham sandwich and drank a Pepsi. After I finished eating, I walked out to the deck.

"Hell of a guy you work for," Mr. Overcash said, putting his arm around my shoulder. I pulled away from him and picked up a beer can. I didn't like it when older men touched me.

"He sure is. Is this your first time out with Captain Jackson, sir?" I asked.

"No, I've been out with him many times. One thing you can be sure of. He doesn't go in until he has a good haul of fish."

"This is my first time out with the captain. I hope you gentlemen are enjoying yourselves."

"We sure are. One of my best trips yet," Mr. Overcash said.

Captain Jackson watched me from the bridge, smiling. He looked very pleased.

When I finished cleaning up, I climbed to the bridge.

"Have a seat, Todd," Captain Jackson said. "You're a good mate. I want you to work for me."

"I'd like that," I said, trying to hide my excitement.

"You have a lot to learn, but I think you'll do well."

"Thank you, sir. I hope I won't let you down."

Captain Jackson skillfully piloted the boat through the mouth of the Cape Fear River into the wide creek that led to the marina at Southport. It had been a beautiful day, the sea was calm, and we caught lots of fish. Captain Jackson seemed glad that my first day was a good one. I felt very much at home on the boat and loved deep-sea fishing.

He pulled up to the dock and gave the fish to two men, who gutted and filleted them in big, galvanized sinks that had spigots draining directly into the creek.

"Great trip, Captain," Mr. Overcash said, tipping Captain Jackson one hundred dollars, on top of the regular charter fee. "Give some to your boy. He did a great job. I understand this was his first trip out?"

"Yeah. I think he'll work out fine."

The men drank beer the entire way in from the Gulf Stream, so they were a little drunk and sleepy. They thanked Captain Jackson and me for a fishing trip they would all remember. Captain Jackson told me he wished they all went as well as this one.

I cleaned up the boat, Captain Jackson locked up, then we gathered our gear and walked across the street to

Bloom's store. It was six o'clock, and the store was closed. I saw my duffel bag, filled with my clothes, sitting outside. The note pinned to it read: Todd, here are your things. If you want to work for Captain Jackson, he can find you a place to live. You're fired.

Captain Jackson read the note out loud.

"Now I don't have a place to stay," I said looking over at Captain Jackson. I felt lost. "I didn't think Mr. Bloom would fire me." I looked down at the oyster-shell pavement.

"My wife and I have a room in the back of our house with a separate entrance. If you don't mind biding by Martha's rules and doing some chores around the house, you're welcome to stay with us. Besides, you're working for me now, anyway."

"But what if you fire me?"

"Then I guess you'll have to find another place to live. Right now, you don't have much choice, do you?"

"No, sir."

We walked down a street lined with live oak trees that were draped with Spanish moss. The pavement wound around several big old trees that were apparently older than the street. Captain Jackson told me most of the one- and two-story frame houses along the street were built over a hundred years ago, by sea captains and channel pilots. Some were newer, and some dated from before the Civil War. The town was beautiful, a little run-down in places, but very proud. It was a tolerant place, and no one was in much of a hurry. There was always time for a good tale, a drink, and a game of cards on the docks. Captain Jackson's house was on Brunswick Street overlooking the water. It was a white frame house with a two-story front porch that

ran the width of the house. He told me it belonged to
Martha's family and was built in the 1870s.

"WHO'S THE YOUNG MAN?" Martha Jackson asked, as she
opened the screen door to let us in. She was a good-looking woman in her mid-thirties, with a ruddy complexion
and short, black hair that was streaked with gray. She had
a beautiful smile that put me at ease right away.

"This is my new mate, Todd Field."

"How do you do?" I asked, nodding my head politely
to Mrs. Jackson.

"You gonna have supper with us, Todd?" Martha asked,
as she would ask anyone visiting this time of day.

"Yes," Captain Jackson said. He put his arm around
his wife's waist and kissed her. "We had a great day today.
Caught over a hundred pounds of mackerel, tuna, dolphin,
and wahoo. Not a wave over five feet tall. Beautiful all
day. Isn't that right, Todd?"

"Yes, sir," I said, taking a chair at the kitchen table.

"Your customers were satisfied, I presume?" she asked,
putting on an apron, facing the stove, and picking up a
pan that sizzled with fried chicken.

"Gave me a hundred dollar tip."

Martha turned around and put her hand out.

"Some of it belongs to Todd," Captain Jackson said.
He then counted out twenty-five dollars, handed it to me,
and gave the rest to his wife. "This is on top of the three
dollars an hour I told you I would pay you, Todd," he said
with a smile.

"Where are you staying, young man?" Martha asked me.

I looked at Captain Jackson.

"He's staying with us."

"Oh, really. Well, I'm glad you told me."

"I was going to tell you after we ate."

"Sure you were," she said to her husband, smiling. "We have plenty of room in this old house," she said to me. "More room than we can ever use. You're welcome to stay in the back room, as long as you mind your manners and abide by my rules."

"Yes, Ma'am. I don't want a free ride. I plan to work for my keep."

The Jacksons had no children, and the house had ten rooms, filled with antique furniture. The house and furniture belonged to Martha's grandfather, a channel pilot, who left it to her when he died.

"You wash up and get a good night's rest," Captain Jackson told me after we ate. "I'll expect to see you at the dock at 5:30 tomorrow morning."

"Where are you from, Todd?" Martha asked.

"Duplin County."

"Do your parents know where you are?"

"They know I'm in Southport."

"Aren't they worried about you, being all alone in a strange place?"

"I don't think so. My mom didn't want me to leave home, but my daddy told me not to come back." I didn't want to say anymore. This was my new home. I wanted to put the past behind me.

"Oh," Martha said, looking at her husband.

The captain looked at her as if to say she had asked enough questions for now.

After we finished eating, I got up, put my things in my room, and took a hot shower. I fell asleep as soon as I hit the bed, I was so tired.

Two

THE WATER MOVED LIKE LIQUID SILVER glazed by the midday sun, as the skiff meandered through the marsh creek behind Bald Head Island. Birds cried out, and the shimmering grass was alive with the sounds of crickets, cicadas, and insects, singing praise to the day. The only man-made sound was the low hum of the outboard motor mounted in a well in the middle of Mitch's flat-bottomed boat. I could smell the salty air, the smell of gasoline, and the odor of the marsh mud.

It was September and the first time I had been in the marshes of Bald Head Island. Mitch Etheridge was my guide. He was seventeen. I had turned eighteen in August. We had met on the docks at the Southport marina. Mitch's father owned a shrimp boat. Everyone who worked the sea in Southport knew each other. Mitch and I struck up a friendship right away. Mitch knew every inch of the marshes. He had been coming to Bald Head for as long as he could remember.

"Is fishing good in the marshes?" I asked, as we made our way up the creek.

"Yeah. The trick is to fish when the tide is coming in. The marsh is where the fish spawn. All kinds of fish come back here, and the shrimping's great, too. We gig for flounder at night, and fish for channel bass, stripped bass, speckled trout, and flounder, during the day." Mitch paused. "The beach is up ahead," he said, pointing to a sandy bank a few hundred yards away.

Birds flew into the air as we passed—snowy egrets, pelicans, ibis, and blue herons. I felt the heat from the sun penetrate my back, soothing my body like a hot bath. But the breeze coming from the ocean was cool and refreshing. I was completely relaxed. We wound our way through the creek until we grounded the boat on a sandy bank on Bald Head.

"From here we walk."

With the motor silent, I could hear the sound of the marsh birds and the distant pounding of the surf. I couldn't wait to see the beach. Mitch put out the anchor, tied the boat to a large piece of driftwood and followed me. We took off toward the beach.

Sea oats and low growth covered the dunes that spread out before us. Between the marsh and the beach lay a flat, sandy area covered with nests of terns. As we crossed the nesting area, the birds flew into the air, squawking and diving at us, trying to protect their nests and keep strangers out. We didn't disturb their nests; all we wanted was to get to the beach as fast as we could. As soon as we left, the birds calmed down and didn't bother us.

"My dad told me pirates buried gold out here on Bald Head," Mitch said. Mitch had a peculiar accent. He is what's called a "hoigh toider," one who says "hoigh toid" for "high tide," an accent native to the Outer Banks. His mother was from Ocracoke, where they spoke a dialect

close to Old English. His father was from Holden Beach.
Mitch knew lots of stories about the Outer Banks.

"Dad told me about the pirate, Stede Bonnet, who was
a buddy of Blackbeard's and is supposed to have buried
gold out here on Bald Head. No one has ever found it.
Some Spanish coins were found on Oak Island across the
river one time, but not on Bald Head yet. Bonnet hung
around here and went to the Caribbean with Blackbeard
to rob the Spanish. But when he started to rob the local
colonists, they got mad. So Captain Rhett sailed up here
from Charleston, captured Bonnet in the harbor at
Southport, and took him to Charleston, where they hanged
him. They never found his treasure though."

"When was that?"

"Back in the 1700s. Lots of people dig for treasure out
here without any luck. I believe it is here somewhere."

"You said he was a friend of Blackbeard?"

"Yeah, him and Blackbeard used to work the coast here.
It was before there was any law and order in the state. They
say Governor Eden, the governor of North Carolina was
in cahoots with them."

"The governor?" I asked.

"Yeah, Blackbeard paid him to keep his mouth shut."

"Tell me about Blackbeard," I asked.

"Blackbeard was the fiercest of all the pirates. He had
long black hair and a black beard that he stuck lit matches
in to scare people with. He would just as soon kill you as
look at you. He killed all of his wives but one, and shot
one of his best friends in the leg while they were playing
cards, just for fun. He was real mean."

"What happened to him?"

"Like I said, the governor of North Carolina was in
cahoots with Blackbeard and the pirates, so he wouldn't

do anything about them. The people got so disgusted with the pirates rampaging, pillaging, and burning, that they asked the governor of Virginia to bring him to justice. The governor of Virginia sent some men down on a warship and caught Blackbeard off Ocracoke Island, at Teach's hole. I've been fishing there with my grandfather," Mitch said, his eyes sparkling.

"The night before the battle, Blackbeard and his men had a wild drunken orgy on the beach at Ocracoke," he continued. "In the morning the governor's men sneaked up on the pirates and surprised them. There was a fierce battle when the pirates boarded their ships in the channel. The Virginians boarded Blackbeard's boat, and a highland Scotsman cut off his head with a single blow of his long sword. They threw Blackbeard's body into the water and they say it swam around the boat three times before it sank. They carried his head back to Virginia stuck on the bow of the boat, as a trophy. The boys in Ocracoke are always digging for Blackbeard's treasure, but they haven't found it yet. At least, no one has told if they did."

"Do you really think there's pirate treasure buried on Bald Head?"

"That's what my dad says."

We climbed the last dune overlooking the beach and looked at the ocean spread out before us as far as we could see. The beach was undisturbed, looking the same, I imagine, as when the pirates found it 250 years ago. It was beautiful—miles of smooth, white, sandy dunes, peppered with sea oats and junipers; the blue sky; and the silver water. A few fishermen stood in the surf casting their rods, with fish pails sitting a few yards away from them. To the south, a group of men dragged a net through the water.

"What are they doing?" I asked.

"They are seining for bait fish."

We walked to the beach. I took my shoes off and rolled my blue jeans up above my ankles.

"Boy, this feels good," I said, pulling my white T-shirt off and tying it around my head like a bandanna.

"Fall is my favorite time on the beach. Not too many people, not too hot, but the sun is warm, and you can still swim in the ocean," Mitch said, squinting as he looked out at the water.

I loved it, too. I didn't want to go back. I wanted to walk, soak in the sun, and relax. I couldn't get enough of it.

We walked to the group of men seining, to see how they were doing.

"What are you all catching?" Mitch asked.

"Mullet," a man in a navy blue cap said. "They are running good today." The man had the same accent as Mitch. There was a stiff breeze blowing from the northeast.

Mitch and I watched the men pull the net onto the beach. The closer the net came to shore, the faster they pulled, trying to get it in before the fish could escape. Once on shore, the men doubled the net over and pulled it away from the water. Then they opened it and picked through the shimmering fish with their hands, putting them in buckets. Whatever was left—seaweed, driftwood, crabs, shells, and small fish—was thrown back into the water.

We headed toward the point of Cape Fear. At the point, the sand jutted out into the ocean. To the east were the rough seas over Frying Pan Shoals. To the south, seas were calmer and you could see Oak Island and the mouth of the Cape Fear River. We walked out to the very end. The waves came from two directions and slapped each other at the point, sending spray high into the air, even though it wasn't a rough day. The waves whitecapped over Frying Pan Shoals as far as you could see.

Frying Pan Shoals extend for miles into the ocean and are part of the reason the Outer Banks are known as the grave-yard of the Atlantic. Many ships have sunk on those treach-erous shoals. We watched a large freighter with foreign markings steam out of the river into the ocean to the south.

"At night you can see the lights from ships far off, com-ing into the Cape Fear River. There's a lighthouse on a tower, like an oil rig, way out on the shoals, but you can't see it from here. The light used to be on a boat, but it wrecked so many times they built a tower," Mitch said.

To the south, on Oak Island, was another lighthouse, tall and straight, painted with three, wide bands—black on the top, white in the middle, and gray on the bottom.

Mitch took me to a place in the dunes where there were little mounds in the sand and the remains of leath-ery egg shells.

"This is where the sea turtles build their nests in the spring. The turtles lay about 150 eggs, then they leave. In July and August the baby turtles swim out to the ocean, guided by the light of the moon. It is exciting to watch. You missed it this year, but next year we'll come watch," Mitch said, poking at the broken eggs with a piece of driftwood.

We walked west along the south beach, until we saw a group of weathered, wooden buildings in the dunes, which looked abandoned.

"That's the old lifesaving station. I used to come out here and play in those houses when I was a kid."

The story-and-a-half houses with front porches and cedar shingle roofs had weathered to a silver gray. They hadn't been painted in years and were surrounded by dunes and sea oats.

"I've seen artists come out here and draw these build-ings because they're so neat. There used to be a light-house here too, but it's been torn down," said Mitch.

Behind the dunes was a thick forest of palmettos, pines, and oak trees. Far down the beach perched on the dunes were some new cottages.

"What's that?"

"A real-estate developer bought most of the island a few years ago and wants to make it a resort. They built a golf course up in the woods, but the state won't let them build a marina. Not many people have built out here. My dad thinks they'll go broke.

"We better start back, or the tide will leave the boat high and dry. I didn't realize what time it was," Mitch said, looking at his watch. "Low tide is at five o'clock and it's four now. High tide isn't until 11:00 P.M."

As we ran back along the shore we noticed that the beach was practically deserted. We crossed the tern nest-ing area and climbed the last dune before the marsh. The boat was completely out of the water. We struggled to free it from the black mud, but it was stuck fast. The wooden boat was light and easy to maneuver in the water, but it was very heavy when it was on land.

"Looks like we're stuck," Mitch said. "Lucky I thought to bring some food and sodas in a cooler. We may as well spend the night out here. I don't like crossing the chan-nel of the Cape Fear at night with all the big ships that use it. We can sleep on the canvas tarp I use to cover the boat."

"I guess it could be worse," I said. "Martha Jackson will wonder where I am. Captain Jackson may even come out looking for us."

"My dad will probably figure out what happened. I did this one other time, and he let me stay out here. Said I needed to learn a lesson. Since we're here for a while, why don't we dig some clams and oysters?" Mitch suggested.

"Sounds good to me."

We rolled up our pants, kept our sneakers on, waded through the shallow water of the creek, and then sat down in the water, feeling through the mud with our hands for clams. Mitch came up with a muddy handful of fat black clams. Soon I found a few myself. It was a little unsettling, feeling your way through the black ooze. I didn't know what I would find in the mud, if I would cut my hand on an oyster shell, or something would grab me. What if I found the bones of an old pirate buried in the mud? This sent shivers down my spine. We soon filled two buckets with clams, cleaned them in the water, and put them in the boat.

"I know where there is a good oyster bed nearby," Mitch said.

I followed him walking through the marsh grass toward the sound. Sometimes the mud came up to our calves. Then we would walk across a firm area where we wouldn't sink into the mud at all. It was slow going, because of the mud and ooze, but we soon came to a place where the dark gray oysters sat on the surface, like clumps of rocks. Mitch picked up an oyster cluster gingerly with his bare hands and put it in a pail.

"Be careful not to cut yourself," Mitch told me, as I stood behind him.

"Don't worry," I said, as I grabbed a cluster. The oyster shells were razor-sharp and cut between my thumb and index finger. Blood ran down my hand.

"What did I tell you?" Mitch said. "Here, wash it off." He took my hand and washed it in the creek water. "The salt water will heal it, just hold it tight until the bleeding stops."

Finally the bleeding stopped, and I was more careful the next time.

Mitch pulled out a pocket knife, pried a shell open, and scraped the slimy, white oyster out with the point of his knife, then popped it in his mouth. "Try one. They're good."

I hadn't eaten an oyster before, and they didn't look very appetizing. But I was not to be outdone by Mitch.

"Sure, I'll have one," I said. Mitch pried one open and offered it to me. I slipped the oyster off the point of the knife with my fingers. It tasted slimy and salty. I liked it. I smiled. "Let me have another one," I said. We both ate several more as we stood knee-deep in the black mud.

We filled our pails with clusters of oysters, then walked back to the boat. We were covered with black mud.

"Let's wash off," Mitch said, back at the boat. We rinsed off in the creek, then decided to go swimming in the ocean.

Mitch ran across the dune toward the beach. I followed. We were the only people on the beach, so when we came to the water, we took off our clothes and dove into the waves. The water felt like a cool bath, it was so refreshing. We splashed and played for some time, riding the waves and swimming in the surf. When we got out, we gathered our clothes, and laid them out to dry on a piece of driftwood. While our clothes were drying, we sat on the beach and talked.

"Have you ever been laid?" Mitch asked me.

"Sure."

"What's it like?" Mitch asked.

"It's like nothing else I've ever done," I said, looking out at the ocean. "It is hard to describe." I told Mitch about the time I made love to a girl named Pamela in high school. We were with my best friend, Andrew, and his girlfriend, Cassandra. Andrew set me up with Pamela. I didn't tell Mitch that Andrew, Cassandra, and Pamela were black.

"Gosh," Mitch said, looking at me. "I can't wait until I get laid."

"Got to find a woman first," I said, standing up, kicking sand at Mitch. I ran into the water and Mitch followed. Mitch tackled me and we rolled in the shallow water, laughing, and splashing each other. Then we ran out of the surf and pulled our jeans on, even though they were still wet. It was warm and the wetness didn't bother us.

As night fell, Mitch and I dragged the canvass tarp onto the beach and built a fire. We ate oysters and cooked clams in a metal bucket over the fire. We walked to the Cape and listened to the ocean. The moon was full. We saw the lights on a large freighter steaming toward the mouth of the Cape Fear River, which was to the west of us.

"A lot of times those big ships are on automatic pilot, with no one at the helm. I wonder what would happen if a smaller boat got in the way," Mitch said.

"I'd hate to be on that small boat," I said, shivering at the thought.

"It sure is beautiful, isn't it?" I said, feeling the breeze blow through my hair, which had grown to my shoulders since I left home.

"Yeah."

"You don't know how lucky you are growing up around all this," I said. "Where I grew up there was nothing but kudzu, tobacco, and pine trees." I looked around at the full moon over the ocean. It made a silvery path that led from the horizon to the breakers a few yards away. The ocean seethed and boiled with white caps over Frying Pan Shoals.

We slept on the beach. I was lulled to sleep by the sound of the waves. The temperature was perfect, about sixty-five, with just enough breeze coming from the ocean to keep the mosquitoes and gnats away. I knew now why I had moved to the coast. I felt more at home there on the beach under the stars, listening to the soothing monotone of the waves, than I ever felt in Duplin county. I couldn't imagine living anywhere else.

Deep in sleep, I dreamt of a huge, dark man with wild black hair, and a beard lit with tiny matches. The man held a large cutlass and threatened to slit my throat from ear to ear. I looked at the man's face. He was a black man—it was Brady Hauss, who worked on my daddy's farm. I screamed, "Get away from me, Brady, you son of a bitch!" Then I woke in a sweat.

"What's the matter?" Mitch asked, waking up.

"Nothing," I said. "A nightmare, that's all. Dreaming about pirates. Go back to sleep. I'll be all right."

"Who's Brady?" Mitch asked.

"No one you would want to know," I said.

I hadn't dreamed about Brady in a long time. I used to have nightmares about him all the time. It had been a while since I'd thought about what Brady did to me when I was fourteen years old, or what my daddy didn't do about it. I didn't want to think about it. I stayed up, holding my knees in my arms, and looked at the ocean until the images in my dream faded. Then I lay down and slept until daybreak.

High tide was at 5:30, so we left as soon as we got up. Water was under the boat, so we gathered our gear, loaded it, and made our way out of the marsh through the winding creek. A line of pelicans flew overhead in perfect formation: When the leader tipped his wing, the others followed suit, then they all, one by one, dove into the water to catch fish. The sound of the birds, crickets, and cicadas in the marsh was as intoxicating, soothing, and beautiful, as the sound of the waves on the beach had been that night. I wanted to learn everything I could about the island and the marshes. I asked Mitch about everything—the names of the birds, fish, the shells, the history of the place, the daily and seasonal changes—I wanted to know it all.

"WHERE HAVE YOU BEEN?" Martha Jackson asked me as I opened the screen door into her kitchen. "I worried about you all night long."

Captain Jackson sat reading his morning newspaper at the kitchen table. "I wasn't worried," Captain Jackson said. "I figured they probably got caught by the tide. A good lesson, right, Todd?"

"Yes, sir," I said, smiling. Then I lifted two buckets of oysters and clams and handed them to Martha. "I brought you something."

"Oh, boy, my favorite," Martha said, taking the pails. "Oysters and clams. I know what we're having for dinner tonight."

THREE

I PULLED THE STRING TIGHT on the hood of my coat to keep the wind out. It was forty-five degrees, and the wind, mixed with rain, blew from the northeast. The boat rocked back and forth, tossed by the waves, as we hauled in the wire fish pots. Mitch and I had put out twenty-five pots at the artificial reef off Long Beach and marked them with yellow, plastic flags. Some time ago the state had sunk several surplus liberty ships from World War II about five miles offshore from Long Beach to create an artificial reef that would attract fish. It worked well. The square wire cages were alive with squirming black sea bass when Mitch and I pulled them into the boat. We opened the pots and let the fish slide onto the deck, sorting the ones we would keep from the ones we would throw back. We only kept them if they were eight inches or longer—which was most of them. The catch was plentiful.

After we emptied the pots we rebaited them with mullet and menhaden, dropped the pots back into the water, and headed to the next drop spot. Captain Jackson piloted the boat from the bridge, which was enclosed with zippered, white canvas and clear vinyl. Still, the rain got through to him, as it drenched Mitch and I below. We loaded the squirming, black fish, their fins bristling when touched, into large coolers filled with ice at the back of the boat. I was ready to take a break and pour a hot cup of coffee in the cabin—the cold and rain cut through me like a knife. The sea was not high, but it was choppy. When we stopped, the boat bounced around like a cork. When we were underway it was much better.

"When I was a kid, my mother told me about a ship that ran aground off Shackleford Banks in the winter," I told Mitch, as we sat on the blue sofa in the cabin, sipping black coffee in Styrofoam cups. Steam rose from the coffee, warming my face. "It was one of the coldest winters ever recorded on the Outer Banks. The crew lashed themselves to the masts of the boat, because waves were crashing over it, and they were afraid of being washed overboard. It was nighttime, and they knew as soon as day broke, help would come from shore. When the rescue crew arrived the next day, they found the men dead, frozen solid, lashed to the masts. Ice coated everything."

"I feel like it's that cold right now," Mitch said, taking a sip of his coffee.

"I know what you mean," I answered.

"This is November. Wait until the northeasters hit in December and January."

"Maybe by then I'll be used to it."

"Yeah, maybe," Mitch said, staring out at the gray sky and driving rain. "My dad has all the luck. He's in Florida, in the Gulf of Mexico, near Key West. He says as long as I'm in school, I have to stay here. He used to take Mom and me to Florida when I was little, but when I was old enough to go to school Mom said I needed to stay here

and grow up like a normal kid. So my dad goes to Florida
in the winter, and we stay here. After I finish school this
year, he said he's going to take me with him. Maybe you
can come, too."

"I want to stay with Captain Jackson until I learn everything I can, then maybe I'll go to Florida with you and
your dad," I said standing up. "Captain Jackson! I forgot
about him. I bet he'd like some coffee." I poured a cup of
black coffee and added some milk, just the way he liked it,
then took it to him on the bridge.

"Cold, isn't it?" Captain Jackson said, taking the steaming coffee from my hand. "This is when we pay for all the
good times we have in the summer—big catches, good
money, warm weather, good-looking girls. But bills have
to be paid, so here we are, putting out fish pots and pulling them up from the bottom." He looked at me and
smiled. "That's the life of a fisherman. I wouldn't trade it
for anything."

"I wouldn't, either," I said, looking out at the ocean as
the rain came at us in sheets across the rolling sea. "I guess
you can't have it good all the time. Besides, I kind of like
fishing in the winter—at least you don't have to please customers, and mind your p's and q's. You can just be yourself—cuss and fart and scratch your ass and not take a
bath—and no one cares. I like that."

"Don't say that to Martha Jackson. She'll have you
scrubbed and cleaned before you know it," Captain Jackson said, laughing.

The captain looked out over the ocean. "In 1942, these
waters were filled with German submarines. They sunk
hundreds of freighters and supply ships that were trying
to make it to port. From January until June it averaged
one sinking a day. There was a news blackout, so no one

read about it in the papers. But those of us who lived on the coast knew. We saw the wreckage, the oil slicks, the bodies lying on the beach, half eaten by sharks or burned beyond recognition. I was just a kid then and remember my dad bringing me out to the beach to see the debris from the ships. One time we saw some men pulling a body from the water. It was horrible—swollen, naked, burned, with chunks of flesh torn out of it, and missing an arm. My dad told me German sailors from the subs came ashore on some of the deserted islands of the Outer Banks, like Bald Head, to sunbathe and play volleyball on the beach. Everyone was terrified. People thought there were spies on shore communicating with the subs. Anyone who was German was suspect." He stopped for a minute, then added, "Even today we get reminders of the war. Sometimes a shrimper will pick up a live shell in his nets."

"Why was all this happening just in 1942?" I asked. "Didn't it continue all throughout the war?"

"No. As soon as the Americans got their act together ships began traveling in convoys with destroyer escorts. Several U-boats were sunk—one off Morehead City and another one off Nags Head. So after the summer of 1942, it wasn't so bad. But that year hundreds of men died."

I looked over the ocean and imagined the German submarines, their torpedoes spinning through the water, boats going down, fire, men struggling in the water. Most of the sailors were young, like Mitch and me. I could see them holding onto rafts and life preservers in the cold water, not knowing whether they would be saved or not, seeing their buddies go down, feeling the terror, and not knowing whether they would ever see the light of day again. Then I could see the German sailors, the same age as the American sailors, pale white, playing volleyball and sunning themselves on the beach after being underwater for months. I thought about Uncle Warren shooting at boys his own age in Vietnam and then being killed by a mortar shell. What was it all for? Was it worth it? The thought sent shivers down my spine.

Captain Jackson and I got home after dark that night. It was still raining and cold. I was ready for a warm meal, a hot shower, and a good night's rest.

"You all look mighty hungry, but you're going to have to get cleaned up before you sit at my table," Martha Jackson said, smiling, as we entered the kitchen. The screen door slammed behind us.

I walked to my room, pulled off everything but my underwear, and sprawled out on the bed. Captain Jackson woke me about thirty minutes later.

"Get up and take a shower. Martha is almost ready for us. You know how she gets when she's ready to feed us."

I stood in the shower, letting the hot water run over my body. It warmed me deeply, gradually displacing the damp cold. I could have stayed under the shower for hours, it felt so good. My muscles ached from the cold, and the work of the day.

"Todd, supper is ready," Captain Jackson called from outside the bathroom. Then he walked in and threw a towel over the shower curtain.

"I'm coming, I'm coming. Can't a guy have some privacy around here?" I got out and dried myself off when the captain left. My body was sore, but I felt good. I glanced at myself in the long mirror on the back of the door. I stood six feet tall, weighed 165 pounds, and was in the best shape I'd ever been in. Commercial fishing during the winter was tough physical labor, backbreaking, and demanded a lot. Even though I'd worked out in the high school gym and spent years on the track team, they were no match for work on a fishing boat when it came to keeping me in shape.

I looked in the mirror again. My hair, which was brown with blonde streaks from the sun, fell to my shoulders, and I had a day-old stubble. Gray-green eyes stared back at me from the mirror. Broad shoulders and a firm chest tapered down to a slim waist and hips, a washboard stomach, and rippled abdominals. My muscles had good definition with hardly an ounce of fat. The biceps were big and crossed with bulging veins, and my legs were strong and firm from hours of work on the boat.

Martha's call interrupted my observations.

"Todd, your supper is getting cold," she yelled from the kitchen.

I dried off quickly, pulled on some jeans and a white T-shirt, and ran out to the kitchen.

"You got a letter from home today, Todd," Martha said when I sat down to eat.

"I did?"

"Yeah, it's on your dresser. I think it's from your mother."

I didn't ask about the letter—I was too busy eating the delicious beef stew Martha served in glazed earthenware bowls. A basket of homemade cornbread sat on the table, along with a bowl of steaming hot corn on the cob, collard greens, and black-eyed peas.

"Have you told your mother anything about us, Todd?" Martha asked.

I didn't answer but kept eating. I didn't want to talk about home or my parents.

"Can't you see the boy is hungry?" Captain Jackson asked, placing his hand on Martha's arm as if to say she shouldn't pry.

She looked up at her husband. "I don't think it's prying to ask Todd if he has written about us. If I were his mother, I would want to know who he is staying with, and whether he is doing well and is being properly cared for. After all, he's only eighteen," Martha said.

Captain Jackson glared at her in silence.

"When I first got here I wrote," I said, not looking up from my stew, "and told her about you all, what I was doing, where I was staying, and that I was all right." I continued to eat, choosing not to tell Martha or Captain Jackson that Mama had begged me to come back home. It was a long time before I wrote Mama again.

"Todd, why don't you want to have anything to do with your family?" Martha asked.

"There's nothing for me back there. This is my home now."

Martha put her arm around me. "You know you're welcome here as long as you want to stay, Todd."

"I'm hungry," Captain Jackson said, picking up a piece of cornbread and the butter plate. After we ate, I went to my room and read the letter from Mama:

November 15, 1975

Dear Todd,

Your sister, Sally, ran off and got married three weeks ago. She found herself a real nice boy. I like him a lot. He sells used cars in Clinton. He's twenty years old. They had to get married. She says she wants to have a home of her own, away from us, like you. June Bug still helps his daddy around the farm. I'm afraid he'll leave too, when he gets old enough.

Your daddy is still drinking pretty bad. If it weren't for Brady Hauss, I don't know how we'd run this farm.

I'm your Mama and I love you. I don't have any hard feelings about your leaving. I want you to know that, no matter what your daddy says.

I still dream about you at night, seeing you on a white boat in the ocean looking just like my daddy. You're a lot like him, you know. I can't ever get the sound of the ocean out of my head. Sometimes I wake up and think I hear it, but it's only the crickets, the katydids, or the wind in the pine trees. I hope you're all right. Tell me what it's like there on the coast. I used to love it when my daddy told me stories about the sea. Let me know how you're doing. Write when you can. I love you.

Love,
Mama

When I finished reading Mama's letter I wrote her and told her about working with Captain Jackson and how well Martha Jackson fed me. I told her about going deep-sea fishing in the summer, and commercial fishing in the winter. I told her about Bald Head Island and the pirate gold. I said I would like to meet Sally's husband if I didn't have to come home and see Daddy.

I loved my mother. I couldn't understand why she stayed with Daddy with his drinking and the way he treated her—the beatings, the fights, the cussing—but that was her business. I also knew that I had to stay as far away from that place as possible, or I would be swallowed up by it and never have a life of my own. After I wrote the letter, I fell asleep.

WHEN WE WEREN'T OUT with Captain Jackson fishing in the ocean, Mitch and I trolled the creeks and inland waterways for shrimp, and harvested oysters when they were in season. Mitch's favorite place to troll for shrimp with his flat-bottomed boat was in the marsh creeks behind Bald Head Island. There the shrimp were big and plentiful.

Mitch and I gradually fed the net into the water. It was held down with lead weights tied to a heavy rope that went around the edge of it. In the middle we had tied strips of plastic, twine, and rope just like the nets on the big shrimp boats, to keep it from chafing on the bottom. After letting it drag the bottom for about thirty minutes, we pulled the net into the boat. It dragged up oyster shells, driftwood, crabs, flounder, other fish, and of course, the slippery, jumping shrimp. After discarding what we didn't want, we caught the shrimp with our hands, which was not easy because the shrimp jumped all over the bottom of the boat. We laughed as they slipped through our fingers more than once.

The shrimp in the marsh creeks are larger than the shrimp caught in the ocean in the winter. Most of the commercial shrimpers from Southport and Holden Beach head to Florida in November and December, where they can catch the big Gulf shrimp. This made the local market for the creek shrimp good. They weren't as plentiful, and the big boats couldn't make it into the creeks, so the only way to catch them was with small boats, like Mitch's.

Soon we loaded the coolers with shrimp. Then we waded into the mud, wearing high rubber waders strapped to our shoulders, to harvest oysters. We gathered them in galvanized pails and quickly filled one end of the boat with oysters. After we took our catch of oysters and shrimp to the market in Southport, we gathered our provisions to go flounder-gigging that night and to spend the night on Bald Head.

It was a full-moon night and not very cold for December, but not warm, either. I hung a Coleman lantern on a stick over the water in front of the boat, as Mitch guided it through the creek. The boat was working against the current as the tide was going out. But this way we would be able to leave at high tide in the morning after sleeping on the island.

We went slowly. I hung over the water, looking for the telltale signs—the ring of sand, the glassy eye looking up into the light. Flounder freeze when they see light at night, so they are easy to stab with the two-pronged gig. We were successful that night, gigging several large flounder, which we put on ice in a cooler.

The moon cast a luminous glow over the marshes. We could see others fishing, too, with lights on the prows of silent wooden boats. The marsh grass glistened with the pale light of the moon, as did the water when a breeze disturbed it. It looked like diamonds thrown on black velvet. At other times the moon reflected smooth and long as the water moved slowly under us. We were very quiet. We used paddles and a pole, not the motor, so we wouldn't scare the fish.

After we filled the ice chest, we pulled the boat up on the sand, walked out to the beach, put up the tent, rolled out two sleeping bags, and hung the Coleman lantern from a piece of driftwood. We weren't hungry, as we ate before we left Southport, but we drank Cokes from the cooler and ate canned sardines spread on saltine crackers.

"Let's walk on the beach," I said. The air was cool, with a gentle breeze blowing from the north. We passed others camping on the beach, preparing to surf fish and seine in the morning. Then we walked to the point where Cape Fear juts out into the ocean. The shoals were white with foam and the sea was glazed by the light of the moon. The high waves crashed against each other at the point, spraying us with a salty mist. We sat on the sand and talked.

"How do you get along with your father?" I asked Mitch.

"Great. We're real close."

"I hate mine."

"I know a lot of guys who don't like their fathers," Mitch said. "My dad's good to me. He leaves me alone when I need to be left alone, but he's there when I need him. We do a lot of things together, like fishing, shrimping, crabbing. Both my mom and dad are good to me. I guess that makes me lucky."

"Yeah," I said. "My dad never did anything like that with me. All he did was yell at me and hit me when he was drunk. I did well to stay out of his way."

"What about Captain Jackson?" Mitch asked.

"I work for him, and he gives me a place to stay."

"You know it's more than that. Martha Jackson falls all over herself for you. It's like you're their adopted son."

"Yeah?" I asked, smiling self-consciously. "Well, they're both real special to me."

"Want to walk to the old lifesaving station?" Mitch asked, standing up.

WE WALKED DOWN the south beach, where the water was warmer and the waves weren't as big. The moon shone so bright that it cast shadows on the sand. Then we climbed the dunes and walked over an area of flat, hard sand where the air was still, but we could still hear the waves on the beach. We walked up to one of the houses and climbed the rickety steps to the wide front porch. The front door stood open, and there was no glass in the windows.

"Let's go inside," Mitch said. We both explored the deserted house.

"Someone told me these houses were haunted. I don't see any ghosts," I said, kicking a door open. The moon lit the gray interior with a pale light.

Outside we sat on the front steps and talked. Mitch turned to me and said. "Todd, you're my best friend."

We sat together on the wooden step.

"You're my best friend too," I said.

"Best friends can talk about anything, can't they?"

"Yeah, I guess so," I said.

"Has anybody ever tried anything with you?" Mitch asked.

"What do you mean?"

"You know, tried anything."

I looked away. I felt uncomfortable and wanted to change the subject.

"When I was in the Boy Scouts, my scoutmaster crawled into my tent one night and tried something with me."

"What did you do?" I asked.

"I was fourteen years old and little for my age. My scoutmaster was in charge of the whole troop—he was a grown-up. I looked up to him. What was I supposed to do?" Mitch turned his head. He looked embarrassed.

"Brady Hauss, a black man who works for my dad, tried something with me," I said. "Every chance he got when I was alone, he would taunt me. I hate his guts. I would have killed him if he wasn't twice me size." I paused and looked out over the dunes. "I told my dad about it. I thought he would fire Brady, but he didn't. He said I was old enough to fend for myself. He said he needed Brady and couldn't run the farm without him." I turned and looked at Mitch with a hard look. "I'll never forgive my dad for that."

"When I told my dad about the scoutmaster, he got real mad. He went to the pack leader and told him. The scoutmaster left town after that."

"I guess that's the difference between your dad and mine," I said.

"Yeah," Mitch said. "I guess so."

"Let's go back to our tent," I said. "I'm tired."

"Me, too," Mitch said.

We both slept well that night, lulled by the sound of the waves on the beach. I was glad to know that at least somewhere there was a father who was a real father to his son, not like mine. It made me rest easier knowing that.

The next morning we woke at sunrise, loaded our tent and sleeping bags into the boat, and motored across the creek and the river to Southport. I felt a lot closer to Mitch after that night. I wasn't one to talk about my feelings, but I'm glad he decided to open up to me, and I'm glad I opened up to him. It was like he knew we had that in common. It made me feel better knowing that I wasn't the only one who had had trouble when they were young, and that the way my family lived wasn't the only way things could be.

MITCH BORROWED HIS father's black Chevrolet Impala, picked me up, and drove to the pier at Yaupon Beach, where we played pinball and shot pool. During the winter there were no tourists at the pier, only locals. There weren't as many good-looking girls as in the summer, but there were a few.

The entrance to the pier was enclosed with a counter that served food, beer, and sodas, and it had pinball machines and pool tables. It was a popular hangout. The fishermen walked through it to fish on the pier and buy supplies from a small stand. It had plywood walls and gas heaters that hung from the ceiling and made a lot of noise. Beer signs hung from the walls and ceiling, and a plastic tiffany-style shade hung over the pool table. Mitch turned eighteen in January so he and I drank beer, played pool and pinball, and flirted with the few women who hung out there, mainly high-school girls. Mitch knew most of them. They seemed to be more interested in me than Mitch. I was new in town; Mitch was a known quantity. I've never had trouble finding girls.

Several times Mitch and I picked up girls at the pier, bought some beer, and took them parking at the end of the beach. As long as I got in at a decent hour, the Jacksons didn't complain. After all, I was a young man on my own. They didn't like for me to drink, but as long as I didn't abuse it, they didn't say anything. Martha's rule was, I couldn't drink in her house, and if I came home drunk I could stay out until I got sober. I never came home drunk—at least not when Martha was awake to catch me. I respected the Jacksons and didn't want to make them mad.

FOUR

THE CHARTER BOAT SEASON began in May. I couldn't wait. It had been a long winter. I enjoyed my trips to Bald Head Island with Mitch, fishing in the marshes, and commercial fishing with Captain Jackson. But the summer was my favorite time of year, when the tourists came and the girls were on the beaches. We were all busy getting ready for the season. Captain Jackson had his boat dry-docked and painted, and the diesels overhauled. He bought a new Loran navigational system and a new depth finder that identified schools of fish much better than the old one did.

Captain Jackson chartered his boat to a Raleigh lawyer and his family, for the second week in June. The captain told me the lawyer had a good-looking daughter who was about my age. But the captain didn't tell me just how good-looking she was. When she stepped out of her father's silver Cadillac and walked toward the boat, I couldn't keep my eyes off her. She had a great body, tiny waist, and thick, shoulder-length blonde hair. Her eyes were so blue they matched the sky. She wore cutoff blue jeans that were tight and very short, and a white blouse that opened just enough to give me a taste of what was inside. Her smile was sweet and modest; she didn't appear to be conceited, despite her good looks. She even looked a little shy.

"Todd, I'd like to introduce you to Edwin Gardner from Raleigh, and his daughter, Elizabeth," Captain Jackson said.

"Pleased to meet you," I said, shaking Mr. Gardner's hand and smiling at Elizabeth. Betty Gardner, Elizabeth's mother, got out of the car, carrying a white canvas bag filled with food, suntan lotion, and towels. Her hair was blonde too, but it looked dyed. She was slightly stooped and wore a pink-and-white-striped sundress and dark glasses.

"Mr. Gardner is a lobbyist," Captain Jackson said. "He knows all the high-powered politicians in Raleigh and Washington. He's paid to know the big dogs."

"I have an active law practice as well, Bill. If you ever need any help, let me know," Mr. Gardner said, smiling, as he helped his daughter and wife on board.

"Todd started working for me last summer. I don't think you've met him. He is the best boy I've had work for me. A real natural," Captain Jackson said, patting me on the back. I wore my favorite outfit—an orange nylon bathing suit and a loose white T-shirt. I had a good tan and my hair had gotten a lot blonder from being in the sun so much. When I stepped off the boat to untie the ropes and cast off, my eyes met Elizabeth's. We both smiled.

I moved quickly and with a confidence that came from experience, as I checked the fishing lines to make sure the proper lures were attached and that other lures were ready to go when the captain wanted them changed. As Elizabeth and her parents talked, I felt her eyes follow me while I worked. I also watched her. She was the most beautiful girl I had ever met. I gathered from the conversation that she had just finished high school and was going to Saint

Mary's College in Raleigh in the fall. I also overheard them say that Elizabeth and her mother planned to stay at their house at Caswell Beach for the summer, and Mr. Gardner would be coming down on the weekends.

It was a beautiful day. The sea was calm and there were a few clouds high in the sky. No storms were predicted. Mr. Gardner didn't want to go to the Gulf Stream because his wife and daughter were aboard. The Gulf Stream was for serious fishermen. He wanted this to be a fun outing for the family. So Captain Jackson took them to the area off Oak Island, south of Cape Fear, to the artificial reefs and wrecks that made for good fishing. We trolled for a while and caught a few Spanish mackerel.

Elizabeth asked me to get her a Coke.

"You should see it when we go sharking," I said, trying to impress her, as I poured Coke from a can into a paper cup filled with ice.

"Have you been sharking?" she asked.

"Yeah, plenty of times." I was exaggerating. I had actually been only once, last fall. The customer insisted we go sharking because we hadn't caught anything else. We caught one shark. "See that place in your dad's seat?" I said, pointing to a chunk that was missing from the thick, wooden chair. "That's where a shark took a bite out of the chair. The shark was eight feet long and once we got him into the boat he got loose. We all jumped back and let him go on the deck until he died. They don't live long out of water."

"Wow, I bet you were scared!" Elizabeth said.

"It was nothing," I said, trying to act tough.

"Elizabeth," Mr. Gardner said, turning to see Elizabeth talking to me. "Are you ready for a sandwich?"

"Todd was telling me about catching sharks."

"Sharking?" He gave me a hard look, seeming to notice me for the first time. "Dangerous sport. Not the kind of thing you would enjoy, Elizabeth. Betty?" he yelled, turning toward his wife. "Where did you put those sandwiches? Elizabeth and I are hungry."

"I put them near the sink in the cabin," she said, getting up. "I'll get them out. Does the young man want anything to eat?" she asked, looking me over.

"No ma'am. Me and Captain Jackson have plenty of food for you all and for us. I'll put everything out. You don't have to do a thing."

"Thank you," she said, smiling appreciatively.

After they ate, I quickly put the lines out again, working with the skill I had learned from scores of trips with Captain Jackson. It was getting hotter, so I took off my shirt.

"Young man, you certainly have a nice tan," Mrs. Gardner remarked, her eyes lingering.

"You must be an athlete," Mr. Gardner said to me. "You certainly have a fine build, but you'd look better with a haircut," he said, condescendingly.

"I was on the track team in high school." I said, ignoring his comment about my hair. "I graduated last June and "I've been working for Captain Jackson ever since."

I felt Elizabeth's eyes follow me as I moved around the boat. We caught each other's eyes several times. I helped her reel in the line when she caught a fish. Her eyes were gorgeous, and the way the sun hit her hair, I couldn't help but notice her breasts as I stood over her—they were so plump and firm. Mr. Gardner noticed all of this, too.

"Do you plan to go to college, son?" Mr. Gardner asked me.

"No, sir. I can't afford it. Besides, I like working for Captain Jackson."

"Didn't you apply for an athletic scholarship?"

"My grades weren't very good. I did well in track, but Coach said I'd have to make better grades to get a scholarship. Then there are living expenses. My folks couldn't afford to pay anything. Some people just aren't meant for college, sir," I said.

"That's right," Mr. Gardner replied, looking at Elizabeth as if he were making a point. "Elizabeth's going to Saint Mary's in September. We are very proud of her. She was in the top of her class."

"I bet you're proud of her," I said, smiling at her.

"Can I get you something to drink, sir?" I asked, noticing him roll his empty beer can between his hands.

"Yes, I'll have another Budweiser."

I brought Mr. Gardner a Budweiser, then put out the lines. We caught several Spanish mackerel.

"Captain Jackson is one of the best captains in Southport, isn't he, Todd?" Mr. Gardner said.

"He's the best, all right. I've learned everything I know from him," I answered.

I relieved the captain from the bridge to let him eat a sandwich and use the head.

"I saw the way you were looking at the Gardner girl," Captain Jackson said, as I sat beside him on the bridge.

"She sure is good-looking," I said.

"If you know what's good for you, you'll stay away from her. Her father's a very powerful man. He's mean, too. If he doesn't like you, he can hurt you. I know he wouldn't let a fisherman go after his daughter."

"They have a house at Caswell Beach and are going to stay here all summer," I said, looking down at Elizabeth.

"I know. That's what I mean—you better watch out. Girls like that are dangerous. They are interested in a sum-

mer fling with a guy like you, then they go home and forget you."

"That can work both ways," I said.

"True." Captain Jackson paused, then continued, "Do
what you want. I can't keep you from making mistakes,
but you can't say I didn't warn you."

"Yes, sir."

MITCH AND I DROVE SLOWLY down Caswell Beach Road, along
the oceanfront. "We should be close," I said, checking the
house number in the phone book.

"What if she doesn't want to see you?" Mitch asked.
"What if her old man answers the door?"

"I don't care—I want to see her," I said.

We stopped in front of a pale green one-story house
on stilts. It had a cedar-shake roof, and a painted wooden
deck in front. I walked up the front steps and knocked on
the sliding glass door. Elizabeth answered the door with
her hair wrapped in a white towel. She had just taken a
shower and wore a white, terry-cloth bathrobe.

"Todd, what are you doing here?" she asked, surprised
to see me.

"I wanted to see you." I hesitated, forgetting for a moment what I had come for. "And I wanted to ask you to go
with me to the Fourth of July celebration in Southport."

"That's sweet, Todd. But I'm already going with my
girlfriend from Raleigh." She paused, then said, "Why don't
you meet us there?"

"Where?" I asked.

"How about at the gazebo in Franklin Square Park?"

"Friday night?"

"Yeah," she said, smiling.

"Elizabeth," her mother called from the kitchen.

"Yes, Mother?"

"Who is it?" Mrs. Gardner asked, walking into the living room. The wood-paneled room which ran the length of the house, had a bright red carpet and bamboo furniture with a floral print on the cushions.

"Oh, Todd, from the boat, right?" Mrs. Gardner said, looking somewhat surprised as she walked to the front door.

"Yes ma'am," I said.

"Honey, we've got to meet Lucretia at The Carousel shop in fifteen minutes. You need to hurry."

"Okay, Mom."

"Nice to see you, Todd," Elizabeth said.

"See you later," I said.

"What is he doing here?" her mother asked Elizabeth as she closed the screen door. I could hear them as I walked down the steps.

"He said he was in the neighborhood and wanted to stop by to say hello," Elizabeth answered.

"I don't think it's a good idea for you to see someone like that," Mrs. Gardner said.

"That's my business."

"Maybe so, but your father's not going to like it."

I got into Mitch's car and said, "Let's get out of here." I remembered what Captain Jackson had said, but I liked Elizabeth. I didn't care what her parents thought. Let her be the judge.

SOUTHPORT HAS CELEBRATED the Fourth of July for as long as anyone can remember. They say the tradition started at Fort Johnson, before the Civil War. Fort Johnson was a group of brick buildings on the waterfront, built in 1810 on the site of an old British fort . Ever since the Revolution, the fort has been owned by the United States government—the Coast Guard used it during World War II; in 1950 the Air Force used it for quarters for a crash rescue team; then in 1955 it was occupied by personnel from the Sunny Point Army Terminal, an installation a few miles from Southport, up the Cape Fear River.

The town was known as Smithville before the Civil War, but the name was changed to Southport in the 1880s, when the town fathers thought it would become the southern end of a railroad, and a new port would be built to rival Charleston. The town fathers hoped the railroad would bring industry and growth, but their hopes never panned out. The railroad didn't come for several years, and Southport remained a sleepy little town that never grew very much. Wilmington got most of the growth, with its better port.

The Fourth of July celebration usually lasted several days and grew each year, according to Captain Jackson. This was July 4, 1976, the Bicentennial year, and it was supposed to be the biggest celebration ever. There were parades, concerts in the park, beauty contests, a calliope concert at Whittlers Bench, a parachute jump by the United States Air Force, an air show over the river, children's field day events, and, of course, the fireworks display that night over the Cape Fear River.

But what really got my attention was a drawing for a seventeen-foot Boston Whaler with an Evinrude motor—perfect for fishing in the river and the marshes around Bald Head. The drawing was a fund-raiser for the Jaycees. I bought ten tickets and Mitch bought several, too, even though he already had a boat. A large crowd of people milled around as the tickets continued to sell for the seven o'clock drawing. About that time I saw Elizabeth and her friend walking toward us.

"Elizabeth, this is Mitch Etheridge," I said as the two girls joined us.

"And this is Lucretia Sloan," Elizabeth answered. "She's visiting me from Raleigh."

Lucretia was very attractive, with long, dark brown hair. She was a little shorter than Elizabeth, with slightly wider hips, a sweet smile and sexy dark eyes. Both she and Elizabeth wore sundresses, since it was hot and humid. The breeze from the river was just starting to cool things off. Mitch and I wore khaki shorts and Izod shirts—more dressed up than usual.

"We're waiting to see who wins the drawing for the boat," I said. "I bought ten tickets. Do you want to buy any? They're a dollar each."

"I don't have any use for a boat, but I'll buy some to support the cause," Elizabeth said. She bought five and handed them to me.

"But they're yours," I said.

"You have more use for a boat than I do."

"No big deal—you're not going to win anyway, Todd," Mitch said, teasing. "Let's get something to eat before the drawing."

Since she insisted, I took the tickets. We walked to a nearby tent and ordered chopped barbecue, coleslaw, and sweet tea.

Mitch and Lucretia talked and seemed to enjoy each other.

"Is your father in town?" I asked Elizabeth.

"Yeah, he came in last night for a long weekend."

"I get the feeling he doesn't like me," I said.

"That's not true. He doesn't know anything about you. I'm sure he would like you if he got to know you," she said.

"Maybe so."

A man announced over the loudspeaker that the drawing was about to begin. Mitch and I and the girls walked to the stage where the president of the Jaycees, a young man with a blonde crewcut and black, horn-rimmed glasses, reached into a big glass jar to draw out the lucky number. The handsome fiberglass boat with its shiny new motor sat on a trailer behind him.

The man read out the first number and no one responded. One of the rules was that you had to be present to win. He called it out several more times, without success. Then he drew another number. It was one of the tickets I held in my hand. I jumped straight up into the air, shouting, before I realized that it was one Elizabeth had given to me. I yelled out to the man on the platform that I had the lucky ticket.

"Elizabeth, this is the one you bought," I said, turning to her.

"I gave it to you, didn't I? It's yours."

I grabbed her and kissed her. Everyone around us clapped. "Thank you," I said, not believing my good luck. "This boat belongs to you."

"I wouldn't know what to do with a boat. It's yours if you promise me one thing."

"Anything," I said, dumbstruck.

"That you'll name it after me."

"Done! I will do it as soon as I get it home. Thank you!" I said as I kissed her again.

The crowd clapped and yelled and whistled their approval. I took Elizabeth up with me to claim the boat. I was ecstatic. My very own boat. I had never owned a thing in my life. I would have given anything to own a boat, and now, because of Elizabeth, I had one. I couldn't believe it.

After all the excitement died down, the four of us walked to the river where a band played music in the street. I danced with Elizabeth. I wasn't much of a dancer, but I loved being with her. When we slow danced, I held her tight and kissed her. We were both swept up in the excitement and beauty of the night. The streets were strung with white lights and crowded with people dancing and celebrating. Mitch and Lucretia danced a few times, but Mitch hated to dance even more than I did, so they took a walk along the riverfront.

Elizabeth and I danced until the fireworks exploded over the river. The night was clear, the moon was a slender crescent, and the sky was alive with the spectacular display. The band played the "Star-Spangled Banner," and everyone joined in the singing.

Walking down to the water's edge, I looked at Elizabeth and asked, "Have you ever been in love?"

"One time, I thought I was, but I realized it was a mistake," she said, looking down.

"I haven't been in love. I've had plenty of girlfriends, but I can't say I was in love with any of them. I guess I'm waiting for the right person."

"You're a very special person, Todd," Elizabeth said, as we took a seat on a nearby bench.

"You're just saying that."

"No. I mean it."

"You're special, too," I said, as she leaned her head on my shoulder. "Can I see you again?"

"Yes, as soon as my dad leaves. I don't think Mom cares, but Daddy's very protective," she said, laughing nervously.

"I can see why."

"I'll call you next week when Daddy leaves for Raleigh, okay?"

"Sounds good. Hey, are you sure you don't want that boat?"

"I gave you the ticket, didn't I? Besides, you're the one who wants a boat."

"You're incredible." I kissed her again. After a while we got up and looked for Mitch and Lucretia. At midnight the girls drove home to Caswell Beach.

FIVE

I GUIDED MY NEW BOAT across the main channel of the Cape Fear River and headed toward Bald Head Island. Elizabeth brought a basket of food, a blanket, and some towels, and we wore bathing suits under our clothes. She and her family had been coming to Caswell Beach for years, but this was the first time she had been to Bald Head. She was excited about seeing the island, and I was excited to be with her. She told her mother she was going to Wrightsville Beach to visit some friends and would be back that night.

The water lay like glass before us, disturbed only by the occasional wake of a boat. The strong reflection of the July sun was almost blinding. In the distance, heat waves hovered in the air above the marshes, distorting the horizon. A large freighter passed down the channel of the Cape Fear River, heading toward the end of Bald Head Island and out to sea.

"This is beautiful, Todd," Elizabeth said, over the loud hum of the engine.

"It sure is," I said, standing in the middle of the boat, holding the wheel.

"I'm glad you kept your promise," she said, looking over the back of the boat at the black letters which spelled her name.

"First thing I did after Captain Jackson and I picked it up was to paint *Elizabeth* on the back."

"It looks great."

"Thank you," I said, as I maneuvered around the sandbars and islands in the wide river. I couldn't have been prouder of my boat. I couldn't believe it was mine.

At the marsh creek I slowed the boat and began to meander through the tall, shimmering grass. We could see the old Bald Head lighthouse to the right of the entrance to the creek. The squat, octagonal tower built of stuccoed brick, stood among some large oak trees. There was a boat dock and few buildings around it where some development had begun.

Once we passed the old lighthouse we were well within the creek. The tide was high. It was ten o'clock in the morning and I figured four hours would be plenty of time on the island. In six hours the tide would be low.

As we made our way through the creek, I told Elizabeth about the pirate treasure supposedly hidden there, and about the Spanish raiders who burned Brunswick Town in the 1700s and camped on Bald Head before they left for the Caribbean. I also told her about the Civil War battle at Fort Fisher to the north, and about the German submarines and the sailors who people say landed on Bald Head during the war, sunning and playing on the beach.

"Have you ever found any pirate treasure?" she asked.

"Mitch and I have dug out here plenty of times without any luck. Somebody found a Spanish doubloon on Oak Island—it's in the museum in town. I'll show it to you sometime."

"I love it out here," she said, the breeze lifting her hair as she watched the birds stand in the water and fly over us. The marsh was alive with the sounds of birds and insects that sang out loudly until we approached. They sat silent until we passed, then they started up again.

At the end of the creek we stopped at a sandbar. I anchored, pulled the boat up, tied it to a big piece of driftwood, and buried the anchor in the sand. Elizabeth carried the towels and blanket and I carried the picnic basket.

We trudged across the soft sand of the island's interior, passing the squawking terns and their nests, until we climbed the dunes to the beach. The ocean was calm, silvered by the sun. The sound of the waves was hypnotic. We walked to the edge of the water and spread out a blanket for our picnic. Then we took off the clothes over our bathing suits and ran splashing into the ocean. We swam, rode the waves, laughed, and played in the water. When we got out, we ate ham sandwiches, drank Cokes, and lay out in the sun on the blanket.

"Do you come out here a lot, Todd?" Elizabeth asked.

"Every chance I get. I love it."

"I can see why."

After a bit, I asked her if she wanted to walk to the cape. I mentioned that we could even see where the sea turtles laid their eggs. Elizabeth pulled on a loose white beach cover-up, and we walked down toward the point.

"The turtle eggs are up there," I said, pointing to a place in the dunes. "It's against the law to disturb them. We're not even supposed to get close to them."

Elizabeth looked at the little mounds of sand near the dunes in the distance.

"In May, the sea turtles come out of the ocean to lay eggs. The turtles are huge." I opened my arms wide to

show her. "Mitch and I saw them swim in this spring.
People come from all around to watch.

"The turtles wash in on the waves at night and waddle
over the sand. Nothing stops them. It's like they're going
to lay their eggs, no matter what. And they take their time
doing it. Each turtle lays over a hundred eggs. When
they're finished they waddle back over the sand and disappear into the waves.

"There's only about an inch of sand covering the eggs,
so that's why they're protected. It's so easy to steal the
eggs. Animals do it all the time. But since each turtle lays
so many, there's still plenty left. In August the baby turtles
hatch. When they start to hatch, the sand begins to bubble
- they call it a turtle boil. Then they all pop up out of the
sand and start waddling toward the ocean. They say the
turtles follow the moon light. On Topsail Beach, north of
here, the beach runs east to west. People have to help
point the baby turtles toward the water or they'll go down
the beach until they're exhausted."

Elizabeth had been listening and quietly watching me.
"I'd love to see the turtles hatch," she said.

"Okay. In August, if you're still here, we'll do that," I
said, smiling at Elizabeth.

We continued walking toward the cape, the only ones
on the beach except for a few fishermen surf casting into
the waves. The sky was pale blue and white clouds drifted
high overhead. The ocean lay on two sides of us,
whitecapped to the east as far as I could see, and as calm
as a lake to the south, where the river met the ocean. The
sound of the waves surrounded us. It was as if we were
alone on a deserted island in the middle of the ocean. I
put my arm around Elizabeth's waist and pulled her close

to me. She looked at me and smiled, brushing her hair out of her eyes. I kissed her.

I held her hand as we walked back to our blanket and picnic basket. "We'd better start back soon, or the tide will be too low for us to make it through the marsh," I said.

"You mean we could be stranded?"

"Yes," I said.

"How exciting," she said, lifting her eyebrows.

"If we get stranded now we won't be able to get back to Southport until tomorrow. I don't think you want to explain that to your mother."

"No," she said, sounding disappointed. "Todd, tell me about your family. Captain Jackson isn't related to you, is he?"

" No," I said, looking away from her.

"Where's your real family?" she asked. "Mitch told Lucretia you grew up in Duplin County."

"That's right."

"Do you have brothers and sisters? Where are your mother and father?"

"I don't want to talk about it, okay?" I said.

"Why?" she asked.

"Because I don't want to," I said firmly. I wasn't in the mood to talk about home. There wasn't anything nice I could say about it, and it would be a downer for both of us. Besides, I wanted Elizabeth to like me. Maybe I would tell her later, when we knew each other better. I just didn't want to talk about it now when I barely knew her.

"Okay," she answered, dropping the subject.

We picked up our clothes and a towel, then walked behind separate dunes to pull off our wet bathing suits and put on dry clothes. After dressing, we picked up the blanket and picnic basket and walked across the sandy flats to the creek. I pointed out the different birds to Elizabeth, and showed her the oyster beds sitting just above the water. I mentioned how Mitch and I fished and shrimped in the marsh.

We got back to Southport that afternoon.

"When can I see you again?" I asked.

"This weekend Lucretia is coming to see me and we are going to a bar in Long Beach. Why don't you and Mitch meet us there Thursday night?"

"Sounds like fun," I said, tying the boat up beside Captain Jackson's boat at the marina.

Elizabeth put her arm around my neck and kissed me.

"Good-bye," she said. Then she ran down the dock to the parking lot where she got into her car. I knew that I was falling in love with her. She was the most beautiful woman I had ever known. I wanted to be with her every day, but I didn't want to seem too anxious.

THE CRICKET LOUNGE WAS NEW. It had a jukebox that played dance music, and they served beer. In North Carolina liquor was only allowed in "private clubs" where you could bring a bottle in a brown bag if you were twenty-one. We were all eighteen, too young to drink liquor, but we could drink beer and wine. Mostly locals went to the bar, but summer people gathered there, too. The jukebox played beach and soul music, mixed with a little rock and roll.

After we danced a little and drank a few beers, Lucretia left with Mitch in his car. It was about eleven, and Elizabeth told me she was ready to leave the bar too, but she didn't want to go home. There was a crescent moon and the night was beautiful. We bought some beer at a convenience store and drove her car to the south end of Long

Beach, which was a great place to go parking. There were no cottages, and there were places in the dunes where we could be private.

Elizabeth parked the car where I told her and turned on the radio. It played "You and Me" by Aretha Franklin. The lights from the dashboard lit her face. The moon covered the dunes with a pale, luminous light. There were no clouds in the sky. We opened the windows to let in the cool night air, then we both opened cold cans of Budweiser.

"Why don't you like to talk about your family, Todd?" Elizabeth asked.

I didn't reply.

"Is there something you're ashamed of? You can tell me." She snuggled up and put her head on my shoulder. "I want you to feel like you can talk me. I try to be open with you."

She paused, laid her head in my lap, and looked up at me. I could see the light from the dash, in the pupils of her eyes. "My mother drinks too much," she said. "I can't say I blame her. My dad is never home—he's always busy at the office. There is always some big deal he has to attend to. A lot of times he doesn't even come home at night. One of my friends told me he's having an affair with a woman in the office—her mother told her. She won't say who with, but I have my suspicions."

"Have you ever asked your father about it?" I asked.

"No," Elizabeth said, looking up at me. "I wouldn't dare."

I was silent for a minute, then began to talk. Elizabeth was opening up to me. I needed to be honest with her. I was taking a chance, but sometimes you have to do that.

My father is an alcoholic," I said. "He beats my mom, and he beat me, my brother, and sister when he could.

One time I got so mad at him, I told him if he laid another hand on my mother I'd kill him. I hate that son of a bitch." I looked out my window. "I don't ever want to see him again."

"What about your mother?"

"I love her very much, but she's not going to leave him. I left when I finally figured that out."

"You said you have a brother and sister?"

"Yeah, June Bug and Sally. They're both younger than me. Sally got married last year and moved to Clinton. June Bug will probably leave too, when he gets older. But he's just a kid now."

"Do you keep up with them?"

"My mother writes me every once in a while, to tell me how things are going."

Elizabeth reached up and touched my hair with her hand. I kissed her hand.

"Want to take a walk?" I asked, looking down at Elizabeth and running my fingers through her hair.

We walked toward the beach, sitting down at the edge of the dunes, looking out at the ocean, and kissed. She wrapped her arms around me and held me close. A cool breeze blew in from the ocean.

"I think I'm falling in love with you, Todd," Elizabeth said.

"You're crazy. You don't even know me. How can you say that?" I couldn't believe that someone as beautiful and wonderful as Elizabeth could ever love someone like me. I was afraid to let myself love her. Afraid of getting hurt.

"I do. I can't explain it," she said, looking down.

I put my arms around her, kissed her again, then said, "We're so different. You're going to college. I'm working on a fishing boat." Captain Jackson's warning kept rattling around in my head. I paused and looked out at the surf. "I think I'm falling in love with you, too. But it scares me. My head tells me we're too different, but my heart tells me I love you." I looked back at her, searching her eyes.

"It scares me, too," Elizabeth said, looking up at me and running her hand through my hair. "I know what you mean. I'm going to Saint Mary's in the fall, and you live in Southport. But somehow that doesn't matter."

We both held each other while the breeze from the ocean tossed Elizabeth's hair, blowing strands of it into my face. I thought again about what Captain Jackson had told me, but I didn't care. I loved Elizabeth and that was all that mattered.

SOON, ELIZABETH AND I were seeing each other every night during the week. When Elizabeth's father came to the beach on weekends, she didn't see me. But I worked weekends on the boat anyway, so that wasn't a problem.

Elizabeth's mother didn't stop us from meeting. I think she liked me. But she didn't tell her husband about us, either. I guess she knew he wouldn't like it, and from what Elizabeth told me, her mom avoided conflict with her husband at all costs. Probably figured what he didn't know wouldn't hurt him.

One night a couple weeks later, after Elizabeth and I had been to Cricket's dancing, we decided to go to Long Beach and park. The moon was full, we had drunk a few beers, and we were tired of the loud music, cigarette smoke, and noise in the bar. We wanted to be alone.

She parked the car and we talked for a while. Then I said, "Let's go swimming."

"I didn't bring my bathing suit," Elizabeth said.

"I didn't, either. Who needs one?"

Elizabeth didn't answer. The dash lit her face with a delicate light while the radio played "Killing Me Softly," by Roberta Flack. Finally, after a long pause, she said, "Okay." She found some towels in the trunk, and we climbed the dunes out to the beach.

It was like daylight, the moon was so bright. The ocean spread out before us as calm as a lake, glazed by the light of the moon, which danced on the surface of the waves. The beauty of the night was intoxicating.

Elizabeth spread the towels on the beach close to the water, then began to take her clothes off. She looked like a goddess. I couldn't take my eyes off her. Her firm, white breasts contrasted against her dark tan in the moonlight. Her waist was so small I could almost reach around it with my two hands. Her hips were not large but were round and sexy.

I took off my clothes with my back to Elizabeth, then turned to face her, with my hands cupped over my crotch. She smiled as her eyes lingered over my body. I felt very vulnerable. Goosebumps formed on my skin as the cool night air passed in little eddies over my body. Elizabeth took my hand and we ran splashing into the waves.

We laughed and giggled in the water. I dove underwater and came up behind Elizabeth to scare her. She didn't want to get her hair wet, but that was impossible. When she turned to look at me, I placed my hand behind her neck and kissed her. Her breasts pressed against me. A wave gently nudged us, making us lose our footing for a moment and almost fall over in the water. Finally, we walked back to the towels to dry off, sat down, and kissed.

I began to run my fingers lightly down her body and legs, kissing her neck and her breasts.

"Todd, I don't know if I'm ready for this."

"If you want me to stop, I will," I said, pulling away.

"Do you have any protection?" she asked.

"Yeah, in my wallet."

"Then I think you'd better get it," she said firmly.

I reached into my pants, took out my wallet, and pulled out the condom I always kept there—a habit I'd gotten into since high school. We kissed again and were soon all over each other.

After we made love we lay on the towels, looking up at the sky. I bent over and kissed her. Her hair was wet and stuck to her forehead in tendrils. I lay against her with my head on her chest and she ran her fingers through my hair. I felt this was the most beautiful moment in my life. I was in love with Elizabeth. She was the most beautiful woman I had ever known and we had just made love. It was perfect. I didn't want to move. The sound of the waves soothed and relaxed us with its quiet rhythm.

"I love you, Elizabeth."

"Will you still love me after what we did?" She had tears in her eyes.

"Of course I will." I stroked her hair, kissed her on the forehead, and lay back down beside her.

After a while we stood up and put on our clothes. I took her hand and we walked down the beach. Tiny spots of green light appeared under our feet where we stepped on the hard sand near the water. "What is that?" Elizabeth asked.

"Bioluminescence," I said. "Captain Jackson told me about it. It comes from tiny organisms that live in the sand. When you step on the sand, they glow. The light comes from within. When you're at sea in the winter you can see it in the water when the water is disturbed—it lights up like a glowing green ghost. It's neat," I said, as I walked toward the water, stomping the sand with my feet.

"You really love it here, don't you?" Elizabeth said.

"Yeah. For someone who grew up on a tobacco farm, they say I'm a natural. This is more home to me than Duplin County ever was."

"I love it here, too. There is something about it. When I'm upset, and I walk on the beach and listen to the ocean, it makes me forget. Do you know what I mean?"

"Yeah. The ocean is strange. It can be the most beautiful thing in the world, but then it can be dangerous and terrifying. It's as if it has a life of its own," I said, looking at the reflection of the moon making a path across the surface of the water.

We walked down the beach a little further, talking as we went, then walked to Elizabeth's car. Sitting in the back seat in each other's arms, we talked some more, then fell asleep.

When I woke up, the sun was barely on the horizon. The sky was a brilliant orange, yellow, and red. The marsh birds cried out and the crickets, cicadas, and insects sang to the new morning. Dew was on the windshield and the air was cool and damp. Elizabeth opened her eyes.

"My God, we fell asleep!" she said. "My mother is going to kill me. I've got to get home right now, before she wakes up, or I'll be in deep trouble."

"Go straight to your parent's house. It will take you too long to drive me into Southport. I'll hitch a ride."

"Are you sure?" she asked.

"Sure."

She drove quickly to her parent's house and parked underneath it. It was still early. She crept up the stairs to the deck in front. Opening the sliding glass door, she waved good-bye to me.

I walked to the highway to hitch a ride to Southport. There weren't many cars on the road that time of day, but I didn't mind. I enjoyed feeling the cool morning air and listening to all the sounds—the birds, the insects, and the distant sound of the ocean. I couldn't stop smiling as I remembered the night on the beach with Elizabeth.

Finally a car stopped. It was a red Mustang convertible driven by a guy in his early twenties who hadn't shaved and looked like he'd been up all night. He let me off a few blocks from the Jackson's house. When I got home, Martha Jackson was waiting for me at the back door.

"Out all night, Todd? What do you have to say for yourself?"

"Nothing, Martha. I'm tired and hungry, though. What's for breakfast?" I said, feeling like I was floating a few inches off the ground.

"I hope you enjoyed yourself, young man, because Captain Jackson has a busy weekend planned for you. Tomorrow he has lined up a charter from Greensboro. I think he needs you all day at the marina today." She let me in, the screen door slamming behind me. "Were you with Elizabeth last night?"

I hesitated, then nodded yes.

"She's mighty pretty. But I'm warning you, don't fall too hard for her. She's only here for the summer, then she's off to college."

"I know, Martha. I'm no dummy."

"Just reminding you. At your age, love is mighty foolish."

"Don't be such a mother hen. I know what I'm doing."

"I just don't want to see you get hurt, that's all," she said.

Six

WE TOOK TRIPS TO WILMINGTON, where we would shop and eat. We went to see the ruins of Brunswick Town, an old English settlement that was abandoned after the Spanish burned it in the early 1700s. One time on the way to Wilmington, we visited Orton Plantation, which was a few miles north of Southport. Another time, we took the ferry from Southport to Fort Fisher.

Fort Fisher was where one of the last great battles of the Civil War was fought. It stood at the end of an island, just north of Bald Head, across a narrow inlet. Huge earthworks guarded the old fort. Yankee cannon fire couldn't destroy them, but they were now being destroyed by the sea. On the southern and eastern sides, the ocean had eroded the fort pretty badly, but there was still plenty to see. There was a little museum, and the grounds were covered with huge oaks draped with Spanish moss. It was a perfect place to take a picnic lunch.

Even the ride to Fort Fisher on the ferry, was fun. Sea gulls flew overhead, following the boat, and sometimes landed on the wide ferry to beg for food. The ferry held about thirty cars, and the trip took about forty minutes.

The cars were parked on the deck below, and the passengers could get out and climb to the observation deck on the second level. It gave a good view of the Cape Fear River, Bald Head Island, and Sunny Point Army Terminal. Sunny Point was an ammunition supply depot for several military bases in North Carolina, including Fort Bragg and Camp Lejeune.

"This is beautiful," Elizabeth said, as we stood on the observation deck admiring the view of the river and the marshes.

"I know. I can never get enough of this scenery," I said. "I love this place so much. I don't ever want to live anywhere else. Don't you love it, Elizabeth?

"Yes, but I love Raleigh, too. There is so much to do in Raleigh. I imagine it gets pretty boring here in the winter. I love it here in the summer, but I don't know about all year round."

I looked at the water, glazed by the summer sun. I knew Elizabeth and I came from different backgrounds, but I didn't want to think about it. I was in love, and that was all I wanted to know. I looked at the marshes and the dunes on Bald Head Island. I wanted to run away with Elizabeth to some place where we could live alone and not worry about the outside world, her going back to school, her father, or anything else but our own happiness.

We were together as much as we could be. During the day we spent time together on the beach when I wasn't working. At night we went out together, except for the weekends her father came, or I was busy on Captain Jackson's boat.

ONE DAY AFTER LUNCH, we drove to the end of Long Beach and instead of going toward the ocean, we headed toward the dunes on the marsh side of the island. There weren't many people around and we brought a blanket to lay on. I knew a place under a thicket of trees in the middle of the dunes, where we would have complete privacy.

We walked across the sand to a secluded place between two dunes and spread our blanket out. We lay on the blankets and kissed. I sat up and took my shirt off. Elizabeth did the same and took off the top of her bathing suit. I kissed her.

We both pulled off our bathing suits and lay on the blanket, naked. Goosebumps covered her body. I reached into the pocket of my bathing suit to get a condom. She put her hand on my arm, signaling me to stop. We made love, but it worried me. She must know what she was doing, I thought.

When we finished I asked, "Aren't you afraid of getting pregnant?"

"No, it isn't that time of the month. I'm sure we're safe." We lay on the blanket, looking up at the clouds drifting overhead.

"You remember when you told me how your father used to beat your mother?" Elizabeth said.

I nodded.

"When my boyfriend, Tim, got mad, he used to hit me too."

"What?!"

"Yeah, he thought he was real macho," she said sarcastically.

"Is he the one you told me you were in love with once?"

"Yes, but I didn't know what love was then. It scares me to death to think that I could have married him."

"How could you?"

"Because I wanted to get out of my parent's house. I wanted to be on my own."

"But living with someone like that isn't the answer."

"I know." She put her hand on my chest, and laid her head on it. "Now that I have you, I don't have to worry about that."

SOON IT WAS AUGUST and time for the baby loggerhead turtles to hatch on Bald Head Island. I took Elizabeth out to the island at dusk so we could watch. We had gone before, without any luck, but this was the night when the turtles were supposed to hatch. The nesting areas were roped off, and a wildlife officer was there to keep the curious out of the way. There must have been fifty people there—older people, young people like Elizabeth and I, and children watching.

I noticed some movement in the sand in one of the nesting areas. The sand began to boil and bubble like hot pea soup on a stove. All of the sudden, hundreds of tiny turtles, the size of my little finger, started bubbling out of the crater in the sand. The moon was full over the water behind us, and the turtles instinctively headed toward the sea. They followed the bright light of the moon, and if someone held a lantern, they followed that too. The wildlife officer told everyone to turn off any bright lights. However, if the turtles got turned around and went the wrong way, we used the lights or flashlights to help point them toward the ocean.

After the first nest boiled over, the others began to do the same. The people cleared a path for each new boil of turtles as they made their way to the sea. It was exciting to see it and to think they have been doing this for millions of years, long before any humans walked the earth.

The beach was thick with the baby turtles, each a few inches long, waddling, as if they were swimming on the sand, toward the moon, which hung over the ocean. They made hundreds of little hatch marks in the sand as they lifted their flippers and pushed to move forward. As soon as they hit the water, they disappeared into the waves.

"I know some grown turtles are over one hundred years old," Elizabeth said. "I wonder how many of these will make it that far?"

"Most of them will be killed by birds, crabs, and fish, but a lot of them will survive."

After we finished watching the turtles, we walked back to my boat. As I was pulling up the anchor, Elizabeth said, "There's something I need to tell you."

"What is it?"

Elizabeth looked down at the sand. Tears began to form in her eyes. "I think I'm pregnant."

"What?!" I said, dropping the anchor.

"I missed my period. I'm afraid to go to the doctor," she said, crying. "I don't know what my father will do. I am afraid, Todd. I'm really afraid," she said, leaning on my shoulder.

I held her and looked at the full moon, now higher in the sky. Then I kissed her and said, "I love you, Elizabeth. No matter what happens, I want you to know that."

"I know you must hate me for being so stupid," she said with tears in her eyes.

"No, I don't," I said, stroking her hair.

"What am I going to do?"

"First of all, you need to go to a doctor to find out whether you really are pregnant. Then we'll decide what to do from there."

We rode back to Southport across the Cape Fear River in silence. Thoughts rushed through my mind like wildfire—Should she have an abortion? Should she have the baby? Was I ready for marriage? Could I support a family? What would her father do? He would probably kill me. How could we be so stupid? I needed time to sort my thoughts out. What did she want to do? I didn't know what to think.

ONE MORNING A FEW DAYS later I walked into Captain Jackson's kitchen after checking on my boat and found Martha and the captain at the breakfast table waiting for me.

"So she's pregnant," Captain Jackson said, glaring at me.

Martha had tears in her eyes. "What did I tell you about that girl? Now look what has happened!"

I didn't know what was going on. I hadn't seen Elizabeth since she told me, the night we went to see the turtles.

"How did you all find out?" I asked.

"Elizabeth's father just left here. He said if he sees you again, he will kill you," Captain Jackson said, visibly shaken. "He is madder than a hornet. He also said that under no circumstances will you be allowed to see his daughter again. He told us he sent her to Raleigh with her mother where she will get an abortion. He is selling his beach house and never coming back here."

"He can't run her life like that. She is eighteen years old. It's my baby too, and I love her."

"Todd, you are not my son, but I'm telling you. You'd better stay away from that girl and that family if you know what's best for you," Captain Jackson said sternly. "I know Edwin Gardner, and I know what he's capable of."

I walked back to my room without another word and lay on my bed. I loved Elizabeth. I couldn't imagine being without her. Surely she wouldn't let her father sepa-

rate us. She must have gone to the doctor and had it con-
firmed. Why didn't she tell me first? I didn't know what to
do. I wanted to go to Raleigh and find her. What if she
didn't want to have an abortion? What if she wanted to
get married? Her parents had no right to keep us apart.

Martha brought me some iced tea and soup. I couldn't
hide my feelings from her. I wept openly. She sat beside
my bed and stroked my forehead.

"Todd, I am so sorry. I know how you feel. I dated a
boy one time whose parents wanted to split us up—said I
wasn't good enough for him—and he let them do it. You're
going to have to let her go."

"But Martha, I love her and she loves me. If I could
just see her. I know she wants to see me. Maybe we can
keep the baby and get married."

"I don't think so, honey," Martha said.

"I have to see her."

"Honey, her father will have you arrested, or worse.
He'll kill you if you show up in Raleigh. You need to forget
about her, I'm telling you."

"I will never forget about Elizabeth, Martha." Then I
laid my head in her lap, crying.

She stroked my head gently.

THAT AFTERNOON I CALLED Elizabeth's house in Caswell Beach.
No one answered. Mitch picked me up and we drove to
the house. No one was there. I called her house in Raleigh. Her father picked up the phone.

"You son of a bitch, don't ever call here again! So help
me, you better be glad I'm not pressing charges against
you."

"But Mr. Gardner, I love Elizabeth. I want to marry her."

"Don't you ever call here again." He hung up.

The next time I called, the number had been discon-
nected and the new number was unlisted. I called Lucretia,
Elizabeth's friend. Lucretia told me Elizabeth would be
with her that night, and to call back then to talk to her. I
called that night. "Elizabeth, I love you. I want to marry
you. I don't want you to lose the baby."

"My father would kill me if I kept the baby. Todd, stay
away and don't call again until my father cools down. He's
crazy. I'm afraid of what he'll do. You've got to stay away."

"But it isn't right," I said. Then I asked her, "Do you
still love me?"

"I don't know what I feel anymore, Todd, I am so confused. All I know is that I can't see you. You've got to stay
away."

"What about the baby?" I asked. "Our baby?"

"I've already had the abortion, Todd."

My heart sank. I had never thought much about being a father before this, but now I was actually excited about
it and was looking forward to it. I felt sick.

"You don't want to see me anymore, Elizabeth?"

"No, Todd. Not now, not anytime soon. You've got to
stay away."

"I thought we loved each other."

"I don't know anymore."

"What do you mean you don't know. What about all
the times we spent together this summer? Our hopes, our
dreams?"

"That was this summer, Todd."

"I see. I guess there's nothing else to say, is there?"

"No, not for now, Todd. Take care. Maybe some day
we'll see each other again. I don't know." She started to
cry and handed the phone to Lucretia.

"I'd better hang up now, Todd," Lucretia said.

When I tried to call again, Lucretia talked to me for a while, but Elizabeth wouldn't talk again. When I wrote, Elizabeth didn't write back.

Mitch and I drove to Raleigh. We found Elizabeth's house and I rang the front door bell. Her mother answered. When she saw who it was, she tried to slam the door in my face, but I put my foot in the door.

"Young man, get your foot out of the doorway before I call the police and have you arrested. You are just lucky Mr. Gardner isn't home, because he would have his shotgun pointed at you, and he is just mad enough to use it."

"Mrs. Gardner, I want to see Elizabeth."

"She doesn't want to see to you. Do you understand? She is trying to get on with her life and put you and what you did to her behind her. My advice to you is to stay away." Then she kicked my foot out of the way and slammed the door shut. In a few minutes a police car drove up, and the policeman asked Mitch and me to leave the property.

"Let's get out of here before Mr. Gardner comes. I'm afraid of what he might do," Mitch said.

We went to St. Mary's College but found out that Elizabeth wasn't enrolled there. She had gone to another school, out of state, but no one would tell me where. Not even Lucretia. I tried to write, but my letters were returned unopened. She completely disappeared from my life.

Mitch tried to get me to go out to the bars with him and date other women, but I refused. I took my boat out to Baldhead, to the place Elizabeth and I had watched the turtles hatch. I walked down to the ocean. It was late in the afternoon. I sat on the sand near the edge of the water, put my head in my hands, and cried. Just as I was learning to love someone for the first time in my life, I lost her.

How could she have been so much in love with me and still reject me so completely? I knew she must still love me. I knew what we had was real. So how could she have turned her back on me? Maybe she didn't love me. Maybe what we had wasn't real. How could I have been so wrong about her? I was completely confused.

I walked to the cape. It was getting darker, and I knew that I would have to return to my boat soon. The sea churned darkly, whitecapping as it fanned out over the shoals. I didn't know what I was going to do, but I did know that it would be a long time before I would ever be able to love again.

SEVEN

For two years I worked hard and kept to myself. Other than the Jacksons, the only person I saw was Mitch. After Elizabeth, I didn't care whether I ever went out with another girl again. Mitch tried to get me to go to the bars and stop thinking about Elizabeth. I wasn't ready for another relationship. If anything, I wanted to kill the part of me that had ever let love in. I was hurt, and I wanted to be hurt.

In the spring of 1978, I decided to go out with Mitch to the Golden Slipper, a beer joint in Holden Beach with pool tables and a jukebox. It was there that Mitch and I met Mark Hamilton. Mark had access to marijuana. We saw him almost every night we were there and soon became friends. I had smoked marijuana a few times when I was in high school, when my Uncle Warren came home from Vietnam, but I didn't particularly like it. Now I wanted to try it again.

One Wednesday night Mitch and I were at the Golden Slipper drinking beer and playing pool, when we saw Mark go outside with Hank Nichols, one of Mark's friends. Mitch and I followed them outside.

"Want some?" Mark asked me, as he lit a joint behind the cinder-block building. Mark had dark brown hair pulled back in a ponytail, and brown eyes. Women found him attractive. A year older than me, he had a round face, broad shoulders, and big arms. But he always had circles under his eyes and looked like he didn't take care of himself.

"Sure," I said, taking the joint.

"It's good stuff," Mark said. "If you like it, there's more where this came from."

I sucked in the smoke and held it in, letting it stay in my lungs as long as I could before blowing it out again. Then Mitch tried it. Soon we were both high. We giggled a lot at silly things.

"Let's go swimming, Mark suggested. "I know someone who has a pool. Come on."

The four of us got into Hank's red, Mazda RX-7 sports car and drove to a house on the inland waterway with a swimming pool. "Jane Whortley lives here, but no one is home. She said I could come here anytime I wanted to," Mark said.

The moon lit the deck around the pool with a pale light. The pool filter made a low hum, and the sound of crickets and cicadas surrounded us. The house was dark.

"I'll turn on the Jacuzzi," Mark said, disappearing behind a row of bushes that hid the equipment room.

"Wow, this is some house," I said. "Jane's folks must be rich." It was a big, new, two-story house with modern glass windows and cedar siding.

"Her dad is big in real estate. He has a ton of money. I make sure she gets all the dope she wants," Mark said, smiling.

Soon the water made a loud roar and bubbled up from a corner of the pool where the Jacuzzi was located. Mark took off his clothes and stepped in, sitting on an underwater ledge. "Come on in, the water's great."

The rest of us took off our clothes and piled into the Jacuzzi where the water was warmer than the rest of the pool.

"This is the life isn't it." Mark said, spreading his arms out across the ledge of the pool and looking up at the sky.

"It would be better if we had some girls with us," Mitch said.

"Yeah," Hank agreed.

Hank and Mark shared a trailer together. Hank was tall and lanky, with stringy, black hair. I felt someone pinch my rear end. I looked around at Mark, who laughed and said, "Buddy check." Then Mark did it to Hank, and Hank reciprocated. They laughed and jumped into the main pool, splashing each other. Hank got a big plastic ball and threw it at Mark.

Mark climbed onto Hank's shoulders. "Let's play chicken," he said. Mitch and I jumped into the main pool. Mitch climbed onto my shoulders and struggled with Mark, trying to throw him down, while Hank and I tried to remain standing while supporting the others on our shoulders. Mitch got the best of Mark and pushed him into the water. Then Mitch and I fell. We all laughed and splashed each other.

"Let's smoke another joint," Mark said, stepping out of the pool. He knew where the Whortleys kept some towels in a cabana. Mark walked in and grabbed a handful of towels.

We all climbed out of the pool, dried off, and sat on lounge chairs with towels wrapped around us. Mark lit a joint, passed it around, then another, and another. Soon we were very high.

"Let's go back to the bar and find some women to bring back here," Hank said.

"Jane doesn't like me to bring other women here," Mark said.

"How's she going to find out?" Hank asked.

"She'll find out. You know how word gets around."

"You've got a point," Hank said. So we smoked another joint, watched the moon, made small talk until after midnight, then left.

MARK RENTED A SINGLE-WIDE mobile home. It was at the end of a dirt road, deep in a pine forest, about a mile from the inland waterway near Holden Beach. Hank rented a room from him. Mark worked at a wholesale seafood-packing house. His dope connection was with the fishermen who went to Florida and brought dope back to North Carolina. He supported himself mainly by selling marijuana. He had no family in the area. Hank was an automobile mechanic. Since their trailer was remote, they had loud, raucous parties that lasted late into the night.

I was drawn to Mark and Hank. Their wildness and spur-of-the-moment craziness was what I thought I needed to forget about Elizabeth. We started to hang out together a lot. We usually met at Mark's place after work, when we started drinking, and then went out to the bars and stayed up until two or three o'clock in the morning, getting drunker and higher as the night went on. Mitch went out with us at first, but he didn't like all the drugs, liquor, and wildness. Mitch started going out with a girl he had known from high school, Theresa Gulledge.

Martha and Captain Jackson told me they were worried about me. I stayed up later and later at night and sometimes didn't come home until the next morning. I wasn't as careful with my work anymore and was drinking a lot and smoking dope, though the Jacksons didn't know about the dope. They could tell I was drinking. I wasn't their son, so they didn't lecture me, but when it affected my work, Captain Jackson didn't hesitate to tell me.

"Todd, you'd better straighten up. I know you are your own man and twenty years old, but you are still living under my roof and working for me. If you don't shape up and do your job, you're out, do you understand?"

"Yes, sir," I answered. This was said one morning when I came in about 10 A.M. after partying all night at Mark's.

ONE NIGHT, MID-WEEK in June, Mark, Hank, and I were at the Golden Slipper. Mark flirted a lot and liked to dance. I was a little more shy. He picked up a girl named Andrea from Shallotte. She was short, with long, black hair, and had a great body. She wore cutoff blue jeans and a red halter top. Mark and Andrea danced and talked, then walked to the bar where I stood talking to Hank and his girlfriend, Lisa White.

"You want to come to my place?" Mark asked Andrea. "I've got some great dope back at the trailer."

"Sure," she said, pulling her hair out of her face.

Hank and Lisa stayed at the Golden Slipper. Mark and I took Andrea to his place. Sitting in the living room of the mobile home, listening to Jimi Hendrix, we smoked pot and drank shooters of vodka and peppermint schnapps.

"Want to have a little fun?" Mark asked Andrea.

"Sure, what you got in mind?" she asked.

He took Andrea's hand and led her into his bedroom. "Come on, Todd," he called to me. I walked to his room and stood in the doorway.

Andrea giggled as she sat on the edge of the bed and took off her halter top and cutoffs. She wasn't wearing any underwear. Mark took off his clothes as I stood in the doorway. They sat on the bed, which was piled with a jumble of sheets and covers. The floor was littered with dirty clothes.

"Three's a crowd," I said, turning to walk back to the living room.

"Three's company," Mark said, as he winked at me and motioned for me to join them. I walked into the living room and turned up the stereo. I could hear them making love in the bedroom over the sound of the music.

After a while Mark walked into the living room, naked. "Let's go swimming," he said.

Andrea stood in the doorway holding a sheet around her.

I looked at the two of them and asked, "Where?"

"Holden Beach."

"It's late and we've been drinking", I said. By this point, I was actually sobering up a bit.

"Andrea and I will take my motorcycle and you follow us in the pickup, okay?"

Andrea giggled. "Sounds like fun." She said.

Mark walked back into the bedroom and came out holding a jean jacket and a black leather jacket. He put on the leather jacket and gave the jean jacket to Andrea. He then took her hand and walked outside, gave her a helmet and put on one himself. They rode off on his Yamaha dirt bike. They were naked except for the jackets and helmets.

I followed them in Mark's black Toyota pickup truck. It was past midnight. The roads were deserted, and the

few cars that passed didn't notice anything unusual, because the two wore helmets and jackets. If they had looked
closer, they would have been surprised. Mark didn't ask
me to bring towels or clothes for them, but I brought them
anyway. It was a bright night, for the moon was almost
full, and there were only a few clouds in the sky. I also
brought a bottle of schnapps, and a bag of Mark's marijuana.

I parked at the deserted end of Holden Beach, away
from the cottages. Mark rode his motorcycle up on one of
the dunes, then down again, and parked it.

He took off his leather jacket and helmet and ran onto
the beach naked, leaving Andrea and me behind. Andrea
looked a little embarrassed, standing beside me wearing
nothing but a jean jacket. We walked over the dune and
saw Mark swimming and splashing in the waves, which
formed wide, silvery bands as they rolled into shore. It was
low tide, and the beach shined like polished leather as it
reflected the moonlight.

"Come on in, you guys! It's great!" Mark waved from
the water. I took off my clothes and ran into the water.
Andrea stayed behind, sitting on a towel. Mark ran out of
the water and tried to pull her off the towel and into the
ocean.

"No, I don't like the water at night. I'm afraid of
sharks. It scares me," she said, holding her knees tightly.

"Okay, let's smoke a joint then." Mark dried off with a
towel, sat down, and pulled a joint out of a pouch. He lit it
and passed it to Andrea. I walked out of the water, dried
off, pulled on my jeans, and took a drag off the joint. I sat
beside Mark, who was still naked on the towel, and took a
swig of schnapps. Andrea held a towel around her.

"This is really living, ain't it," Mark said.

"Yeah," I said, taking another swig from the bottle of schnapps.

"I don't know about you guys, but I have to get to work in the morning," Andrea said. "This has been fun, but I need to get back to my car, before it gets any later."

Mark jumped up and ran down the beach, disappearing behind the dunes. Andrea and I didn't know where he went. I put on my shirt and we walked to the dunes near the car, and Mark jumped out from the top of a dune. Andrea screamed.

"Scared you, didn't I?" he said. Then he opened the door to the pickup. "Get in, Andrea. I'll take you to your car."

"What about the motorcycle?" I asked.

"You take it. I'll take Andrea back to the Golden Slipper in the pickup."

"Okay," I said, taking Mark's helmet from the sand where he had thrown it. They put on the dry clothes I brought, and I rode the bike back to Mark's house, waiting for him to come back. An hour passed and Mark didn't show up. I went inside, took my clothes off and fell asleep on the sofa with a sheet over me.

When I woke up the next morning, Mark stood over me smiling. "Andrea was great, wasn't she?"

"Did you spend the night with her?" I asked.

"I followed her home and we made love all night long. She couldn't get enough."

Mark walked into his bedroom and collapsed on the bed. I knew he wouldn't wake up until after noon, so I borrowed Mark's bike to go home to Southport.

The next week I rode with Mark in his pickup to the Golden Slipper. Hank wasn't with us.

"That was a blast with Andrea wasn't it?" Mark said, looking at me. I wish you could have joined in. It would have been that much better.

I didn't say anything.

"You know Jane Whortley, the girl who owns the swimming pool? I made love to her in front of her boyfriend one time. First he watched, then he joined in. It was wild." Mark looked out the windshield at the street lights passing by. "You know Lisa, Hank's girlfriend?"

"Yeah," I said, looking at Mark's face lit by the bluish light of the street lights.

"I made love to her, too." He looked at me for a reaction. "Hank was gone, and Lisa came over one night looking for him. I asked her to stay and smoke a joint with me. Well, one thing led to another and before long we were in bed." He laughed. "All the women want me," he bragged, with a big grin on his face.

I liked the excitement and thrill of being with Mark. I never knew what he would do next. That was fun. But I didn't like his cockiness and bragging. I didn't want to hear all the gory details of his escapades, either, especially with his best friend's girlfriend. There was something very dangerous about Mark.

Late one night, after a party at the mobile home, everyone had left but Mark and me. Hank was spending the night with Lisa. Mark and I stayed up, drinking peppermint schnapps and vodka. We got very drunk, and our conversation was not very coherent.

We talked for a while, sitting on the sofa in the living room. Then Mark turned to me and put his hand on my thigh.

"Todd, you're my good buddy," he said. Beer cans and cigarette butts littered the floor and every flat surface in the room. James Brown played "I Feel Good" on the stereo. "You're about as crazy as I am, and that's pretty damn crazy."

I didn't say anything. He passed the peppermint schnapps to me, and we both drank straight from the bottle. Mark moved his hand up my thigh, then suddenly grabbed my crotch.

"What are you doing?" I asked, pushing his hand away.

"I just thought you were game for a little fun," he said, grinning.

"Not that kind of fun." I said, standing up. I took the keys of his motorcycle from the kitchen counter and left, driving home to the Jacksons house.

WHEN I WALKED INTO the kitchen that morning, both Martha and Captain Jackson were sitting at the breakfast table.

"Where were you last night?" Martha asked me.

"At Mark's."

"Were you doing drugs?"

"That's none of your business."

"Like hell it isn't." Captain Jackson said, sternly.

"You're not my parents. I don't have to report my every move to you. I'm twenty years old," I said, defensively.

"I don't care how old you are. As long as you are living under my roof, you play by my rules. Didn't I tell you that when you first came to live here?" Martha said, sternly.

"Yes ma'am," I said, looking down at the tablecloth.

"Martha found a marijuana cigarette in your pants pocket when she was doing the wash," Captain Jackson said. "I knew that Hamilton boy was a bad influence. From what I hear, he sells dope all up and down the beach." Captain Jackson looked me straight in the eye. "Todd, I haven't decided what I'm going to do with you yet. We can't allow dope in this house, and I can't have a doper working for me. I'm mad as hell, and I don't even want to look at you right now. Get out of my sight."

Martha began to cry.

I walked back to my bedroom. Then I remembered that Captain Jackson kept a .38 in a table beside his bed. I quietly slipped into the captain's bedroom and got the pistol and some bullets and walked out the back door.

The Jacksons were like parents to me, despite what I said to them. I couldn't imagine working for anyone but Captain Jackson. I rode Mark's motorcycle to my boat, the *Elizabeth*. I took the pistol with me.

I raced across the river in my boat, to Bald Head Island. Tears streamed down my face. I have really screwed up, I thought. All I knew was that I needed to go to the island to get my thoughts together. Maybe I'd use the gun, maybe not.

I couldn't understand what happened that night with Mark. When I was with him, there was always something exciting going on. I really enjoyed being with him, but sex? Was it somehow my fault? Had I led him on? It was like with Brady Hauss. Was there something wrong with me that attracted this sort of thing, just like Daddy had said? I thought Mark was such a ladies man, bragging all the time about his conquests. He really went after women, much more than I did, and they liked him. I didn't know what to think. One moment Mark was my friend, then this. I must be really screwed up, I thought.

I thought about Elizabeth and the pain of losing her, the abortion, not knowing where she was. The Jacksons finding the marijuana. Now they wanted me out. I would lose my job. I didn't know where to turn or what to do.

At the end of the creek, I pulled up the boat and walked out to the beach. There weren't many people on the island. I loaded the gun and shoved it down my pants. Tears streamed down my face—I couldn't stop crying. I walked to the edge of the ocean, took my shoes off, and walked toward the cape. The breeze from the ocean was cool and refreshing, and the sound of the waves was soothing. I looked at the ocean—it sparkled with sunlight. I loved the beach and the ocean. My mind was in a confusion. I decided to stop thinking and listen to the sounds of the ocean, the birds, and the breeze.

The image of Elizabeth arose in my mind. I still loved her. I thought about the baby we would have had. I stopped and sat cross-legged on the sand. No one was around. I pulled the gun out of my pants and pointed it at my temple. The steel felt cool and refreshing against my skin. I looked out over the ocean again, then lowered the gun slowly and laid it in the sand in front of me.

"Todd, don't."

The voice came from behind me. I turned and saw Captain Jackson and Martha running across the sand toward me. Soon Captain Jackson had the gun in his hand and unloaded it. Martha threw her arms around me.

"Nothing is worth this, Todd," Captain Jackson said.

I stood up. Captain Jackson put his arms around me and squeezed me hard. He was crying. "Come home, boy. Don't worry, we aren't going to put you out."

Martha put her arms around me. Tears streamed down my cheeks. I felt as though I was melting in Martha' arms. I needed them. I didn't realize just how much they meant to me until that moment.

"When I found my pistol was gone, I looked and saw you had taken the skiff and figured you headed out here. I sure am glad we found you," the captain said.

"I love you both," I said to them.

"And we love you, Todd," Martha said.

We walked slowly over the dune to Captain Jackson's skiff. I rode with the captain. Martha followed in my boat. Once on shore I took Mark's motorcycle back to his trailer. Captain Jackson followed me. Mark wasn't home. I rode with Captain Jackson back to our house.

THE NEXT WEEK I WAS at the marina working on some lures for Captain Jackson and cleaning up the boat. Mark rode up on his motorcycle and stopped.

"Where have you been, Todd? I haven't seen you at the Golden Slipper?" he asked, after he parked his motorcycle and walked out onto the pier.

"I've been around," I said, not looking up.

"Want to ride out to my place and smoke some dope? Two good-looking girls are going to meet me there in half an hour."

"No thanks, Mark. I've got work to do. We're going out on a fishing trip tomorrow. Captain Jackson wants everything to be spic and span," I said, looking at him. Mark looked worse than the last time I'd seen him—he looked pudgier, wore dark glasses, and hadn't shaved in a few days.

"Just thought I'd ask," Mark said, walking away. "See you later, maybe."

"Yeah, later, maybe."

EIGHT

I WORKED HARD FOR THE NEXT two years to save enough money
to buy a car. I continued to live with the Jacksons and
didn't go out much at night any more. Mitch and I went
out occasionally, but Mitch was dating Theresa Gulledge,
and I felt like a third wheel. It had been hard for me to
date anyone after Elizabeth. I couldn't get her out of my
mind. I was afraid to get close to a woman, because I was
afraid of getting hurt again. During that time all I wanted
to do was work and save money.

In the spring of 1980 I bought a black 1976 Chevrolet
Malibu with a red vinyl interior. I was really proud of it.
Mitch and Theresa broke up, so he and I began to hang
out with each other again. I heard Mark Hamilton had
gotten married, gained weight, and moved to Morehead
City, where he was selling cars for a Porsche dealer. I only
saw Mark once or twice after the time on the dock. I didn't
care if I ever saw him again.

A new discotheque, Tramps, opened in North Myrtle
Beach, across the state line in South Carolina. It was a
forty-five minute drive to North Myrtle from Southport. I

asked Mitch if he wanted to check it out. Mitch didn't like to dance, but I told him there were lots of women there looking for a good time. It had been four years since I dated Elizabeth. Maybe it was time to start to looking again, and what better place than "Tramps."

The disco was in a strip shopping center, in what had been an old A & P grocery store on Highway 17. Inside, the walls were covered with chrome and brushed aluminum. Potted palm trees were placed around the entrances and the tables. The dance floor was at the center of the club, bathed in moving lights and pulsating music. Tramps had a dress code and sometimes there was a long line to get in. But Mitch and I got to know the bouncer at the front door, a college student from Charlotte named Branson, who was living at the beach for the summer. Branson let us in without having to stand in line. He was a big guy, a weight lifter, and a college football player. Not someone you would want to get into a fight with. But he was friendly to Mitch and me. He invited us to parties and told us about the women he knew at the bar—which ones had boyfriends and which ones didn't; which ones were worth talking to and which ones weren't.

Mitch and I picked up girls, went to parties, and generally had a great time that summer. Often we didn't get home until late at night. Captain Jackson and Martha didn't mind, because they knew I was with Mitch and they trusted him, and they wanted me to go out and have fun. I was twenty-two years old, I wasn't doing drugs, and I was more careful with alcohol than I had been before. It was okay with them.

THE THIRD WEEK IN JUNE, a large college crowd gathered at the beach. Tramps was packed with people and filled with cigarette smoke. A perky little girl with short, brown hair and horn-rimmed glasses, walked up to me and asked me to dance.

Usually I asked the girls to dance, not the other way around. She was a little homely and she talked like a farm girl, but she had a great body and she looked like fun so I said yes.

She was a good dancer and I enjoyed being with her. Unlike most of the girls, who tried hard to look bored on the dance floor, she actually smiled and seemed to enjoy herself. When we slow-danced, we held each other real close and kissed a long, sexy kiss. After dancing, she asked me to join her at a table with some of her friends. Her girlfriends were good-looking and went to the same college that she went to, Winthrop, in Rock Hill, South Carolina.

"What's your name?" I asked.

"Cynthia."

When I told her my name, we got into a conversation.

"Todd, has anyone ever told you how good-looking you are?" Cynthia said, sipping a wine cooler.

"No.

"You are so good-looking it makes me tingle inside just to look at you," she said, with her eyes sparkling.

This kind of plain talk from a country girl like Cynthia took me by surprise. But it also turned me on. I liked it. I hadn't been talked to this way since high school. She had been drinking, but she wasn't drunk. She told me she had just broken up with her boyfriend—they had been engaged to be married—but she was glad to get rid of him.

"He's a son of a bitch. A farmer. He thinks women were made for having babies and cleaning house. That's all. Is that what you think, Todd?"

"No," I said, holding my hands up and smiling. I didn't want to walk into that trap.

"What do you think of women?"

"Well, I would like to have children some day, but not now, mind you. I guess when I love somebody I want them to be my best friend, too."

"I like that answer," she said. "Would you get me a drink, please?"

I walked to the bar and ordered a beer for myself and a wine cooler for Cynthia. Branson was working the bar.

"Branson, do you know that girl?" I asked, pointing to Cynthia.

"I've seen her in here before with this big guy—looks like a linebacker."

"Must be her fiancee. She told me she broke up with him."

"That's good," Branson said. "Because he looked like the kind of guy who would just as soon kill you as look at you." He paused, then looked up at me. "I saw you two dancing. Have a good time, but be careful."

"I will," I said.

Branson shook his head, smiled, then handed me a Budweiser and a wine cooler. I walked back to the table. Cynthia's friends were dancing so this left us alone.

"I'm staying at an apartment in Myrtle Beach. Would you like to come home with me tonight, Todd?"

"Sure. Let me find Mitch and tell him where we're going." I found Mitch, gave him the keys to my car, and followed Cynthia to her car. In her car, she leaned over and kissed me, then she put her hand on my crotch.

"What's that, a gun in your pocket, or are you just happy to see me?" she said, in her best Mae West voice.

I smiled and continued to kiss her.

She drove me to a one-story brick apartment building a few blocks away from Ocean Boulevard. The apartment was in a grove of pine trees. There was no grass. Sand and pine needles covered the ground. Inside, the walls of the apartment were paneled with knotty pine, which had aged to a dark blonde color.

She offered me a Budweiser and took a wine cooler for herself from the refrigerator.

"I'm from Clio, a few miles east of here. My daddy is a farmer," she said.

I told her that I'd grown up on a farm, but now I worked on a charter fishing boat in Southport.

We sat on the sofa, and she edged closer to me, saying, "Shit, Todd, let's forget the preliminaries and get down to business. I want to go to bed with you right now."

I thought she was aggressive at Tramps, but nothing prepared me for this. She stood up, took my hand, and marched me into her bedroom. Turning off the lights, she slipped out of her dress, and started to take off her bra and panties.

"What's the matter, you afraid of me? Go ahead and take your clothes off," she said as I stood in the doorway watching her. She did have a good body.

When I started to take my clothes off, she jumped into the unmade double bed and covered herself with a sheet smiling as she stared at me.

"Just as gorgeous as I thought. I can usually tell what a man looks like naked even with his clothes on," she said, reaching for me as I slid under the covers.

She smothered me with kisses, running her fingernails over my chest, my shoulders, and my back. I kissed her neck and nibbled her ear lobes, lightly running my fingers over her body until goosebumps appeared. She shivered all over. We were really just beginning to enjoy ourselves when we heard a knock at the front door.

"Oh, shit! Quick, get into the closet!" she said, jumping out of bed and pulling her clothes on. She yanked me out of bed, pushed me into the closet, threw my clothes at me, and shut the closet door.

"You have someone in here, don't you," a husky voice said after Cynthia opened the front door.

I quickly pulled my clothes on and crept out of the closet to peek into the living room. The guy in the living room stood about six-five and looked like he weighed 250 pounds. He was very muscular and had an enormous chest and neck.

"Where is the son of a bitch? I'll kill him," he said.

"There isn't anyone here, Eddie. I swear," Cynthia said, pushing him down onto the sofa with one hand. "Have a seat. Listen, Eddie, I told you I don't want to see you again. Do you understand?"

"But Cynthia, I love you." Eddie began to cry, holding his head in his hands. "Please, I'll do anything. I can't stand the thought of losing you."

"You can start by leaving me alone and letting me live my own life."

"But I can't."

She asked him what he did that day, to calm him down. He said he worked for his daddy all day, and the cucumbers were too ripe so he had to plow them under with the disk harrow.

I could see ripe green cucumbers being sliced to pieces by sharp metal disks. It made me hurt to think about it. I thought I'd better get out of there before Eddie decided to search the house. Cynthia was fun, but not that much fun. I had just met her and I figured she had known Eddie for years. I couldn't blame Eddie for being upset. All I knew was that I needed to get out of there before something serious happened. A back door led outside through the kitchen so I slipped into the dark kitchen, quietly opened the door, and left. As I walked down the road, I saw that Eddie was still there.

I walked to a pay phone and called Mitch at Tramps. Branson answered. Mitch was still there but was getting ready to leave. Just in time. Mitch picked me up on the highway, a few blocks from Cynthia's apartment.

ONE WEEKNIGHT, LATE in July, Mitch and I were at Tramps and saw a few guys handing out engraved invitations to a party at the "Alexander Cottage," 1010 Ocean Boulevard, North Myrtle Beach. The guys were college students. They handed the cards out to good-looking girls and to some guys they knew. They gave one to Branson, and he asked Mitch and me to come along with him. Things were slow at Tramps, and Branson said the Alexanders had good parties, so we decided to go.

The Alexander Cottage was a beautiful, cypress-paneled beach house in the Tilghman section of North Myrtle Beach, on the oceanfront. On that stretch of beach, most of the houses are real expensive. The house had a cathedral ceiling, with an exposed brick fireplace that rose from the floor to the ceiling. I overheard one of the Alexander boys tell a guest that all the paneling in the house was made of single boards—there were no two boards joined together. Each board had been hand rubbed with a driftwood-colored stain and custom-made for the house. Original paintings decorated the walls, and fancy bamboo furniture was mixed with English antiques. There was a recessed screened porch in front and a wide, cypress deck that led to a walkway over the dunes. It ended at a wooden gazebo that overlooked the ocean.

All the houses in the section sat a few hundred feet from the dune line. The dunes were undisturbed because the houses were built on stilts. This one was built on concrete pilings, anchored deep in the ground.

I had never been in such a beautiful house at the beach. I overheard one of the Alexanders tell a girl about going to a party at the Dunes Club in Myrtle Beach put on by one of the Belk family, where a real carnival carousel was set up to entertain the guests in the back yard.

The Alexander boys were about the same age as Mitch and I. Both went to college in North Carolina. Their parents were in Europe. Branson knew them from Charlotte, where they lived.

"Make yourselves at home. There is plenty of beer in the kitchen and liquor on the bar. Branson, who are your friends?" Frank Alexander asked.

"Todd Field and Mitch Etheridge, from Southport," Branson said.

"Branson's my buddy," Frank said, putting his arm around Branson's shoulder. "He always lets me in when there is a line at Tramps. Any friend of Branson's is a friend of mine."

Frank's younger brother, J. P., was in a fraternity at East Carolina, and most of the guys at the party were J. P.'s fraternity brothers. Frank didn't belong to a fraternity. He was in the architecture school at N.C. State.

"Do you know any girls who went to St. Mary's?" I asked.

"When you're in the school of design, you don't have time to see anyone other than the girls in your classes at State," Frank answered politely.

"I used to date a girl who went to St. Mary's," I said.

"Really?" Frank looked a little surprised.

"Yeah, her name is Elizabeth Gardner, Edwin Gardner's daughter."

"I've heard about Edwin Gardner. Isn't he a political bigwig in Raleigh."

"That's what they say." I hesitated, then added, "He's a son of a bitch."

"I wasn't going to say that, but that's what I'd heard. He does a lot a work for the Congressional Club." Frank said.

"That's right," I answered.

Frank then introduced us to some of the others at the party. Mitch introduced himself to a good-looking blonde on the front porch. She wore a tight tank top and cutoff blue jeans that were so tight and cut so high they didn't leave much to the imagination. She smiled and talked to Mitch. Then a big-chested, muscular guy walked up, holding two drinks.

"Is this guy bothering you?" the big guy asked.

"No, Ralph, we were just talking," she said. "This is Mitch Etheridge from Southport. Mitch, this is Ralph Eckles from High Point."

"I don't give a damn where you're from. Bug off, buddy," Ralph said, in an angry voice.

"Cool it, buddy, I was just talking," Mitch said.

I stepped up to see what was going on. A few guys began to gather behind Ralph.

"Who invited you here anyway? This is a private party, invitation only," Ralph said.

"We were invited," Mitch said.

I took Mitch's arm and said, "Let's get out of here. I don't want to get into a fight."

"Yeah, get going, buddy," Ralph said, pulling his fist back like he was going to hit Mitch. Ralph was very drunk.

Mitch and I walked through the large group of young people in the living room, dancing to beach music on the stereo. Frank saw us at the back door.

"You all aren't staying?"

"No, some of your buddies don't like us rednecks crashing their party," Mitch said.

"It's my party and I want you to stay."

"Thanks, but we better leave before there's some trouble," I said.

"Okay," Frank said, looking perplexed.

"Tell Branson we went back to Tramps. And thank you, Frank. It was nice meeting you," I said.

"Nice to meet you, too," Frank said.

WE WENT BACK TO TRAMPS, where we drank some more and danced. After midnight we headed back to Southport on Highway 17. Mitch, usually the calmer of the two of us, was acting pretty silly and kept trying to fool around by grabbing the steering wheel. I put up with it for a while because he was rarely this drunk, and I figured he'd put up with enough of my antics. But I finally had to yell at him to knock it off. From there, we drove on in silence.

Shortly after that we came to a road block. Several highway patrol cars sat in the road with their lights flashing. Nearby was an ambulance. As we came closer, we saw a car turned upside down beside the road.

"Todd," Mitch said, looking very agitated. "I know that car."

Given Mitch's state, I was skeptical. But when we stopped and got out, I could see it was Branson's car. Mitch and I rushed to the back of the ambulance just as the doors were being shut. We could see Branson strapped on a stretcher. There was white tape over his forehead to hold his head steady, and he appeared to be unconscious.

"What happened?" I asked one of the ambulance attendants. "He's a friend of ours." Mitch was standing next to me. He suddenly seemed very sober.

"He was driving alone," the ambulance attendant said, as he shut the door. "He must have fallen asleep and run off the road. Not sure if he was drinking or not. Listen, you guys better move. We've got to get him to the hospital."

THE NEXT DAY, we found out Branson had massive head injuries and was in a coma. The doctors didn't know if he would ever come out of it, so they sent him to Durham to a better hospital. Later I heard from one of the guys at Tramps that Branson's condition hadn't changed, so his parents moved him to a hospital in Charlotte, on the other side of the state. It was closer to where they lived. We never saw him again.

NINE

THE END OF AUGUST 1982, on my twenty-fifth birthday,
Mitch asked me if I wanted to go shrimping with him and
his father in Florida. I had never been shrimping except
with Mitch, and then only in the marsh creeks. I had never
been to Florida, but had heard about the beautiful water
and the great fishing. I asked Captain Jackson if I could go.

"Who is going to stay here and help me?" Captain Jackson asked, not too happy about it.

"Let him go. He'll have a great time," Martha said.
"The boy's not your slave, you know."

"He's my best mate," Captain Jackson said angrily, turning to Martha.

"You can find someone else to help you this winter."

"Oh, all right. Go then, dammit. Only don't decide
you like shrimping better than deep-sea fishing and stay
with Captain Etheridge, you hear?"

"Yes, sir," I said, smiling.

I helped train a new boy, Victor Slade, to work with
Captain Jackson. I stayed in Southport until late October
when the boats left for Florida. At the end of October,

when it was beginning to get cooler and the sea was getting rougher, I joined Mitch, his father, and his father's crew, and traveled south along the inland waterway, to Florida. We followed several other shrimpers from Southport, Holden Beach, and Calabash going in a caravan down the waterway. Our destination was Key West.

I DRANK MY THIRD SHOT of Cuervo Gold, sucked the juice out of a fresh lemon, and licked salt from between my thumb and index finger. I was with Mitch at Harry's Bar. Harry's was just off Duval Street in Key West, in a pink stuccoed building. Ceiling fans purred overhead, keeping the heat moving as it rose from all the people in the crowded establishment.

I leaned against the antique mahogany bar, rested my foot on the brass rail, and looked at the stained-glass bar back, which was framed with large, beveled mirrors. The place was so packed that Mitch and I could hardly move. A band played loud rock music in one corner. The lead guitarist was a guy in his twenties with blonde hair that hung to his waist. He wore blue jeans and no shirt. As he took the microphone to announce another song, I reflected on things over another a shot of tequila.

This was the first time I had been in the Gulf of Mexico, and it was my first time in Key West. Mitch and I had worked all day on the boat, getting ready to go shrimping. That night we decided to go into town for some fun. I loved the tropical weather in Key West. I liked the bars, the people, and the good-looking women there too. I couldn't believe so many beautiful women could be in one place at one time.

Turning, I noticed a very attractive young woman standing close to me. I started talking to her and found out her name was Jennifer. As we talked, I noticed Mitch signaling me that he was going to look around for a girl for himself. I called over to him and said I would meet him on the boat later that night, or in the morning, if we got separated. Then I went back to my conversation with Jennifer.

She told me she was a waitress at a seafood restaurant. She was in her late twenties, and lived with a friend. As she talked, I noticed she wore khaki pants, a loose, white blouse, and no bra. Her light brown hair was short and bouncy, as were her large breasts, which I could easily see through her thin blouse. She had a sexy smile.

"Would you like to dance?" I asked her.

"Sure."

We danced, then walked back to the bar, and I bought her a gin and tonic.

"Want to dance?" A husky young man with curly black hair and a thick mustache was standing beside us at the bar. He was talking to Jennifer.

"No thanks," she said.

The guy grabbed her arm and tried to pull her toward the dance floor.

"She said she didn't want to dance," I said, standing between him and Jennifer. The guy looked like a weight lifter—big and muscular—and sported a few days' growth of beard. He was very drunk.

"Says who?" the guy said, pushing me.

"I said so."

"Well, who are you?" the guy said, pulling his fist back, ready to punch me.

The bar was crowded and there was barely enough room to swing a fist without hitting someone else. The guy was very slow. I threw a quick punch to his stomach, and he doubled over in pain.

"Let's get out of here," I said, taking Jennifer's hand as the guy groaned.

"Suits me. I'm ready for some fresh air," she said.

WE MADE OUR WAY through the crowd to the street. A warm breeze blew from the south, rustling the palm branches in a yard across the street. We walked down Duval Street for several blocks. The streets were filled with tourists, locals, and people from the boats in the harbor and the marina. I saw two men kissing. One had a black beard and wore a short, black, leather skirt, black net stockings, and high-heeled shoes. The other man wore a leather vest, a black cap, tight jeans, and no shirt. He had a tattoo of a rose on his chest.

"Did you see those two guys?" I asked Jennifer.

"Listen, this is Key West. Anything goes here. The attitude is, if you don't bother me I won't bother you."

"Sounds good to me," I shrugged.

"Would you like to go to my place?" Jennifer asked with an alluring smile.

"Sure," I said, putting my arm around her waist.

We walked down a side street, past several Victorian houses with gingerbread front porches, and green shutters that had top hinges that allowed them to swing out from the bottom. Lush growth of tropical plants and palms crowded the small front yards, filling the air with a sweet fragrance. It seemed like spring to me, not November. We stopped at a two-story, white Victorian house and walked up the side stairs to a shuttered porch that overlooked a tropical garden in back. The lights were on in the apartment.

"Damn, my roommate," Jennifer said, looking around at the messy apartment. "It helps having a roommate when it comes to paying rent, but as far as turning out lights and cleaning up, forget it," Jennifer said.

"Would you like something to drink?" she asked, walking to the kitchen counter which opened to the living room. She opened a cabinet and pulled out a bottle of Cuervo and a bottle of Dewars Gin.

"Do you have any lemon and salt?" I asked.

"Sure," she said, opening the refrigerator and pulling out a dish of lemon slices.

We took our drinks to the porch and sat on a white bamboo sofa. A fan purred overhead, and light shone through the window that opened to the living room. The sound of crickets, tree frogs, and tropical birds filled the air. I thought I could hear the sound of the surf in the distance, but I wasn't sure. She put on a Billie Holiday record. The night was beautiful—the moon lit the cloudless sky, and there was a nice breeze blowing from the southeast.

"So this is your first time in Key West?" Jennifer asked, stretching out on the sofa. "Do you like it?" She motioned for me to sit beside her. She started to kissed my neck and rub my chest.

"I like it a lot," I said, turning to kiss her.

Soon she was moving her hands all over me, unbuttoning my shirt, and running her fingers across my chest and back. The sweet smell of the flowers and the sounds of the night mixed with the drink and conversation to create an intoxicating brew.

She took my hand and led me into her bedroom. I felt like I was floating on air as we walked into the moonlit room. I couldn't keep my hands off of her, and she couldn't stop touching me. We made love on top of the sheets. A ceiling fan hummed overhead, evaporating the sweat from our bodies.

I sat up fast when I heard the front door open. "Who is that?"

"It's just Jerry, my roommate."

"Does he mind if you have a guy here?"

"No, he's used to it. We're just friends, nothing more."

Jerry stayed in the living room and turned on the television. We made love again, then I fell asleep, or rather, passed out from the tequila. When I woke the next morning, Jennifer was asleep beside me. Her hand rested on my thigh, and her head was tucked under my arm. I moved her hand and quietly slipped out of bed. I walked past Jerry, who was sleeping on the sofa in the living room, and left a note on the table telling her I had to go and hoped to see her again.

After I left her apartment, I walked past the Victorian cottages and the lush tropical greenery of the side streets, into the harsh sunlight of the harbor. I had a terrible hangover. It was 7:30 A.M. and I knew Captain Etheridge would be looking for me. I was supposed to be on the boat by eight o'clock. We had a lot of work to do, preparing for our shrimping trip.

"Where have you been, young man?" Captain Etheridge asked me sternly at 8:15 when I came running up. He was standing on the dock beside his shrimp boat, the *Laura Ann.*

"I'm sorry I'm late, sir. I promise it won't happen again," I said, not able to keep back a smile as memories of the night still lingered.

"You're forgiven. Get to work. We have a lot to do to get ready for tomorrow."

Captain Etheridge was fifty-three, tanned, trim and fit, about six feet tall, with wavy black hair, and an infectious smile. He loved people and life on the sea. He had known me since I first met Mitch in Southport. He wasn't too mad. As long as I worked hard and did what I was told, Captain Etheridge was pretty tolerant.

THAT NIGHT CAPTAIN ETHERIDGE decided to take the crew out to eat at a seafood restaurant near the harbor. He knew we were all in for a hard week of shrimping in the Gulf, with little sleep and backbreaking work. Most of us ordered fish, two of us ordered steaks, but no one ordered shrimp. We'd had our fill of shrimp from working with them all day. We didn't feel like we had to support the industry— there were plenty of tourists to do that. Shrimp was always popular. Demand wasn't a problem; if anything reliability of the source and competition with other shrimpers were the problems.

Eight of us sat at a long table covered with a red-and-white-checked oilcloth. The restaurant was a fisherman's place—nothing fancy, just good eating. The walls were covered with photographs of fish caught by sportsmen, a variety of mounted fish—sailfish, marlin, cobia, dolphin, barracuda—fish nets, and glass and cork floats. The walls were built of rough cut lumber, and there were exposed beams overhead. The place smelled of fried seafood, beer, and sawdust. The seafood was served on platters heaped with French fries. Green sawdust covered the floor—easy to sweep, clean, and disinfect.

"Mitch told me you picked up a good-looking girl last night, Todd," Captain Etheridge said, as he picked at his grilled swordfish with a fork.

"Yeah, I met her at Harry's Bar. Mitch left when I started to talk to her. He tried to pick up somebody, but didn't have any luck, so he left." I paused. "I woke up this morning at her place," I said, bragging a little.

"Someday you'll grow up, Todd," the captain said with a laugh.

"What do you mean?"

"I mean, someday you'll be ready to settle down."

I thought about Elizabeth. I had tried to settle down once and look what happened. It still hurt to think about her.

"Do you still think about that girl from Raleigh, Todd?" Captain Etheridge had this look on his face like he could read me like a book. I guess maybe he could—Mitch and I were best friends, and I was like another son to the captain.

"Yes."

"You were really in love with her, weren't you?"

I looked down and picked at the pile of French fries on my plate covering the flounder. "Yes, sir."

"There'll be someone else. Mark my word. When the time is right, you'll know."

"I hope so," I said, still looking down.

"It will happen." He paused, then added, "That is, if you don't screw yourself up in the meantime." Then he laughed.

After we ate, Captain Etheridge asked Mitch and me if we wanted to go into town for a little while. This was only the second time Mitch had gone with his father on a shrimping trip to the Gulf and of course it was my first trip. The other men went back to the boat—they had seen the town and wanted to get some sleep.

Captain Etheridge took us to Sloppy Joe's, where we had margaritas. Then we walked past the house where Ernest Hemingway had lived. The house was one of the largest on the island, surrounded by a beautiful tropical garden. It was built of stucco, with corners that looked like stone blocks, and had a two-story, wrought-iron porch across the front and sides. The captain told us a little about Hemingway, and what a great fisherman and writer he was. Mitch didn't know much about him, but I remembered reading the *Nick Adams Stories* in high school and liking them. However, as interesting as all this was, I just wanted to go back to Harry's Bar.

THE SAME ROCK BAND was playing in the corner of Harry's. Smoke hung everywhere and the place was packed with people of all ages. Some were dancing while others just stood around, and the only way to get from one end of the bar to the other was to follow someone else.

I walked to the bar to get drinks. Mitch managed to find an unoccupied table, right beside the speakers, in front of the band. He and his dad sat down.

I saw Jennifer standing at one end of the bar, talking to a guy who handed her a drink. She didn't see me. I watched as she laughed and flirted with him. She put her hand on his neck and kissed him. I also noticed for the first time that Jerry stood nearby, watching Jennifer and the young man. Jennifer didn't look at Jerry and he never went up to her. I wondered if Jerry had been there when I met Jennifer. Then I noticed Jennifer wink at Jerry when the guy Jennifer was talking to, turned his head. Did Jerry follow us to the apartment? Did he watch us make love? What did Jennifer and Jerry do when I passed out? It sent shivers down my spine. I made my way back through the crowd to Mitch and Captain Etheridge.

"Let's go," I said, yelling over the noise of the band.

"We just got here," Mitch said, enjoying the music.

"This place is too loud. I can't hear myself think, much less carry on a conversation." I said.

Captain Etheridge nodded in agreement.

On the way back to the boat we stopped at a coffeehouse. A gentle breeze blew over the tables lining the sidewalk where we sat. We heard music coming from the bars nearby, which mingled with the sound of conversation, birds, crickets, and cicadas.

"Isn't Key West great?" Captain Etheridge said, looking around.

"Yeah, it's like another world," I said. "Everything is so laid back. No one is in a hurry, and the weather—I hear it's like this year round. I could get used to living here."

"Me, too," said Mitch. "The women are great, too."

"You can say that again," I agreed. Then I remembered Jennifer picking up the young man . . . while Jerry watched.

THE NEXT DAY, SUNDAY morning, we all got up early to prepare the nets, clean the boat, work on the motor, and get ready for a week at sea. We would leave at dusk. Since Captain Etheridge was superstitious about shrimping on the Sabbath, we would wait until midnight to put out the nets.

It didn't matter. In the Gulf we shrimped at night anyway. We would shrimp until four in the morning, then put the anchor out and sleep while someone stood watch. We usually prepared for the catch in the afternoon, then put the nets out as soon as night fell.

As we sailed out of the harbor, I stood at the back of the boat watching the sun turn the water a pale rose as it set in the western sky. The water was calm, looking like wavy glass. Rippled waves of heat rose on the horizon, creating slender ribbons of pink and silver where the sun met the water. The sun was big and red as it sank into the ocean.

Captain Etheridge's comments about finding a woman and settling down, kept running through my head. I had picked up plenty of girls in bars, but I knew that wasn't the answer. Sighing, I headed off to get ready for the night's work. In a week, we'd be back to unload our catch.

TEN

FOR TWO DAYS WE SHRIMPED in the Gulf of Mexico, trawling at night, and repairing nets and cleaning up by day. As soon as the would sun disappear, we'd put out a test net to find a good bed of shrimp. If the depth finder indicated a smooth bottom, a necessity so the nets wouldn't snag, we'd lower them into the water. Captain Etheridge checked often to see if the depth finder showed rough spots that indicated a wreck or a rocky place. We would shrimp until four or five in the morning, depending on how well things were going, then we'd set anchor and sleep for a few hours.

That evening, the sky was cobalt blue, except at the horizon where the sun colored the bottoms of the clouds with fiery streaks of red and pink. Slowly, the light disappeared. The sea was calm and the air was warm, smelling of salt mist and fish from the boat. The moon would appear later. The water moved slowly, like ink sloshing in a bottle. Glazed by the lights of the boat, it glowed.

The lights were strung everywhere on the wooden shrimp boat so the crew could see the catch when the nets came in. The boat looked like a Christmas tree. Toward the middle of the boat were two booms towering overhead. There was one on each side of the boat, and they were used to haul in the nets when we finished trawling. The two main nets they held were huge—each was sixty feet wide and a hundred feet long. At the opening of each net was a wooden "door," which kept the mouth of the net open as it dragged the bottom. The bottoms of the nets were threaded with pieces of plastic and cloth that made them look like hula skirts. That kept them from chafing on the bottom.

After we pulled in the test net that evening and found the shrimping to be good, we let out the big nets and trawled for two hours before hauling them in. Each boom swung around to the center of the boat, unloading a mass of squirming, flailing sea life onto the deck. The deck teemed with big Gulf shrimp that jumped and snapped, trying to escape to the sea before we could catch them. The nets also brought up seaweed, sponge, tropical fish, crabs, and coral.

We kept the fish we wanted, concentrating on the slippery shrimp. The rest we threw back into the water. Though it was hard to do, we caught the shrimp with our hands and put them in buckets. These were dumped into the large iced compartment in the hold. A large cork-filled hatch covered the opening.

I looked up from my work for a moment. Everyone was working hard. If the catch was good, all the men benefited. It was a tradition that went back two hundred years. We were not paid a salary but were paid in shares of the catch. After the catch was sold at the market and the overhead paid, the money was divided among the men. So it was in everyone's best interest to get as much shrimp into the hold as possible.

The second time we pulled in the net, a sea turtle was tangled in it and we had to cut it out. One of the men repaired the net after we removed the dead turtle. Turtles drown when they get tangled in the nets and are dragged through the water. They need air to survive.

Behind us, seagulls and porpoises could be seen. They followed the boat, picking up the fish that we threw back into the water. As long as the porpoises were there, there would be no sharks. Porpoises are smarter and stronger than sharks and keep them away.

We had a good catch that night so we worked very late, taking shifts. I wore a red bandanna around my head to hold my hair back and keep the sweat out of my eyes.

Shrimping was much better here in the Gulf, than in North Carolina, I thought. The shrimp were bigger and there were more of them. The big Gulf shrimp were discovered in the 1950s, almost by accident, near an oil rig in the Gulf of Mexico at night. During the day they are inactive and burrow under the mud on the bottom, but at night they are active and can be caught by the nets.

During a break I noticed the moon over the water. Its reflection created a silvery path that ran across the sea from the horizon to the boat. I imagined myself walking across that path to the horizon, reaching up and touching the moon. The path was made of millions of tiny crescents of light dancing on the surface of the water like sparkling diamonds. It was beautiful. I knew my home would never be far from the sea.

I climbed into my bunk at five o'clock that morning, tired. We had worked hard and caught several hundred pounds of shrimp. Since he was the youngest, Mitch kept watch on the bridge. The older you were, the less likely you were to be called for watch duty. Mitch got it a lot. His father owned the boat and didn't want Mitch to have it easier than anyone else. Mitch was twenty-four years old, tall and skinny, but he was strong and worked as hard as the other men.

Captain Etheridge stayed up with Mitch for a while, talking, until the others went to bed. Then the captain went to his bunk. The sun would soon rise in the east. The captain had set anchor just outside of a major shipping lane. All the lights were left burning to warn ships of our location.

I dreamed about Key West, and Jennifer. I dreamed about Elizabeth, making love in the dunes at Holden Beach, her father not letting her see me, the letters I wrote that she never answered. I dreamed about taking the skiff from Southport to Bald Head Island. The sound of the engines of the skiff became louder and louder, drowning out all thoughts, all dreams. Then I woke up. The sound of engines was very real and very close. I ran to the deck and saw a huge black freighter bearing down on our starboard side. It towered over us.

"Mitch!" I yelled up to the bridge. I could see Mitch had fallen asleep. He awoke just in time to see the prow of the freighter cut into the deck of our boat. I was knocked into the water by the power of the impact. The turbulence caused by the huge propellers of the freighter passing overhead, dragged me down and tumbled me head over heels through the water. I struggled to swim away toward the surface, away from the turbulence. I looked down and saw the lights of the shrimp boat sinking below me, looking like a broken Christmas tree suspended in the water. Then the lights went out.

I thought about Mitch, Captain Etheridge, and the other men, as I struggled to free myself from the terrible suction of the water under the freighter. I wasn't sure how to get to the surface as I'd lost my sense of balance and direction. It seemed like I was underwater for hours, though it must have been only seconds.

I thought I heard a familiar voice. It was the voice of my Uncle Warren, who had been killed in Vietnam so many years ago. Then I saw what looked like a hand reaching out to me from above. I swam toward it until I saw the shimmering silver glow of the surface. The hand disappeared.

I swam as hard as I could until I broke the surface. I gulped the air, sucking it deep inside of me, happy to be alive. I looked around trying to find signs of life. It was very dark. Did anyone have a chance? All the men must be dead. They were sleeping when the freighter hit.
The freighter continued on its way, without stopping or slowing down. I heard a moan come from the dark sea in front of me and swam toward it. The water was oily, covered with diesel fuel from the sunken boat.

"Who's there?" I called out. "It's me, Todd."

I heard a moan again, several yards away, and continued to swim toward it. It was Mitch. I found him holding onto a white, plastic cooler. He moaned and didn't speak at first. I felt a large bump on his forehead.

"Are you all right?" I asked, looking for any other hurt places. He didn't answer.

I put my hand under his chin to keep him from slipping under the water and held onto the cooler with my other hand. Mitch didn't sound coherent. I was afraid he had a concussion. Finally he opened his eyes.

"What happened?" Mitch asked. "What am I doing in the water? Were we knocked overboard? Where's the boat?"

"It sank. A freighter cut it in two. I can't find anybody else."

Mitch moaned and closed his eyes, putting one arm around my shoulder.

The sky began to lighten. I saw a few coolers and the big cork hatch that had covered the hold, floating nearby. I swam with Mitch toward the hatch, climbed onto it, pulled him up, and pulled several coolers out of the water. The hatch was big enough to hold both of us. I saw a few life preservers floating in the water. Swimming over to them, I put one on myself and slipped another around Mitch's neck. Mitch lay on the hatch with his eyes closed. I wore only the white boxer shorts I'd slept in that night. I had no shirt. Mitch wore a pair of khaki shorts and a white T-shirt.

I was thirsty, but I knew I couldn't drink the seawater. One of the coolers held some freshly gutted fish on ice. The ice was bloody and smelled of raw fish, but I put a piece of it in my mouth and sucked on it. It got hotter as the sun rose in the sky. A gentle breeze blew as the sea rose around us in swells. The sky was clear, but I thought I saw a cloud bank forming to the south.

When Mitch woke he did not talk much but complained about his head hurting.

"Don't talk. You need to keep your strength," I told him. "No telling when someone will find us."

It was getting hotter. We were lucky we had the coolers, I thought. I rubbed some ice on Mitch's forehead. Mitch went in and out of consciousness.

"That should make you feel better," I told him as I put a piece of ice in his mouth. Mitch smiled. I looked out over the ocean. The swells were higher than the night

before, but the ocean was calm. I thought about how well
the ocean hides its mysteries—How could anyone tell from
the peacefulness of the water that such violence had taken
place in that same spot the night before?

I thought about the men who were sleeping on the
boat, and Mitch's father. It was so awful, but there wasn't
anything I could do about them now. I couldn't dwell on
it. I had to think about Mitch and myself. Then I remembered being in the water under the freighter and hearing
Uncle Warren's voice and seeing his hand. Uncle Warren
was killed in Vietnam in November 1973, exactly nine years
ago. Did he save me? It would be like him to do that. It
was all so crazy. But I couldn't think about it. I had to
think about surviving and being rescued.

The sun shone directly above us at midday, relentlessly
hot. There was no avoiding it. I got in the water a few
times to cool off, but I was afraid of attracting sharks, and
I needed to hold onto Mitch. Then Mitch opened his eyes
and pulled himself up on his elbows. The sea was calm as
we rode the gentle swells. The clouds I had seen earlier
scattered. The thin clouds that floated far above us, did
not shield us from the sun. I took a piece of ice from the
chest and put it in my mouth. It tasted awful. I washed it
in the ocean and ate it.

"Do you think any of the others survived?" Mitch asked,
looking over the water.

"I don't know. They could have gotten separated from
us. The freighter cut the boat in two. Some could have
been swept to the other side out of sight."

Mitch cupped his hand and called out for several minutes. There was no response. I didn't think anyone else
survived, but I didn't want to discourage Mitch. Mitch felt

better and was alert now. I heard an airplane. I pulled off my shorts and waved them over me, but the plane passed without acknowledging us.

"We could be out here for days," Mitch said.

"I know."

We sat on the hatch for a while in silence, with the sun beating down on us. I was hungry but not hungry enough to eat the raw fish in the cooler. We talked about home to keep from thinking about our predicament.

"If we ever get back home, what will you do, Todd?" Mitch asked.

"I guess I'll go back to work for Captain Jackson, like I always have."

"I want to save some money and buy my own boat," Mitch said. "Except, I don't want to run a shrimp boat. I saw this tourist boat in Wilmington, a big double hulled boat that takes people out cruising at night. They serve dinner and everything. It's great. I would like to own a boat like that."

I thought for a while, then said, "Someday I'd like to be my own boss, too. Maybe I could own a charter fishing boat like Captain Jackson. But how could I afford it? It will be a long time before that happens." I smiled and shook my head.

"Do you think you'll ever have children?" Mitch asked.

"I don't know. After Elizabeth, I haven't thought much about children. I always thought one day I'd get married and have children. But I don't know."

"I want to have five children, all boys, like stair steps. I can't wait to play ball with them and take them out on a boat and teach them everything I know about the marshes, the beach, and fishing."

"If I have children, I want to be a better father than my father was. He never did anything with us. Mom was the only one who even noticed we were there."

"I want to be just like my father," Mitch said. "He's the greatest man I've ever known. Sure, he was gone a lot on fishing trips, but when he was home, he was always there for us." Then Mitch began to cry. He put his hands over his eyes. "I wonder if I'll ever see him again."

I put my arm around him and let him cry. I loved his dad, too. He really cared about Mitch and his men. I would never forget him. He and Captain Jackson showed me what a real father could be. I swore that if I was lucky enough to survive and have children of my own I would be there for them, like Captain Etheridge and Captain Jackson had been there for Mitch and I.

We floated in the water for several hours, until the sun started to go down. The sea was glazed on top like black jelly. The colors of the sunset were beautiful—orange, red, violet, then a deep sapphire blue. The sun hovered over the water until it disappeared into its own reflection, leaving the sky lit and the sea dark.

"I'm hungry," Mitch said, opening the ice chest. The ice had melted and the gutted fish floated in the bloody water. "If the Japanese can eat raw fish, I can too." He took a piece of raw meat, rinsed it in sea water, then took a bite. "Yuck," he said, wrinkling up his face. Then he took another bite. "Try it—it's better than nothing," he said, handing me a piece of raw fish.

I took a bite, spit it out, wiped my mouth, then tried another piece. I chewed it, not liking it, but it was moist and helped my hunger. The water in the cooler smelled bad and made me sick to drink, but I wet my lips with it.

As the night wore on, I found myself fighting sleep. Finally I closed my eyes and slipped into a deep sleep. I saw a beautiful, light-filled room. It was in a house with a bay window near the water. White lace curtains billowed out from the open windows. It was spring time. I was happier than I'd ever been in my life. I stretched my arms out and spun around. There were other people in the house— were they my wife and children? I couldn't see them, but I knew they were there. I felt the most profound peace and happiness I'd ever known.

"Todd," Mitch said, shaking me. "You fell asleep. We've got to stay awake, or we could roll off the hatch."

I looked around and realized I was back in the ocean. The dream was gone. "Let's take turns sleeping and watching each other, okay?" I suggested. "You sleep first, since I already got a nap. I'll wake you when I feel tired again."

"Okay." Mitch said. He then unhooked some straps from the life preservers, tied one end to his belt loop, and the other to a ring on the hatch. Mitch lay down and closed his eyes. I sat beside him with my arm around his waist, looking up at the sky. The sea was calm, but a storm could blow up any time. Mitch began to snore lightly. The image of my dream remained with me. I wondered if it was heaven, my future, or just another dream.

The wind began to rise and the waves rose with it. I held onto Mitch so he wouldn't roll off the hatch. Then Mitch woke. We sat up talking for a while, looking at the stars. In the distance I saw lights moving on the ocean.

"A ship" I said.

"There's no way they can see us in the dark and we don't have a flare."

We sat and watched, as the lights moved away from us, growing fainter and fainter.

At sunrise, I slept and Mitch stayed awake. When I woke, Mitch and I tried to eat another piece of fish. It tasted terrible, but at least it was moist and gave us some nourishment. I noticed a large fish stirring the water beside the hatch.

"Shark!" I cried out.

"Oh, shit!" Mitch said, pulling his feet up from the edge of the raft. A lone shark about eight feet long swam around us several times. It nudged the hatch, then disappeared under the water.

"I sure hope he doesn't come back with friends."

I was not very religious, but I prayed then. Silently I prayed that we would both be rescued and make it home safely. I thought about Captain Jackson and Martha. I thought about Elizabeth, and my whole life in recent years—the drifting without purpose, the drinking, the sex, the drugs, and the depression. I thought about Branson, and how that could have been me. I thought about how he'd love to have the opportunities I have, and how I was wasting them. I resolved to change. If only I could make it back home.

Another several hours passed. It was noon again. The sun burned me as I had no protection from it. Mitch's skin began to turn red, too. We chewed some more fish and rubbed the water on our lips and face. Then I saw an airplane. I took off my underwear and waved it over my head again. Mitch took off his shirt and waved it. The plane came back, then circled overhead.

An hour later we heard a boat. I looked up. It wasn't a Coast Guard cutter, it was a charter fishing boat. I waved my boxers again. When the boat came near us I put my shorts back on and waved with my hands. I saw two young men and a woman in bathing suits on the bow.

The captain put the engines in neutral after pulling up beside us. Then one of the young men, wearing a rainbow-colored bathing suit, reached out to us with a long aluminum pole with a gaff at the end of it. I grabbed the gaff and pulled the hatch to the boat. Mitch grabbed the hand of the other young man who was standing on the ladder at the back of the boat. After Mitch stepped onto the ladder, I climbed aboard.

"Here," the young woman said, handing me a beach towel to cover myself, for my boxers didn't hide much. We looked terrible, with salt crusted on our lips and hair and our faces and hands red and swollen from the sun. But we both smiled broad grins.

"Thank you," I said.

The young woman wore a white blouse over her black bikini and looked about twenty years old. She smiled and said, "You look pretty bad."

Homer Bates, the charter captain, was in his late forties and wore a red baseball cap on his balding head. He led us to the cabin below, gave us some water and sandwiches, a change of clothes, and let us shower. He then radioed the Coast Guard that he had picked up the two men who had been spotted in the water by the plane an hour earlier.

After we showered and changed clothes, Mitch and I told the captain and his guests what had happened when the freighter ran over the shrimp boat.

"I can't believe a boat passed right over you without stopping or radioing for help. They must have been on automatic pilot and no one noticed. It's incredible. You said you weren't in a major shipping lane?" Bates asked.

"No, we were just outside of it. Captain Etheridge, was a good skipper," I said. "He wouldn't put us in danger like that. He must have thought we were safe. Mitch is the captain's son."

"Has anybody else been found?" Mitch asked.

"Not that I know of," Captain Bates said. "But now that they know about it, the Coast Guard will comb the area pretty well. If there's anybody alive they'll find them."

Mitch began to cry. He knew there was probably no hope that his father was alive, but as long as he was on the raft, he didn't think about it—all he could think about was survival. He couldn't control himself. He was embarrassed. I put my arm around him.

"That's all right, son," Captain Bates said, putting his arm on Mitch's shoulder. "Why don't you all go back upside?" Captain Bates said to his other passengers. "These boys have been through a lot." The two young men and woman walked out on the deck.

Captain Bates told Mitch and me to climb into the V-berth in the bow of the boat to get some rest. We were exhausted. Captain Bates covered us with a blanket and left us alone.

I lay in the V-berth, unable to sleep at first. My thoughts went back to Duplin County. I hadn't thought about home in a long time. It wasn't easy. But I guess it was time.

ELEVEN

I CAN'T REMEMBER A DAY DADDY didn't drink. Mama tried to get him to go to church with the rest of the family, but he wouldn't.

Daddy owned 120 acres, 50 of which were in tobacco. It paid him well. He had a good allotment—the number of acres the government let him plant in tobacco. The land was rich, and his crop did well. His tobacco was in demand at the market in Clinton. He hired extra hands during the summer to help him pick the tobacco and set it up in the barn to cure. All his help was black. He had some full-time help, like Brady Hauss and his family. Brady practically ran the farm, especially when Daddy got to drinking bad.

Daddy inherited the land from his granddaddy. There used to be an old house on the property that Daddy grew up in, but he didn't like it. So he bought a new mobile home and pulled it up in front of the old house. After a while he got tired of looking at the old place and had it torn down. June Bug, Sally and I used to love to play in the old house with its big rooms, fireplaces, wide pine floors,

and heavy wooden doors. Someone told me later it was
built before the Civil War. I couldn't understand why
Daddy tore down the old house. I thought at the time
that he did it just because we liked to play in it so much. I
didn't like the mobile home with its loud air conditioner,
smelly shag carpet, cheap paneling, and low ceilings.

I'LL NEVER FORGET THE DAY Martin Luther King was shot.
Daddy and four of his buddies sat in the living room of
our mobile home in Duplin County, watching a rodeo on
television and drinking long-neck Budweisers, when an an-
nouncer interrupted the show. Daddy was thirty-eight then.
He was a large man with broad shoulders, big hands, and
hard eyes. The room was stuffy and filled with cigarette
smoke. I walked out of the bedroom where I was helping
Mama fold clothes when I heard Daddy and his friends
yell, "Yahoo!" I was ten years old.

"What is it, Henry?" Mama asked Daddy, stepping into
the hall.

Mama was thirty-two but she looked older. She held a
folded sheet in one hand. My sister Sally, who was eight,
held Mama's apron, hiding from Daddy. Sally had curly,
blonde hair that hung to her shoulders. June Bug, my
brother who was seven, played outside, hitting a tree with
a stick, yelling at it like the tree was a ferocious monster.

"Somebody shot Martin Luther King in a motel in
Memphis, Tennessee. They just announced it over the television," Daddy said, with a wide grin on his face.

"Who is Martin Luther King?" I asked Mama.

"He's a nigger preacher from Georgia," she replied.

I didn't understand why Daddy and his buddies were
so happy that a nigger preacher had been killed. I loved

to listen to the music coming from the Shady Grove Primitive Baptist Church down the road from our house. The church was a simple white frame building with a narrow, pointed steeple. The preacher was always friendly and asked me to join the service. I never did, because I knew my father would wear me out with a leather strap if I did. Daddy hated niggers. But I liked preacher Mason and his wife, who always dressed in a starched, white cotton dress. When I fished at the pond a half mile from our house, I often saw the preacher's son, Andrew Mason, and we talked about fishing. Andrew was coming to my school that year. Integration had closed the black school, and the blacks were coming to the white school now.

"Frances, get me another beer. This is interesting," Daddy said to Mama. He had been drinking since he got up that morning.

"Can't you see I'm folding clothes?"

"I said, get me a beer," Daddy said, his tone becoming harsh. This was for the benefit of his buddies. Daddy wanted his friends to think he was tough. "Women," Daddy said to Luther Holshouser, a fat, balding man wearing overalls and a white T-shirt, who was sitting in the recliner beside him.

"Did you hear me?" Daddy asked, his voice rising.

I walked to the refrigerator and pulled out a bottle of Budweiser for Daddy.

"I thought I told your mother to get that," Daddy said, taking the beer from me.

"She's busy," I said, looking down at the orange shag carpet.

"You're always looking out for your Mama. You got to learn that women are supposed to obey men, not get us to do their work," Daddy said, not taking his eyes off the black-and-white television screen.

"Yes, sir," I said, walking back to the bedroom to finish helping Mama fold clothes and put them in the bureaus in the bedrooms.

When I finished helping Mama, I got my fishing rod and walked down the road in front of our home, to the pond. As I passed the black Baptist church, I could hear crying, wailing, and moaning coming from inside. I also heard the preacher's voice rise in a sad, harsh tone that I had not heard him use before. I wondered if they were talking about Martin Luther King.

After I had been fishing for a while, I saw Andrew walk up on the opposite bank. "Hey, Andrew! What's up?" I asked, waving at him.

Andrew didn't reply. He glared at me and walked away, carrying his fishing rod. "I'm going somewhere else to fish," he said.

I couldn't understand. Andrew had never been that way to me before. We were friends.

That night the family sat around the television set as the news reports covered the riots and fires that spread through Washington, Newark, New York, Los Angeles, and other cities. I had never seen anything like it before.

"Damn niggers! Civil rights started all this and look what it's led to—rioting in the streets, cities burning. Is this what all them liberals and Jews in New York and Washington want? Well, they got it now," Daddy said to Mama.

She did not respond.

I went to bed that night with images of fire, riots, and people who were looting stores, burning buildings, and being shot at by the police, running through my head. It was what I imagined hell to look like.

THE DAY THE ASTRONAUTS LANDED on the moon, July 20, 1969, Sally, June Bug, and I watched television all day long.

"I think the whole thing is fake, filmed in some movie studio in Hollywood." Daddy said, sitting in his recliner, drinking a beer.

I didn't say a word. I watched the men in white space suits run, jump, and play like kids, on the moon. It was incredible. Unlike Daddy, I believed the men *were* on the moon. My whole body tingled with excitement.

"I read in a magazine at the supermarket that if they bring home so much as a rock from the moon it will put the whole universe out of balance, and set off earthquakes, volcanoes, and all kinds of disasters here on earth," Mama said, watching intently.

"We'll know when they come back, won't we?" Daddy said. "Damn waste of money, I say. I could think of a lot of things I'd rather see that money spent on."

"Let's go outside and see the astronauts on the moon," Sally said, as night fell.

We all went outside. Mama and Daddy stood in the doorway and watched. It was a clear night and the moon was bright. I looked up and squinted, trying to see something, anything, but I couldn't.

"I see em!" Sally said.

"You do not," June Bug said.

"Let her alone. Maybe she can see," I said.

"Ya'll get back in here. It's time for bed," Daddy called from the doorway.

"Yeah, come on in. You can't see anything from out there, even if there is somebody on the moon," Mama said.

When I went to bed I couldn't get the images of the astronauts out of my mind—grown men, laughing, jumping, and playing on the moon, just like kids. I hoped when I was a grown-up, I could have that much joy in what I did.

IT WAS SPRING TIME. I was fourteen, small for my age, and just beginning to mature physically. Early one morning as I walked in the woods near the house I saw Brady Hauss peeing on a tree. Brady turned around, still holding himself.

"You like this?" Brady asked, with a sarcastic grin. "You want to touch it?" It looked like a big brown uncut cigar. I turned and ran through the woods to the house. I didn't say a thing to my parents. Brady was a big, black, muscular man, three times my size.

A few days later I stood in the woods bending over a log, cutting off a branch to whittle. I thought I heard someone behind me. Then I felt a hand on my leg. I looked around quickly and saw Brady's face smiling a few inches from mine.

Brady slipped his hand around my thigh and grabbed me. "Come on, Todd. Let ole Brady see what you got," he said, in a high-pitched, mocking voice. Roughly he grabbed at my pants and tried to pull them down. He held me tight. It was hard to shake loose.

"No!" I cried out, finally pulling away from him. I was terrified and wanted to get as far away from him as I could. I ran down the road to the fishing pond, where I sat balled up on the muddy bank, looking out at the water.

I was afraid to tell my parents. I was afraid Daddy would go into a rage and shoot Brady or run him out of town. Then Brady would be after me. I could see Brady sneaking up at night, with a knife clenched between his teeth, and killing the whole family as we slept, but only after he

had slit my throat from ear to ear. I was scared to death of
Brady, but I had to tell my parents.

When it started to get dark I walked home and found
my parents sitting in the living room, watching television.

"Daddy, I need to tell you something."

"What is it?" Daddy said, looking at the television.

I told them what Brady did to me.

"What?!" Mama said with her mouth wide open.

"What did you do to make him do something like that?"
he asked.

"Nothing." I said.

"Listen here, Todd. You're fourteen years old and big
enough to defend yourself. Don't ask me to fight your
battles for you." Daddy's eyes never left the television
screen.

"Aren't you going to do anything about this?" Mama
asked, looking at Daddy.

"Brady is my best man. I can't replace him. Todd's
got to learn to defend himself. He's a big boy now. He's
got to learn he can't come running to Mama or Daddy
every time he gets into trouble."

I turned and walked out the front door. I kept walking
until I got to the fishing pond, where I sat in the grass
looking at the water. About that time Andrew walked up
and sat down beside me.

"What's wrong?"

"What's it to ya?" I said. I was mad.

"Just curious."

"You know what curious did to the cat?"

"Whoa, you are mad!"

"I sure am. I'm not in the mood to talk to no nigger
about it, either."

"I thought we were friends."

"We are."

"Well, what are you calling me a nigger for?"

I turned to Andrew and saw I was being unfair to him. It wasn't his fault what Brady Hauss did to me, and what Daddy did or didn't do afterwards. "I'm sorry. I didn't mean nothing. I just can't talk about it, okay?"

"Okay. I can respect that," Andrew said. "How about going for a swim?"

We both ran down the road to a place we liked to swim, under a highway bridge on the creek that fed the fishing pond. We took all our clothes off, except our underwear, then jumped off the steel truss bridge into the muddy water below. We laughed and splashed each other, then dove and swam. After a while we both stretched out on the bank of the creek on our backs, with our hands behind our heads, looking up at the sky.

"Does your daddy ever beat your mama?" I asked Andrew.

"No. Does yours?" Andrew asked.

"When he gets drunk, he does. He's mean."

Andrew didn't respond. Then he stood up and pulled on his clothes. "I gotta go. It's about supper time. My Mama is going to be looking for me pretty soon."

I didn't move. "I'm going to stay here a while longer," I said.

After Andrew left, I pulled my clothes on and slowly walked down the road. It was getting late and dark outside. I didn't want to go home, but I knew I had to. I didn't have anywhere else to go. I thought maybe Daddy was right, maybe I brought it on myself. Was I really a mama's boy like Daddy said? Was it my fault that Brady did what he did? Did I somehow lead him on? I was confused, hurt, and angry. I went to my parents for protection and they let me down. Finally, when there was no light left in the day, I turned around and walked home. It was about nine o'clock at night.

"Where the hell have you been?" Daddy barked at me when I came through the front door. He was drunk. I knew to avoid him when he'd been drinking. I tried to walk past him to my bedroom, but he caught my shirt.

"Don't walk by me and not answer when I ask you a question!" He yanked me around until I faced him.

I looked down at the floor and mumbled, "Yes, sir."

"Speak up! I can't hear you!"

Mama walked into the living room from the rear of the house, with a basketful of laundry to be folded. Sally stood in the doorway of her bedroom, wearing her pajamas and holding a teddy bear.

"I said, yes sir." I looked Daddy straight in the eye. The odor of alcohol on his breath was sickening. Then Daddy swung his big, strong arm and slapped me with all his strength, knocking me to the floor.

"That's for being late!" he said.

Mama dropped the clothes basket. "Stop it!" she said, standing between Daddy and me. Daddy then hit her across the face. The force of the blow threw her against the wall behind her.

She glared at him in silence, wiping the blood off her mouth. Then she bent down to help me off the floor. "Todd, go to your room."

"Protecting your sissy son? Isn't he man enough to protect himself?"

"Not against you, he's not."

Daddy struck her across the face again.

Sally began to cry as she stood beside her bedroom door. June Bug, who had been asleep, walked out of his bedroom, too. He wore a big T-shirt over his underwear and stared at Mama and Daddy and me in the living room, rubbing the sleep out of his eyes.

"Ya'll go to bed now," Mama said to us, wiping her face with a paper towel.

"What's the matter? You ashamed of your husband?" Daddy asked.

"Go on," Mama said, pushing me toward my bedroom.

"You're a mean old man," I said, turning to face him.

"You shut up and go to bed like your mama said, before I knock you so hard you'll wish you never heard my name before."

"I already wish that," I said.

"Hush," Mama said, holding her hand over my mouth. "He's drunk. There's no use fighting him now. It won't do any good. Go on to bed, all of you."

Sally was crying as she went into her room. June Bug watched silently. He and I went into our bedroom and locked the door. I could hear my parents arguing after I closed the door. I heard Daddy slap Mama again. Then I heard the front door slam and Daddy storm out of the house. I could hear Mama quietly sobbing in the living room. Daddy would be back in the morning. He had done this before. I took off my clothes and stretched out on top of the bed, looking up at the pattern in the ceiling tiles above me. Tears streamed down my face. I repeated over and over again in my mind, I hate Daddy, I hate Daddy, I hate Daddy.

A FEW MONTHS LATER, when the rest of the family was gone and I was alone in the mobile home, I walked into the living room and found Brady sitting in Mama's chair with his pants undone.

"Come here, Todd? You afraid of me, boy?" Brady said, with a big grin on his face.

I turned and ran out the door. I could hear Brady laughing. Surely Daddy would fire Brady this time, I thought.

"ALL RIGHT, I'LL SAY something to him and ask him to leave you alone," Daddy said, when I told him about the latest incident.

Mama was outraged. "Sitting in my chair in the living room, no less! Henry, you better do something about this. What about Sally and June Bug?"

"All right, all right I'll talk to him. You all don't know how hard it is to find a good farm hand these days. Brady's the best," he said. He looked at me with a hard look, like it really put him out to deal with it, and like it was my fault he was having to deal with it at all.

BRADY STAYED AWAY FROM me for a while after that. But he still worked for us and whenever he caught my eye, he'd smile at me with a mocking smile, and mumble to himself.

Andrew got on the track team at school and asked me to try out. I was a good runner and made the team. I started to work out with weights at the school gym. If no one else would stand up for me, I decided I would have to stand up for myself. I was small for my age and more underdeveloped than my friends. But I learned how to fight, and with running and lifting weights, I developed speed and coordination. No one at school messed with me, because I wouldn't back down from a fight, even if I was small.

On my fifteenth birthday, Andrew and me got an older boy to buy us a bottle of Boone's Farm apple wine. We sat behind Andrew's father's church that night, drinking the wine and talking.

"Andrew, have you ever gone all the way with a girl?"

"Lord, yes, haven't you?"

"No."

"Well, we'll have to do something about that," Andrew said.

"What's it like?"

"It's like being in heaven." Andrew smiled. "The first time I did it was with this girl that goes to my daddy's church. She's a couple years older than me. After church one day she asked me if I would show her around. We were in the choir loft and everybody had left. She said she was hot and did I mind if she took off her dress. When she started to take off her dress, I got hard. She saw it and smiled. Then she asked me if I had ever made love to a girl before. When I said no, she said she would teach me how."

"No shit!"

"We did it right there in the choir loft." Then he laughed. "I'll never forget that day. I used to think I was tough shit until that girl showed me a thing or two. I was a babe in the woods. She took me in her hands and taught me all she knew. Do you want me to ask if she'll line you up with one of her friends?"

"Me, date a nigger?"

"I wish you'd stop using that word. I'm damn tired of it. What in hell makes you think you're better than me? If I had a daddy like yours, I wouldn't be so proud."

I chuckled. "You got me there. You know I don't mean anything by it, but I won't say it again if it means that much to you. It's just that things are so screwed up—topsy-turvy. Whites and blacks being friends and then dating each other. It's strange, that's all."

"You don't think that hasn't been going on for a long time? Nothing new about that, boy. You just got your head in the sand. Just because people don't talk about it, don't mean they don't do it. Look at me," he said, pointing to his light skin. "You think I ain't got no white blood in me? Shit, who you fooling?" He took a swig of wine and passed it to me.

"You got a point there," I said, taking a drink.

TWELVE

I MET ANDREW BEHIND HIS FATHER'S church, one night late in June. The moon was just a sliver and the dark sky was filled with stars. The night air was crisp and cool, filled with the mournful sound of crickets and cicadas, which rose and fell in waves around us.

"Todd, I'd like to introduce you to Cassandra and Pamela." Two young black girls stepped out of the darkness, and smiled shyly. Andrew put his arm around Cassandra.

"How are you doing?" Pamela said, walking up to me.

Andrew told me that Pamela attended his church but lived in Bitter Lake, a community a few miles away. Cassandra lived near Andrew. Cassandra went to school with Andrew and me. Pamela didn't.

I sat close to Pamela on a bench behind the church. Andrew and Cassandra started to kiss, leaning against the white frame building. Pamela was light-skinned, like Andrew, and had a shy smile, and sparkling eyes.

"My mama gave me a quarter before I left," Pamela told me.

"You don't need any money.   Me and Andrew are going to treat tonight."

"She said I'd need it if you all leave me out in the country somewhere, and I have to call home for her to pick me up."

I laughed, thinking she was joking, but she was serious. "Did you tell her where you're going?" I asked.

"She knows Andrew.   I told her we'd be back before twelve."

"Do you think Andrew and I would leave you in the country with no way to get home?"

"I don't know."

"Well, we won't.   I promise."

"I'm not used to white men keeping their promises."

Pamela was very proud.   I was attracted to her.   She was also very pretty and had a deep, sexy voice.

We sat in silence for a moment, then she asked, "Well, what are you waiting for?"

"What do you mean?"

"Aren't you going to kiss me?"

I hesitated, then said, "Sure."   I wrapped my arm around her neck and kissed her.   She was delicious.   I didn't want to stop.

Andrew got my attention and motioned for me and Pamela to follow them to a dark blue Buick Electra, parked behind the church.   It was Andrew's father's car.   Pamela and I slid across the big back seat.   As Andrew drove out of the driveway, Pamela put her hand on my leg.   I was going to be sixteen in August.   Andrew had just turned seventeen.

"Do you like me?" Pamela asked in a soft voice so Andrew and Cassandra couldn't hear.

"Yes," I answered, as I felt her breasts squeeze against my chest.   I put my arm around her neck and kissed her.

Andrew drove to a narrow dirt road near our fishing pond. At the pond he stopped the car and turned off the lights but kept the radio on. It played "My Girl" by the Temptations.

Pamela was all over me. I had never gone out with a girl who was as aggressively sensual as she was. Girls usually waited for me to start the action, then acted like I moved too fast. Not Pamela, though. She moved first, kissing me, nibbling my ears, rubbing my back hard with her fingernails. She wasn't the least bit shy. My body felt like it was charged with electricity. I became so sensitive that all she had to do was touch me with a finger, or threaten to kiss me, and I winced with pleasure.

She unbuttoned my shirt and pulled down my pants. I undid her blouse and bra and slipped my hand inside her panties. When she kissed me, she didn't stop at my mouth. Her hard tongue moved over my face, my ears, my neck, my chest . . . I felt like I was a chocolate bar and she was eating me up.

She played me like a musical instrument. She was in complete control. After we made love we sat there, melted into each other's arms, covered in sweat.

Pamela pulled the quarter out of her pocket. "Am I going to have to use this?" she asked, smiling coyly.

"I don't think so," I said, feeling as if I were floating a few inches above the car seat. I thought I knew something about women before I met Pamela. I didn't know anything. I had no idea my body was capable of so much pleasure until I met her. It was incredible.

MY UNCLE WARREN CAME HOME from Vietnam on leave that summer, to visit Daddy and our family. Uncle Warren was twenty-seven, good-looking, with a crew cut, square jaw, broad shoulders, and muscles as hard as a rock. He always wore a smile. I loved him. He used to ride me on his shoulders in the yard of the old house when I was a little boy. I can still remember the smell of his sweat and the feel of his strong shoulders moving beneath me. Uncle Warren was more like an older brother than an uncle.

He grew up at the home place, but when Daddy got the farm because he was the oldest, Uncle Warren wandered off until the war took him. When he got leave, he came to our house—that was his home. He wasn't married and didn't have any children. When Uncle Warren visited it was one of the few times I saw Daddy smile. Everyone loved Uncle Warren.

One night, me, Daddy, Uncle Warren, and two of Daddy's friends—Luther Holshouser and Earl Dangerfield—sat on lawn chairs in the yard outside our mobile home, in front of a bonfire Daddy had built. At dusk, the sun sat big and red on the horizon as it sank slowly into the cool night air. Daddy and his friends passed around a bottle of peach brandy as Uncle Warren told us stories about Vietnam.

"One time our unit entered a village on the coast with a Catholic church in it - a lot of Vietnamese are Catholic," he explained. "The village was deserted. We searched every house and building, looking for gooks. I was standing outside the church with my rifle, while two guys went inside. They found a young woman in the church, hiding behind the altar. One of the guys tried to rape her but she slashed him with a knife. He screamed bloody murder and before I could do anything, he shot her in the face. Just kept shooting her, over and over. It was awful. I'm telling you, I seen a lot over there, but I ain't puked like I did when I seen that. Terrible place."

Everybody listened, spellbound.

"You can't sleep at night over there—you never rest," Uncle Warren continued. "You don't know who is your enemy and who is your friend. All you know is that you can't trust the slant eyes, no matter whose side they're on."

Uncle Warren reached into his shirt pocket and pulled out a hand-rolled cigarette. I'd never seen one that thin before. Uncle Warren lit it and passed it to Luther Holshouser, who sat beside him. I could smell the sweet odor of the smoke and knew it was not tobacco. After Luther took a drag from it, Uncle Warren handed it to Daddy.

Daddy looked at him and whispered something about "the boy," then took it and smoked it.

Later, Uncle Warren told me it was marijuana. He said all the guys in Vietnam smoked it. It was the only way they could get through the war.

All the men around the fire tried it and soon began to laugh at the silliest things. Luther handed the bottle of peach brandy to me. I took a drink. It warmed my throat as it went down. I saw Daddy watching me, but he didn't try to stop me.

A FEW DAYS LATER, I took Uncle Warren fishing with me at the pond and talked to him about my daddy, the family, and Vietnam.

"Uncle Warren, if you had a son and someone tried something with him, would you stand up for him and protect him?"

"I sure would. What's wrong? Has somebody tried to hurt you, Todd?"

"No," I said, insincerely. "I just wish you were my daddy, not him."

"Henry is a good man, Todd. He had it rough growing up. Our daddy used to get drunk and beat the hell out of us." He paused, then asked, "Does Henry beat you?"

"Sometimes, when he gets mad or drunk. He beats Mama when he gets drunk—a lot of times for no reason at all. But I know when to stay away from him," I said, not telling the whole truth. I hesitated, then said, "A couple years ago, Brady Hauss tried something with me."

"What do you mean?"

I told him what Brady did to me in the woods. "I told Daddy about it and all he could say was, 'you can protect yourself.' I was scared to death."

Uncle Warren looked at me with sad eyes and said, "When I was your age, we had a black man living on the farm with his wife and kids. He practically ran the farm, what with Daddy drinking and all. I'll never forget his name - James Hazeltine. He done me the same way," Uncle Warren said, then looked away. "I would have killed him if I could, but I was too little. It seemed like he was eight feet tall and weighed three hundred pounds. I told my daddy what happened, and he didn't believe me. I think he was more interested in what James could do for him than in what he did to me." Uncle Warren turned and looked at me. "I'm going to say something to Henry."

"No. It's too late. Brady hasn't tried anything in a long time. I'm bigger now. He knows I'd kill him if he tried anything again. But when he did it, I was too little to protect myself."

"I suspect James Hazeltine tried something with Henry too, but I don't know. Henry never told me, but he was just as afraid of James as I was."

"Uncle Warren, I wish you were my daddy."

"No, you don't. I'm just a wild buck, trying to have a good time. I'm not a family man." He grabbed me around the neck and rubbed his knuckles on the top of my head.

Then he stood up, grabbed my shirt, and threatened to push me in the pond.

"No! Don't, Uncle Warren!" I laughed, with my adolescent voice cracking.

"You promise you won't ask me to be your daddy anymore?"

"I promise, I promise. Just don't push me in the pond with my clothes on," I said, trying to wiggle loose.

Warren let go. "Is that better?" he asked.

"Yeah, that's a lot better."

Later, after not catching any fish, we both stripped down to our underwear and went swimming in the pond. Uncle Warren and I splashed and played around, trying to dunk each other. I swung from a vine that hung from the tree over us, and dropped into the water. Uncle Warren dove off the bank. I laughed and giggled. He chased me onto the bank, picked me up, and threw me in the water. Tired, we climbed out and lay in the grass beside the pond.

"One time when I was near Da Nang, deep in the jungle," Uncle Warren began, with his arms folded behind him as he looked up at the sky, "we discovered the ruins of an ancient city. There was this tall stone tower, covered with carvings of elephants, tigers, monkeys, and people all lined up to bring presents to a king who sat on a throne in a beautiful palace. The locals said their ancestors built the city hundreds of years ago. If you think about it, when our ancestors were living in thatched huts in Europe, their ancestors were building palaces and stone temples. They had writing and learning. Now they live off the land, mostly farmers. Before we came, there were the French, and before that, the Japanese. When we leave, it will just be them again. They know life will go on, no matter what happens today." Warren paused.

"I hope you don't have to go to Vietnam," Uncle Warren said, looking at me. "If the war is still going on when you're old enough to go, and they call you up, go the Canada, go anywhere, but don't go there. I've heard of guys breaking a hand with a hammer. Do whatever you have to do to stay out of that war. It doesn't make any sense, and it sure as hell isn't worth losing your life over."

"I thought you were proud to be a soldier?" I asked.

"I was proud. When I first went there, I volunteered. And I've gone back when I didn't have to. I wanted to make the army a career. But I'm not proud anymore. I've seen too much, like what that guy did in the church. Now I just want to stay alive long enough to make it back home for good. This is a politician's war. We have no business being there. Those people want to be left alone to live their lives, just like you and me."

We talked a little more about Vietnam, then I changed the subject.

"Have you ever been in love, Uncle Warren?"

"Yep. It was a long time ago. She was a preacher's daughter. I thought she was the prettiest thing I'd ever seen. She liked me too, but her daddy wouldn't let me see her. He told her I was trash, with my daddy's drinking and our family not going to church and all. After that I've been with the kind of women you wouldn't exactly want to settle down with." He laughed and threw back his head. "Maybe someday I'll find someone and settle down. Who knows. I might even become a daddy some day myself." He turned on his side and roughed up my hair. "But I'm not going to be your daddy!"

"When was the first time you screwed a girl?" I asked.

"Now this ain't something a boy is supposed to talk to his uncle about, is it? I'm supposed to talk about uplifting

things with you, not things like that." He laughed, lay back
in the grass and looked into the hazy blue sky. "Well, it
sure wasn't with the preacher's daughter."

"I did it with a black girl."

"You what?!"

"She's one of Andrew's friends."

"It wasn't this way when I was growing up. Before you
know it, we'll all be intermarrying and having brown babies." He paused, leaned on his elbow, and smiled. "I've
been with a black woman, too. Some of my best buddies
in Nam are black. I have more in common with them than
I do with the white guys from up north. Ain't nothing
wrong with seeing a black girl. Except don't tell your daddy.
He'd skin you alive."

"Don't worry about that," I said. "Andrew is my best
friend. He told me he is going to college and then on to
law school. I admire him. You think I could do something
like that? Shoot no! But he can, and he will if he wants to
bad enough."

"Todd, you can do whatever you put your mind to.
Don't ever forget that," he said, getting real serious. "You're
smart and you got a lot a sense. You can go far if you work
hard, and it's something you really want."

"Uncle Warren," I said, changing the subject. "You and
Daddy grew up in the old house that used to be on the
farm, didn't you?"

"Yeah."

"Why did he tear it down? He could have fixed it up
for what it cost to buy that ugly old trailer."

"I know. You don't know the memories he had of that
old house—the beatings, the way our daddy treated our
mama. I'm surprised he wanted to stay here at all."

UNCLE WARREN'S LAST NIGHT was in the middle of September.
We held a big celebration. Daddy asked his buddies and
several of Uncle Warren's old friends to come over. They
drank beer, peach brandy, and passed marijuana cigarettes
around. I listened as the men laughed, told stories, and
cut up around the bonfire. I wanted to stay up all night
with them, but at midnight my mother said I had to go to
bed, because of school in the morning. I watched from
my bedroom window. I had never seen Daddy laugh so
much or be so happy as he was when Uncle Warren was
around. Uncle Warren and Daddy had their arms around
each other most of the night. They were very close. Every
once in a while I caught Daddy just looking at Uncle Warren, while Uncle Warren was talking to someone. Daddy
had tears in his eyes.

TWO MONTHS LATER, November 15, 1973, a telegram was delivered to the our house. Uncle Warren was dead. He'd
been killed in a strange sounding place in the highlands
of Vietnam, blown up by a mortar shell.

When Mama read the telegram to us, I ran to the fishing pond, sat on the bank, and buried my head in my
hands, crying. I heard someone behind me. It was Andrew.

"I heard about Warren," Andrew said, sitting down beside me on the grass.

I didn't respond or look up. I wanted to tell him to
leave me alone. But Andrew was my best friend.

He put his arm around me. "I'm sorry, man. I know
how much you loved him."

I still couldn't speak.

"Why is it that God seems to take some of the best
people before their time," Andrew asked, "but lets drunks,
crooks and no-goods live on and on? You know what my

daddy would say don't you? He'd say, son, it's because God wants his angels up in heaven. Let all them nasty old drunks and crooks stay on earth; he wants the good folks first. But then my daddy's a preacher, and he's always got to get in a plug for God."

I smiled. "It isn't fair. Uncle Warren was so good. He was more a father to me than my own daddy."

"I know," Andrew said.

DADDY STARTED DRINKING real bad after we got the telegram. For a whole day no one could find him. Finally Mama and me found him in the woods, his hair matted, his clothes muddy, his lips crusted, and his skin powdery white. He was so drunk he couldn't talk. Mama put him in a hospital in Clinton to dry out. They let him go to the funeral, but then he had to go back for a few more weeks. When he finally came home, he didn't say much to anybody for weeks. On Christmas he sat in his chair and didn't say anything as the family opened presents.

When they brought the body home for the funeral, they wouldn't let anybody see it. They said the body wasn't fit for viewing. They buried him in the family graveyard, which was a few hundred feet from the mobile home. They put him under a big oak tree, beside his mom and dad. He was given a full military funeral with a group of soldiers from Fort Bragg. When they folded the flag to give it to the family, they gave it to me. Daddy was too broken up.

After Christmas, Daddy started drinking again, heavily. He said little to Mama and us kids, and when he got drunk he became violent. We stayed out of his way.

ANDREW AND I WERE BOTH good athletes. I was not a very good student but I did well at track. Andrew was better at

the short runs that took a fast explosion of energy. I was
better at the longer races that took stamina and endur-
ance. I was soon winning county-wide races and made a
name for my school's track team. I played baseball and
basketball, too. After all the workouts with the weights,
I'd built up a pretty good body.

Mama came to the track-and-field events and brought
my brother and sister, but Daddy never came. I thought,
if Uncle Warren was around he would come to see me.

One day that spring, as Mama was hanging laundry
on the clothes line in the side yard in a sundress, I noticed
that she had a big bruise on her shoulder.

"Did he do this to you?" I asked. My voice was changing and was deeper than it had been six months before. It
was the end of my junior year in high school. I had grown
to be six feet tall. I had broad shoulders and a lean body.

"Don't, Todd," Mama said.

"I asked you if he did this?"

She didn't answer but continued to hang clothes on
the line. I took her arm and made her face me.

"Todd, you're hurting me."

"Did he hit you?"

"Yes, he hit me, but it won't do any good for you to get
mad. This is between your daddy and me, Todd. It's not
your concern."

"Oh yes it is." I said. Then I walked to the trailer,
opened the door, and stood in front of Daddy who was
drinking a beer in his recliner in front of the television.

"Big man aren't you, beating up a woman. I bet that
makes you feel real tough."

"What the hell!" he said, looking around at me with a
wild look in his eyes. "Get out of here, you little son of a
bitch!"

I swung at him, slapping his face and knocking the beer out of his hand. Daddy stood up. I was as tall as he was, but Daddy was bigger and stronger. He punched me hard in the stomach. I doubled over in pain.

"That'll teach you to talk back to me!"

I straightened up and my eyes filled with anger. I swung at Daddy again. He caught my arm and punched me again in the stomach. Mama appeared in the doorway.

"Stop it," she said, looking hard at Daddy. "Both of you, stop it. Todd, go to your room. This is between your daddy and me. I can take care of myself."

I looked at her, feeling betrayed. "Yeah, that's why you have that bruise on your back."

Daddy grabbed my arm and twisted it behind me until it hurt. "You heard your mama. Go to your room—this ain't none of your business!"

"It is too my business. You let go of me, you son of a bitch!" I said, shaking loose from Daddy's grip and standing back. "If you so much as lay a finger on me or Mama again, so help me, I'll kill you!"

There was silence. Even I was surprised by the anger in my voice. I had never spoken to Daddy like that before. But I meant every word of it.

"Get out of here!" Daddy yelled, waving me to the back of the mobile home.

I walked out the front, slamming the screen door behind me.

THIRTEEN

WHEN I WAS A LITTLE BOY my mama used to tell me stories about the Outer Banks—about ghost ships, the Gray Man foretelling the coming of hurricanes, and the mystery of Theodosia Burr. I had never been to the Outer Banks, but I loved to hear her stories.

During the spring of my freshman year in high school, my class took a field trip to Shackleford Banks, a deserted island near Beaufort. It was a national park. I loved the island, the ocean, the dunes, the sea life, and the birds. I didn't want to leave. I wanted to learn everything I could about the coast, so I asked Mama more about it. She had grown up in Beaufort.

"Tell me about what it was like to live in Beaufort," I asked Mama one day when she was cooking dinner.

"We lived on the waterfront," she began, standing over the stove, checking the vegetables as they cooked. "There were several small islands between Beaufort and the inlet. Shackleford Banks is on one side of the inlet and Fort Macon on the other. I could hear the ocean from our house. We lived in a two-story, white frame house with a double front porch. My favorite place was on the upper porch, where I could see over the islands, to the inlet. It was beautiful. Seabirds flew by our house all the time— egrets, pelicans, seagulls, herons, and cranes.

"You could smell the ocean in the air, and when a storm blew up, the water got choppy and rough, just like the sea. Storms came in quickly. A beautiful sunny day could change suddenly. Black clouds and a hard-blowing rain would roll in from the sea and you wouldn't be able to see five feet in front of you."

She picked up the lid on a pot of hot, steaming corn on the cob. "Daddy was a fisherman. He made his living from the sea." She opened the refrigerator to get some hamburger meat.

"Tell me again what happened to Granddaddy," I asked.

"His boat was lost in a storm. All they found were a few life jackets, an ice chest with the boat's name, and some other debris. Back then it wasn't easy to tell when bad weather was coming. You didn't have much notice when a hurricane came, only a day or two. When that storm came through Beaufort, it nearly blew our house down, or so it seemed. Me and Mama hid in a closet under the stairway. We didn't budge all night long. Daddy took the boat to ride out the storm, otherwise it would have been pounded at the docks. When it finally passed, the house was filled with glass where the front windows blew out. We didn't have electricity for weeks, and for the longest time we had to boil the water before we could use it. Trees were all over the roads, telephone poles were down, houses were blown off their foundations, boats were up on the road in front of our house. It was awful. You don't ever want to live through one of them, I'm here to tell you."

"They didn't find a trace of Granddaddy? How did you know it was the storm and not the engine blowing up, or something?"

"We didn't. There wasn't any way of knowing."

"You met Daddy after that, didn't you?"

"Yeah, my daddy didn't have any insurance. Mama wanted to keep the house, but she had to sell it before long. So she and I moved to Morehead City, where she got a job as a waitress in a seafood restaurant. I got a job there too, when I was old enough. I met your daddy at that seafood restaurant—the Sanitary Fish Market. That was before he got the farm from his daddy. He was in Morehead City on business for him."

"Why did you marry him, Mama?"

"He was a lot of fun, drinking and carrying on. Said he had a big tobacco farm he was going to inherit from his daddy. He looked like he was on top of the world to me. I was eighteen years old and I was looking for any way out of Morehead City and living with my mother in that crowded little apartment. He promised he'd take care of me, so that I wouldn't have to work."

"He's taken care of you, all right," I said, with bitterness.

"You don't understand, Todd. I love your daddy."

"You're right. I don't understand."

DURING MY SENIOR YEAR in high school, I was a star athlete. Not only was I interested in girls, but they were interested in me.

One night at a football game I sat with a group of classmates. Sally Koontz, a pretty girl with long, wavy, blonde hair, sat beside me. She was a doctor's daughter. I knew she wouldn't go out with me—I didn't even have a car—but we flirted a lot in school and I liked her.

"Todd, what are you going to do when you get out of high school? Have you given it any thought?"

"No, not much."

"I'm going to Meredith College in Raleigh and find me a rich man to marry," Sally said.

"Sounds good," I said, not taking my eyes off the football game.

"Do you think you'll work on your daddy's farm?"

"Hell, no. As soon as I get out of school, I'm going as far away from this place as I can. I don't know where yet, but I'm going somewhere."

"Do you think you'll go to college?"

"Are you kidding? With what? If my daddy had any money, he wouldn't spend it on college."

"What about a track scholarship?"

"My grades aren't good enough, and I would still have to have money. It's just not there."

"Just thought I'd ask."

"Andrew's going to college," I said. "He's already been accepted at Chapel Hill. He said he's going to go to law school after college. They say he could go to any school he wants with his grades and him being such a good athlete."

I was proud of him. Andrew was vice president of our class and was real smart. Even though I was not a good student or a student leader, he kept his friendship with me. I was a good athlete, though, and we stayed close.

"You and your nigger friends. I never have understood that," she said, looking at me with disgust.

"Andrew isn't a nigger. He's my friend, a good friend, better than most white friends I have. You wait and see. He'll make more money than any guy you meet in Raleigh." I stood up. "Excuse me. I'll be back in a few minutes."

I walked through the crowded stadium, and stopped at the refreshment stand, where I saw Pamela. I hadn't seen her in a year. Andrew and I went out a few times with Cassandra and Pamela, but then Andrew lost interest in Cassandra. I didn't have a car and Pamela went to a different school, so I didn't see Pamela any more.

"Hey, white boy. I see you got yourself a cute little blonde date. Too good for Pamela nowadays?" she teased.

"We're just friends, not dating. How are you? I haven't seen you since Cassandra and Andrew split up."

"I still got that quarter."

"Have you used it yet?"

"No," she smiled.

I would never forget the time we made love. I couldn't say I loved her, but she taught me a lot and I sure was attracted to her.

"What are you doing tonight?" I asked.

"You don't want to know, white boy," she said. Then her date, a tall, muscular black guy from her school, walked up holding two Cokes. He handed her one.

"Who's he?" Pamela's date asked her.

"An old friend," she said, looking at me like she could see right through my clothes.

"Let's go."

"Okay," she said and left with him, looking back at me with her sexy smile. I went to the restroom, then walked back to the stands, where I sat down beside Sally.

"I saw you talking to that Black girl," Sally said, acting a little jealous.

"You did?"

"Yeah, I don't miss a trick. Who is she?"

"Someone I met with Andrew."

"The way she looked at you, she seemed to be more than just someone you met."

"That's none of your business."

"I suppose not," Sally said, looking at me, then out to the players on the field.

APRIL 30, 1975. Mama was cooking supper and Daddy was sitting in his recliner watching television, while the June Bug and Sally played ball outside. I was walking down the hallway after taking a shower, drying my hair with a towel.

"Frances, come here, look," Daddy said. On the news there were people scrambling up a ladder to get into a helicopter on the roof of the American Embassy in Saigon.

"Kids, come inside and see what's on TV," Daddy called to June Bug and Sally.

They ran inside and we all sat in front of the television set. The news reported the fall of Saigon. The television changed to a scene on an American aircraft carrier where helicopters flew onto the deck unloading passengers. Then the empty helicopters were pushed into the ocean. There was a report of a cargo plane loaded with orphans from Saigon that had crashed as it tried to take off from the airport.

"Remember this, children. This is history," Daddy said, as we all watched in amazement. Each member of the family was struck silent by what we watched—a war that had taken so many lives ending in such humiliation and defeat.

"I can't believe it," Daddy said. "This is what Warren gave his life for."

I had the same thought, but I didn't say it. I was too amazed by what I was watching. We heard the president say it was a victory, but everyone knew better. It was at that point that I decided I would never believe a politician. I remembered what Uncle Warren had said about politicians and the War. I didn't understand politics, but I knew I wanted to keep as far away from it as possible.

IN MAY, TOWARD THE END of our senior year, Andrew and I decided to hop a freight train. I had heard about some of the guys from school doing it. Not to be outdone, I dared Andrew to go with me. So one Saturday we walked about a mile from where I lived, to a place on the tracks where trains had to slow for a curve. We knew the 10 A.M. train usually passed on time.

About 10:15 we heard the whistle blow, then saw the train coming from around a tall pine forest. The train slowed but was still going fast enough so that we had to run to keep up. Andrew jumped on first, catching a ladder next to the open door of an empty boxcar. Then I caught the ladder and jumped on. We both sat in the boxcar, which smelled like wood and oil.

"We shouldn't stay long. I don't want to get stuck," Andrew said.

"We can get off at the river bridge. It's about five miles from here."

"Okay."

We sat and watched the lush, green landscape of eastern North Carolina go by slowly—red clay banks covered with kudzu, pine forests, oak trees hung with Spanish moss, rusted warehouses, wooden tobacco barns in fields, and old houses in various states of decay.

"After graduation I'm moving to Durham to live with my aunt and uncle. I have a job at Duke Hospital cleaning bedpans and changing sheets. My uncle, who's a preacher, got me the job. I need to work to stay in school. That scholarship I got will only pay for my tuition. I also have to take out a student loan."

I could see that Andrew was excited about going to Chapel Hill in the fall.

"Have you decided what you're going to do?" Andrew asked.

"No," I said, looking at the passing landscape. "All I know is that I want to get out of here. I'd like to go to the coast, maybe work on a fishing boat. I'm sick of tobacco country."

"I know what you mean. I'm ready to get out of here, too. The only way I would come back is if I could make a lot of money or go into politics."

"Politics!" I said. "The politicians gave us Vietnam."

"The only way I would get involved in politics is if I can change things, really make a difference."

"Well, I'm glad of that. If I can help you, let me know. Something tells me, things aren't going to change, though."

"Maybe, but not if I have anything to do with it."

"Hey, I think the river bridge is coming up. We'd better get out of here."

The train was going faster than when we picked it up. Soon the train would be going even faster and wouldn't stop until it got to Clinton, which was thirty miles away. I jumped out, rolling down the gravel embankment, then Andrew followed. We were both bruised a little, but okay. We stood up, brushed off the dirt as much as we could, and started to walk home. On the way home we stopped at the fishing pond and went swimming to wash the railroad dirt off. After the swim we sat on the grassy bank. It was getting dark.

"Todd, you're my best friend," Andrew said. "When I go off to school and you go wherever you're going, I hope we don't forget each other."

"Aw, we'll see each other plenty," I said.

"Things change. Unless we try to keep up, we might never see each other again."

I turned and looked at Andrew. "When you go off and become a high-powered lawyer and make lots of money, get into politics and run for president, are you still going to want to be my friend? For all I know, I'll be working on a shrimp boat in Beaufort. You sure you want to be friends with someone like me?"

"I sure do. I don't care what you're doing, you're my friend and friends stick together, right?"

"Yeah."

"Okay then, will you promise to write and stay in touch? I promise I will stay in touch with you."

"Sure, I promise," I said. It was only beginning to sink in that my whole world was about to change forever.

A WEEK BEFORE GRADUATION, I walked in on my mother putting Sally to bed.

"Mama tell me some ghost stories," Sally said. June Bug came in and sat on the edge of the bed. Daddy wasn't home. He was out playing poker with some of his buddies.

"Yeah, Mama," June Bug said. Tell us about the ghost ship, and about the men who strapped themselves to the mast and froze to death."

I loved to hear the stories, too. I sat down beside June Bug, on the bed.

"Okay, let me start with the ghost ship." Mama sat on the bed beside Sally, who was tucked in. "A long time ago, a lady named Theodosia Burr lived in New York. Her daddy, Aaron Burr, was the vice president of the United States. She was the most beautiful woman in the city. The governor of South Carolina, Mr. Alston, was visiting some friends in New York and met Theodosia at a ball. It was love a first sight. He asked her to marry him, and she moved with him to his plantation in Georgetown, South Carolina. After a few years, she became homesick for her daddy and decided to visit him. She sailed up the coast to New York, taking her finest silk and satin dresses and a beautiful portrait of herself as a present for him.

"Off the coast of North Carolina," she continued, "something happened. Some fishermen found the boat with all the sails set, but it was blowing around like no one was at the helm. The fishermen boarded the ship and found everything in order, but no one was on board. They found hot food still on the table. The only living thing on the boat was a cat, which one of the men took. They also took the portrait of Theodosia. They towed the boat to shore, but a storm came and grounded it on the shoals. Before long another storm came and the ship broke up. Now all that's left of the ghost ship of Theodosia Burr, is a few timbers on the beach at Nags Head."

"Did they ever find Theodosia Burr, Mama?" Sally asked.

"No, not a trace. But someone on the Outer Banks still has her portrait."

"Tell about the men on the frozen ship," June Bug asked.

"A fine sailing ship made its way up the coast from South America one December, when they hit a bad winter storm, a northeaster, off the coast of North Carolina. The storm got worse and worse and the waves almost knocked the ship on its side. Then the main mast snapped, and the crew were at the mercy of the waves. They were off Shackleford Banks, and the storm drove them onto the shoals. It was the coldest month the Outer Banks had ever known back in the 1880s. As the waves broke over the ship, the water froze on deck. The captain told his crew to lash themselves to the masts until daybreak when some- one from shore could rescue them. This they did, but it got colder and colder. The next day, when a rescue ship came, they found the men dead, frozen solid, covered with ice, still tied to the masts."

We listened intently as Mama told the stories. Some were real tales from the Outer Banks, others were a combi- nation of stories she had heard.

After she put Sally to bed and said good night to June Bug, I told her I wanted to talk to her.

"Mama, I'm leaving home after I graduate."

"You know your daddy needs you around here to help on the farm."

"I know, but I have to leave. Daddy will be fine. He has Brady Hauss," I said, with a trace of bitterness.

"I know, but we need you, too. Someday this farm will be yours."

"I don't want this farm. I want to move to the coast. I've made up my mind."

"But you don't have any place to go. What family I had in Beaufort has long since died or moved away. You'll be completely on your own."

"I know. That's what I want."

"You're seventeen, son, going to be eighteen in Au- gust. You're getting ready to graduate from high school and free to go and do as you please, but I wish you'd stay."

"I've made up my mind."

"Are you going to tell your daddy?"

"Yeah."

"He's not going to like it."

"I know."

I decided to tell Daddy a few days before graduation. He was standing in the yard talking to Brady Hauss, giving him instructions about the day's work.

"When you're through I've got something I want to tell you," I said to him.

Daddy looked at me, finished talking to Brady, then walked back to the mobile home with me. "What is it?"

"I'm leaving home when I graduate."

"You're what?"

"I'm leaving home. I'm going to hitch a ride to the coast and get me a job. I want to work on a fishing boat."

"What the hell do you know about fishing?"

"Nothing, but I'll learn."

"Well, if you leave, don't bother to come back."

I saw Brady watch us talk, with a smirk on his face.

"If I ever come back, it won't be to see you, you can count on that," I said.

I DECIDED TO LEAVE EARLY in the morning after graduation. That night I talked to Sally and June Bug. I asked them to walk to the pond with me. Leaving them was the hardest part.

"Don't leave, Todd. We love you," Sally said, after I told her my plans. There were tears in her eyes.

"Yeah," June Bug agreed.

"I've been thinking about this for a long time. I need to make my own way. I'll write Mama, and tell her where I am and what I'm doing. I'm moving to the coast. If you ever need me, I won't be far away."

"Are you going to see the ghost ship?" Sally asked.

"I guess so, if it's still there," I laughed. "Listen, if Daddy ever tries to hurt you, let me know. And another thing. If Brady Hauss ever tries anything with either of you, let me know. I'm serious about this. He tried something with me when I was your age, and if he tries anything with either of you I'll kill him. And I'm going to tell him that."

THAT NIGHT I WENT to Brady's house and asked him to come outside.

"Your dad said you're leaving home," Brady said, smiling as he walked off the porch. "What's the matter, this place too much for you?"

"I have my reasons," I said. "Listen, if you ever touch my brother or sister, I'll cut your nuts off and cram' em down your throat." I'd grown a lot bigger since the last time Brady gave me trouble. Brady no longer looked as threatening to me, but he was still a big man.

"I don't know what you're talking about," Brady said, with a sarcastic smile.

"Brady?" Virginia Hauss said, poking her head out the front door. "Oh, it's you, Todd," she said. "When you're through out there I need you inside, Brady."

"Okay, I'm coming," he said to his wife. "If that's all you wanted to tell me, wasn't any use you coming out here," Brady said, after his wife shut the door.

"I'll be the judge of that," I said, my voice filling with anger.

EARLY IN THE MORNING after graduation, I gathered my clothes and a few belongings into Uncle Warren's old duffel bag and walked into the living room of the mobile home.

Daddy was asleep. Mama was in the kitchen fixing me a breakfast of ham, fried eggs, and grits.

"You'll need something for the road," she said, handing me a hundred-dollar bill.

I had also saved about two hundred dollars. I took my mother's money and hugged her. "It's not you, Mama. I love you. I need to go out on my own."

"I know, son," she said.

I ate breakfast, then started toward the door.

"Write," Mama said, walking with me to the door. "Let me know where you are, so I can write you. You know you're welcome home anytime."

"I'll stay in touch," I said.

Then June Bug and Sally appeared in the kitchen. I hugged them both.

"I love you," I said, as I kissed Sally and hugged June Bug. "Let me know how you're getting along. If you do good in school, June Bug, you might be able to go to college like Andrew."

Then I walked out the front door into the early morning light. It was cool and I heard the mourning doves call their mournful song. I walked for some time on the blacktop road with my thumb out, until a farmer stopped and picked me up.

"Where you headed?"

"To the coast," I said.

"I'm going to Southport. Will that do?"

"Sure," I replied, climbing into the back of the truck, finding a place to sit among the cabbages, collard greens, onions, radishes, and lettuce.

FOURTEEN

AFTER THE WRECK OF THE SHRIMP BOAT, there was an investigation. The captain of the freighter, licensed in Panama, was found to be negligent. He'd left the automatic pilot on without a night watch, and the ship had wandered out of the shipping lane. Mitch and his mother received a large insurance settlement, though I was not told how much. But Mitch still blamed himself.

When we got home, I took Mitch out to Bald Head Island. We walked on the beach and talked. It was late November, and a stiff cold wind blew from the northeast roughing up the ocean. It was mid-afternoon and there were few people on the beach.

"It's my fault they're dead, Todd," Mitch said, pulling up the hood of his parka against the cold.

"That's not true. It was the freighter captain's fault," I replied.

"If I had stayed awake, I could have seen the freighter coming," Mitch said. "I could have warned everybody."

"You don't know that. There is nothing you or I can do to bring them back," I said, sticking my hands in the big pockets of my coat. "Your father wouldn't want you to blame yourself. He'd want you to get on with your life. There are some things we just can't help."

"If I'd only stayed awake," Mitch said, tears forming in his eyes.

"It's okay, Mitch," I said, putting my arm around his shoulder.

"I'll never be able to forgive myself, Todd."

"Give yourself time."

ONE DAY, IN THE MIDDLE of March, when I'd returned from fishing with Captain Jackson,
Martha told me my mother had called. That was unusual. Mama never called. She wrote every once in a while, but she didn't call. I figured something must be wrong.

"What was it, did she tell you?" I asked Martha.

"She needs to tell you herself," Martha said.

I could tell by the tone of her voice that it was serious.

"YOUR DADDY IS DEAD, Todd," Mama told me when I called her.

"What happened?"

"He was driving the tractor, plowing a field with the disk harrow behind it. We don't know exactly what happened, but he must have fallen off. He had been drinking. I don't know. He shouldn't have been out there, but I couldn't stop him." She paused. "It was pretty awful— the disk harrow cut him to pieces. The casket will be closed. The funeral's going to be day after tomorrow if you can get here." She began to cry. "I need you, Todd."

"I'll be there, Mama."

IT'D BEEN ALMOST EIGHT years since I'd been home. When I drove up to the mobile home it looked smaller and shabbier than I remembered it. There wasn't much grass in the front yard, and the white metal siding was streaked with rust. When I pulled up in my shiny black Malibu, June Bug ran out to greet me. My mother stood in the doorway, looking much older than when I last saw her.

"How the hell are you?" June Bug asked me, holding the door to my car.

June Bug was twenty-one years old. When I had left in 1975, he was fourteen. He had grown a lot since then. He was a good-looking boy; tall, well-built, with wide shoulders, and big arms. He stayed home to help Mama and Daddy on the farm. I got out of the car and wrapped my arms around him.

"How the hell are you?" I asked, "You look great. Looks like farm life agrees with you."

"Looks like life on the coast agrees with you," June Bug said, looking me over. "I see you've gained weight in all the right places." He squeezed my shoulder.

I walked to the house where my mother stood.

"Mama, it's been a long time." I paused, then said, "I'm sorry about Daddy." As I put my arm around her, I could see tears forming in her eyes.

"I've missed you, son," she said.

"I missed you too, Mama."

I walked with June Bug and Mama into the mobile home. We sat down and talked, bringing each other up to date on events. June Bug told me about finding Daddy's body in a pool of blood in the field, cut to pieces. The tractor circled around it without a driver.

"I knew his drinking would get him one of these days," June Bug said. "But I never thought it would be like this."

Soon Sally arrived with her husband and two children— six-year-old Clarence, Jr. and three-year-old Tiffany. Sally was twenty-two now. Her husband, Clarence Sifford, a beefy car salesman from Clinton, was four years older than her. Sally had gained weight and was too busy keeping up with her children to pay much attention to me.

"You left us all alone," she said to me, in a quiet moment in the kitchen. "We stayed here with Daddy drinking and all." She looked down at the floor. "It was bad. I had to get out. June Bug stayed, but he won't touch a drink. I think he really likes this old place." She looked around. "I couldn't get out of here fast enough."

"Then you can understand why I left," I said.

"I can see why, now, but at the time I thought you'd deserted us. It took a long time before I could forgive you for leaving. I'm still not sure I've forgiven you completely. You were the only one who stood up to him, and you left."

THE FUNERAL WAS HELD in the Baptist church that we belonged to, but never attended. It was a gloomy day and threatened rain, but the weather held. The preacher searched for something nice to say. He talked about Daddy's family—Mama, us kids, and the grandchildren.

We buried him beside Uncle Warren in the family graveyard near where the old house had stood. A cold wind blew across the green Astroturf, under the funeral home tent where we sat in plastic folding chairs.

I didn't cry. I didn't feel anything but emptiness at the thought of Daddy's death. I am who I am in spite of him, not because of him, I thought to myself. I felt sorry for Mama and my sister and brother, for having to put up with him for so long. For them, and for us as a family, I found tears, as they lowered the casket into the ground. I wept for the dad I'd never had. But I had no tears for him. I did not weep for Henry Field. He was given so

much and did so little with it. The only time I remembered Daddy being even remotely human was when Uncle
Warren died—he grieved so deeply. That was the first time
I'd seen Daddy show any emotion other than anger. I
could've almost loved him then.

I looked at Uncle Warren's grave. The white marble
government-issue stone had weathered with streaks of gray.
I thought about being underwater when I heard Uncle
Warren's voice. I knew it was Uncle Warren who'd saved
me from drowning. It would be just like him to do something like that, come back as a ghost and save me. It's too
bad he couldn't do anything for Daddy. But you have to
want to live before even a ghost can help you.

AFTER THE FUNERAL, when the relatives and family friends
came by to visit, I noticed that   Brady Hauss wasn't anywhere to be seen. Brady's wife, Virginia, was at the funeral,
and at the house afterward, but not Brady.

"Mama, where's Brady Hauss?" I asked, after the guests
left and only the family was at the house.

"I didn't tell you because I knew how you felt about
him. Brady has cancer. The doctor first found it about six
months ago. It was too late to do anything by then. He's
at home. They're just trying to keep him comfortable.
He's on morphine. You wouldn't recognize him—he's all
skin and bones," Mama said.

Mama and I walked to Brady's house the next morning. Brady and his wife lived on our farm in an old, one-
story house that had been there for as long as anybody
could remember. They say it was the house our family lived
in before the old house that I remember. It took a while
for my eyes to adjust after I entered the house—it was so
bright outside and dark inside. Virginia Hauss explained

that all the windows were draped with blankets because the sunlight hurt Brady's eyes.

Mama and I walked back to the bedroom with Virginia. Brady lay in the bed under an old quilt. His once huge body, was shriveled almost to nothing. I could hear his labored breathing. There was hardly a lump in the bed made by the gaunt man. The only way you could tell a man was in the bed was to see his face and the lumps under the covers where his feet stuck up. His face looked like a living skeleton.

Virginia asked me to help her turn him over. She had to turn him every so often to keep bedsores from developing. As Virginia and I turned him, I saw Brady's eyes follow me. There was a look of terror in them. Even though he didn't speak—he was too weak—I could tell he recognized me. I was big enough to break Brady like a stick.

We spoke to Virginia in the living room after we left the bedroom.

"How long does he have?" I asked.

"I don't know. A few weeks, a few days. I'm just trying to keep him comfortable and keep him from catching a cold or pneumonia." She paused for a moment, looked at Mama, and asked, "Mrs. Field, have you said anything to Todd about the house?" She looked worried.

"No, I haven't had a chance to talk to him about it yet."

"Oh, I'm sorry," Virginia said. "I shouldn't have said anything."

I looked at Mama, wondering what Virginia was talking about. Mama said good-bye to Virginia and walked out the front door with me. On the way to the house, she explained.

"Your daddy didn't leave a will. As you know, he inherited the farm from his daddy. He never put my name on

it, so it belongs to all of us—you, me, Sally, and June Bug.
Your daddy always said he wanted to give Brady that old
house and a few acres around it for all the years of service
he gave us, but he never got around to doing it. I want
you to sign the deed. June Bug and Sally have already said
they would," Mama said.

"I'm going to have to think about that, Mama," I said.
"You know how I feel about Brady Hauss."

"I know, son, but he is dying, and his widow will have
nothing. It's the least we can do for him. It was what your
daddy wanted."

"Daddy always protected Brady Hauss."

"It's because he needed him to run the farm."

"What did he care more about—his children or having someone else do his work for him? If he hadn't stayed
drunk so much of the time, he could have done the work
himself."

"Todd, there isn't anything we can do to change that.
You are going to have to put that behind you. It's only fair
that we help those who help us."

I didn't give my mother an answer right then, but I
did finally agree to sign a deed giving Virginia Hauss the
house and five acres around it. I made it clear though,
that I was doing it for Virginia, not for Brady.

The family also discussed the rest of the property. I
asked Mama to come live with me in Southport. She said
no, she'd been away from the coast for so long, she had
forgotten what it was like. She wanted to live with Sally to
help raise her grandchildren. Sally needed her, and she
had plenty of room. That left June Bug and the farm.

June Bug was good at farming, and he loved the farm.
He wanted it. He went to the bank and they agreed to
loan him the money to buy out Sally and me. Mama would

co-sign and keep her share of the farm. But it was agreed
that if June Bug worked it, she would write a will and leave
her share to him.

WE MET IN ANDREW Mason's law office in Clinton to conduct
the closing and exchange the deeds. Andrew was working
for another attorney. He had only been out of the Chapel
Hill law school for a year. He had graduated near the top
of his class. I was glad to see him.

"I see you've done well for yourself, Andrew. I'm just a
fisherman, and here you are, a lawyer," I said, entering
Andrew's office.

Andrew threw his arms around me and hugged me.
"You look great, Todd. How are you doing?" Andrew said.

He looked trim and business-like, wearing a dark gray
suit and red striped tie. He looked very distinguished. He
was less than a year older than me.

"I'm sorry about your father," Andrew said.

"Thank you." To change the subject, I brought up a
couple of old acquaintances. "Do you remember Pamela
and Cassandra?" I asked.

"I sure do," Andrew said, looking embarrassed. "We
had some great times, didn't we."

"We sure did."

At that point, Andrew called us together and started
on the closing. He had worked out all the details. Daddy
didn't own anything else other than the farm, and it was
worth one hundred eighty-thousand dollars. He did have
a federal loan on it, but since the government required
him to have life insurance, the mortgage was paid off when
he died. Mama owned one-third and the other two-thirds
were divided between the children. June Bug kept his
share, and he paid me and Sally for our shares, with the

loan from the bank. That gave the two of us forty thousand dollars each. June Bug would pay Mama rent for the use of her share of the property. That would help pay her bills and not be a burden on Sally financially.

After the closing, I rode with Andrew to Kenansville, the county seat, to record the deeds. Then he asked me to meet him for a beer after work so we could talk about old times.

WE MET IN THE BAR of the Holiday Inn in Clinton. I told Andrew about living in Southport, about Elizabeth, and about the ship wreck. Andrew told me about law school and private practice. He planned to run for city council in November. Andrew was twenty-six. His mother had died a few years ago, but his father was still alive.

"Come visit me in Southport," I said. "I'll take you out on Captain Jackson's boat. They are building a new development on Bald Head Island. If you get rich enough, you'll have to buy a house out there and come see me every summer." I took a sip from my long-neck Budweiser. "I'll never forget Pamela. How is she doing?"

"I heard she got married and has a few kids now. She lives in the country. Her husband owns a poultry farm. I see her sometimes at church. I'll tell her you asked about her."

"I'd appreciate that." I paused, then said, "Tell me something, Andrew. When you were in high school, did you think it would turn out like this?"

"What do you mean?"

"You on the top and me on the bottom."

"Who's at the bottom? You're just twenty-five years old, and you have a whole lifetime in front of you, Todd. I knew what I wanted early on, mainly because my father pushed me. Not everybody is like that. You can do anything you want to do. If you want to go to college, go. If you want to own a boat, buy one with your new money. The only one who can hold you back is you."

I looked down. "I wish I could believe all that," I said, then looked away. "Maybe you're right. Not that stuff about going to college. You couldn't pay me a million bucks to go to college," I said, laughing and giving Andrew a punch in the arm. "But I can own my own boat and build from there."

"It's up to you, Todd."

SALLY, JUNE BUG, MAMA, and I sat down to eat dinner that night after we got home from the real estate closing. Mama had prepared a big turkey dinner. I planned to leave in a few days for Southport.

After we ate, we heard someone knock at the front door. It was Virginia Hauss.

"I don't mean to interrupt, Mrs. Field, but Brady wants to speak to you all. I'm not sure how much longer he has."

We followed Virginia to the one-story, frame house. It was nighttime and the house was not well lit. We walked into Brady's room.

"Brady wants to say thank you," Virginia said. "He can only whisper, so you'll have to lean close to the bed."

June Bug and Sally each bent down to hear Brady thank them. I was next.

I leaned close to Brady. The skin stretched tightly over his face. His eye sockets looked hollow. Brady whispered something I couldn't understand.

"You need to get a little closer, Todd," Virginia told me.

I felt like I was staring death in the face. The closer I got, the more sickening it became. I could smell the sweet odor of the morphine.

Brady spoke again. This time my ear was right against his mouth.

"Thank you, Todd," Brady whispered. "I know what you done." Brady held out his hand.

When I took it, it felt like the hand of a skeleton. I whispered, "Thank you for keeping the farm going, Brady."

A peaceful smile crept across Brady's face.

Then he thanked Mama. He said some things to her that no one could hear. She began to cry.

Brady's face relaxed and he looked peaceful. Virginia asked us to leave. The next day, Virginia told us Brady died during the night.

I stayed to help Mama pack and move her things to Clinton.

I WAS ABOUT READY to leave Sally's house after I got Mama settled in, when Mama followed me to my car.

"Get in. Let's drive around the block. I want to talk to you, Todd," she said.

I got in my car and drove us around the neighborhood, while we talked.

"Todd, when you get married I want you to invite me to the wedding. I want to come see those grandbabies, too. Will you promise you won't forget me?"

I nodded.

"I know I haven't been much of a mama to you these past few years, and I know you have another family in Southport. It isn't hard to see that you care about them a lot. But I'm still your mama, and I love you very much."

I was silent, then I said. "Mama, there's one thing I don't understand. Why did you stay with Daddy for so long, the way he treated you?" I looked her straight in the eye.

"Honey, there are some things you don't understand and won't understand until you have a family of your own."

"Maybe so," I said.

"It doesn't do any good to let yourself be eaten up with hatred, Todd. You don't hurt anybody but yourself. You've got to learn to put things you can't change behind you and get on with your life, or you'll never be happy," she said, looking out the side window.

WHEN I GOT BACK to the mobile home I had a chance to visit with June Bug. June Bug was excited about running the farm. He was going to miss Mama, but he was looking forward to the challenge.

"Why don't you stay on the farm with me, Todd? We can make this place really blossom.

"You don't need me. You can do just fine by yourself. I have a life in Southport, now. There are too many memories here for me. I hope you understand."

"After you left, things got better, really. Daddy didn't beat Mama near as much, and he even cut down on his drinking for a while. I remember what you told us about Brady Hauss—he never tried anything with me or Sally."

"I had to leave, June Bug. You might not understand. I couldn't stay. You can make this place into anything you want it to be—it's yours now. You don't have to worry about Daddy, or Brady, or anybody else messing you up. I wish you luck." I looked away, then said, "I have another home."

"If that's your decision, I respect it," June Bug said.

I threw my arms around him and got in my car, ready to leave. As I was driving off, June Bug said, "Write. Let me know when you get married. Don't be a stranger."

"You, too. You'll be needing a good woman to help run this place, and plenty of young-uns to help with the chores. Don't forget me when the invitations go out for the wedding. I wouldn't miss it for the world." Then I drove off, heading back home to Southport.

FIFTEEN

WHEN I DROVE INTO SOUTHPORT after my trip to Duplin County, it looked strangely different. I noticed how beautiful the town was. It was like seeing it for the first time.

Heading down Howe Street, which led to the water, I looked at the old churches with their white spires, the quaint downtown with its old, brick storefronts, and the old oaks lining the street. Some of the oaks, whose leaves stay green all year round, were so old that the road and sidewalks curved around them. Most of the trees were draped with Spanish moss. The ground was sandy white, except where patches of grass grew.

At the end of the wide street was the shimmering water of the Cape Fear River. Across the river, alive with light, I could see the lighthouse at Oak Island, and the old buildings at Fort Caswell. There was no question in my mind—Southport was a magical place. It was home.

As I drove up to the Jackson's house near the marina, I noticed the old houses, each one filled with different stories about people who knew the sea. The Jacksons' house faced the old Yacht Basin and the boats docked along

Brunswick Street. On the second story porch hung a
Pawley's Island Hammock. Captain Jackson loved to stretch
out in it in the middle of the day when he wasn't working.
He found it relaxing, feeling the breeze from the harbor,
and listening to the birds and cicadas.

MITCH AND HIS MOTHER decided to use the insurance money
they got from the shipwreck, to buy a big boat. Not a
shrimp boat, but a boat to take tourists fishing and on
nighttime cruises, just like he told me he wanted to do when
we were in the Gulf. The boat had a large dining room
and kitchen. He named it the *Carolina.*

First he tried to operate it out of Wilmington, without
much luck. Then he decided to move it to North Myrtle
Beach, where it became very successful. Mitch didn't want
to move from Southport and commuted for a while, but as
more of his time was spent away from home, he bought a
condo in North Myrtle Beach. His mother stayed in
Southport.

I put the money I got from the sale of the farm in the
bank and decided to wait for a good deal on a boat. I told
Captain Jackson that when I found the right boat I would
go out on my own. The captain told me he would help me
as much as he could. Far from seeing me as competition,
he felt another good charter captain would help establish
the reputation of Southport as a great place for charter
fishing. All the charter captains helped each other out in
Southport, as long as there was plenty of business to go
around. I continued to live with the Jacksons and work for
the captain, but I knew it was only a matter of time until I
bought my own boat and started my own business. Victor
Slade, the young man who worked for Captain Jackson
when I went to Key West, continued to work for him. Vic-

tor was twenty years old and lived with his family at Holden Beach.

Captain Jackson heard about a good deal on a five-year-old, thirty-six-foot Silverton built in New Jersey. I had enough money to pay for it in cash and keep some money in reserve. It was docked at a marina in Norfolk, Virginia. Captain Jackson wanted to go with me to pick it up, so we flew to Norfolk to get the boat.

It took a few days to make the trip down the inland waterway from Norfolk to Southport, but it gave Captain Jackson and I a good chance to visit. There were long stretches of the trip where there wasn't anything to do but talk.

Captain Jackson told me about when he first went into business. He told me how he kept his books and kept track of expenses. He said he would refer any customers he couldn't handle, to me. The best advertising was word of mouth, but I still had to have cards printed and flyers made. At first, it would be better if I kept my living expenses to a minimum. The captain was glad to let me continue to live with him and Martha for a small rent.

When we got to Southport I had cards and flyers printed and bought a telephone answering machine. I bought fishing rods, ice chests, life vests, lures, and line. Captain Jackson told me to go light on the fancy equipment, but I did buy a Loran unit and a few pieces of equipment I thought I really needed. I named the boat the *Martha Frances* after the two women who had meant the most to me in my life. My Boston Whaler kept the name, Elizabeth, true to my promise. I hired a high-school boy to help me for the summer. Business was slow at first, but then as I developed a reputation, and because there was plenty of work to go around, I was soon doing very well. In the winter I continued to fish commercially with Captain Jackson, but during the summer, I was on my own.

I stayed so busy during the summer of 1983 and the winter of 1984 that I had little time to play or date. Mitch was working hard in North Myrtle Beach establishing his business, and we didn't see much of each other. I went to bed early and got up before sunrise every morning. I stopped drinking almost completely, because I didn't have the time. The few times I got away from work, I visited Mitch in North Myrtle Beach.

ONE DAY IN THE MIDDLE of June 1984, while I was working on my boat at the marina, I looked up and saw Elizabeth walking down the dock. I couldn't believe my eyes.

"They told me I could find you here," Elizabeth said, as I stood in my boat hosing it down.

She wore a white cotton shorts outfit, sunglasses, and a tan "Bald Head" visor. She had gained a little weight, but still had a good figure and looked great. I was so surprised to see her that I didn't know what to say at first.

"How are you doing?" she asked.

My khaki shorts were dirty, my white T-shirt was soaked with sweat, and my hands were smeared with grease. I looked terrible.

"I'm doing fine. How are you?" I answered finally, staring at her as if she had returned from the dead.

"I'm staying with Lucretia and her husband on Bald Head Island. They just bought a house on the golf course."

The development of Bald Head Island was slow during the 1970s. But after a lawsuit, filed by several conservation groups, was settled in 1976 and a marina permit was issued, development took off. Part of the settlement stated that the developers would protect the marshlands and outlying islands from development and would leave them natural. Development of the island was restricted—there were no phones and no cars, only electric golf carts. It was very exclusive. The locals didn't mind too much because it left the marshes intact, and they could still fish on the east beach. The south beach was never very good for fishing anyway because of the Cape Fear River, and that was where most of the houses were built. The developers put money into the town, too. A few new restaurants, some antique shops, and an ice cream parlor opened.

"David's coming tomorrow. My daughter, Heather, is on the island with Lucretia. I told Lucretia I wanted to go shopping in Southport. I hoped I would find you."

"I don't know what to say, Elizabeth."

"Want to go for a cup of coffee?"

"Sure. Let me get cleaned up, and I'll be right with you."

I washed myself as best I could in the sink on the boat, changed pants, and put on a fresh shirt. Elizabeth waited on the dock. We walked to a restaurant near the marina that served breakfast and sat in a window booth overlooking the water.

"When did you get married?" I asked, as I sipped a cup of coffee.

"I got married after my sophomore year at Hollins. Oh, that's right. You didn't know I went to Hollins, did you? David went to UVA. David's father is an attorney and knows my father. We met at a fraternity party," she said, sipping her coffee.

"And your little girl?" I asked.

"Heather is three. We're trying for another one. We'd like to have a boy."

"What does your husband do?"

"He's a broker with E. F. Hutton in Raleigh." She sipped her coffee. "What about you, Todd? Was that your boat? They told me at the marina office that you had one."

"Yeah."

"What happened to Captain Jackson?"

"I'm still living with him and Martha until I get my business going. We're still good friends. He sends me business and I work with him during the winter."

"I read about Mitch's father and the accident in the Gulf, in the *News and Observer*. How is he doing?"

"I was there, too. Mitch and I were the only ones who made it." I paused. "Mitch is doing great. He has a boat in North Myrtle Beach, the *Carolina*. He takes tourists out for midnight cruises, then takes fishermen out during the day. His family got an insurance settlement that gave them enough money to buy it."

"How could you afford a boat?" she asked.

"My dad died."

"I'm sorry."

"He was drunk, fell off a tractor, and was killed. When he died all four of us got the farm. My brother, June Bug, bought out me and my sister, Sally. She has a house in Clinton so my mother moved in with her. I bought the boat with my share. Happy ending, huh?" I said, laughing sarcastically.

"Looks like life is agreeing with you. You look better than ever. I see you're not married," she said, looking at my ring finger.

"No."

"Do you have a girlfriend?"

"I don't have time for such foolishness," I laughed.

"A man like you needs a good woman, Todd."

"You're telling me?"

"You're a very special person," she continued. "You will make someone very happy."

"Don't you think it's cruel to talk to me that way after what happened to us?" I said, looking at her straight in the eye. "You know how much I loved you." I paused. "The cruelest thing you did was to send my letters back unopened, not letting me know where you were. It would have been better if you had told me to go to hell. I could have lived with that. When I couldn't see you, I kept alive the hope that you still loved me. That was why I went so crazy."

"It was hard for me too, Todd. My father wouldn't let me talk to you. I couldn't tell you to go to hell, because," she looked down at her coffee. Tears welled up in her eyes. "I would have been lying."

"You got an abortion, and you let your father keep us apart," I said. "Don't tell me that."

"It was impossible. I wasn't ready to get married or have children. I love my parents. I didn't want to make them mad."

"You sure didn't wait very long to get married."

She started to cry. "I knew this was a bad idea."

I put my hand on hers. "I'm sorry, Elizabeth. I've been through so much since then. I haven't loved anyone since I loved you."

"I'm sorry. I couldn't stand up to my father, and I let him run my life." She was still crying. "After the abortion, I started to eat like crazy, eating until I threw up. I gained a lot of weight and didn't want you or anybody to see me. It took a long time to get over that. I still haven't gotten over it completely."

"Elizabeth, will you tell me something, honestly," I asked, holding her hands. "Did you love me?"

"Yes."

"Did you love me even after you moved to Raleigh?"

"Yes."

"Are you happy now?"

"I love my little girl, and David is very good to me," she said, looking out the window at the water. "We have a nice house and we take trips. He works late at night and is away from home a lot, but we have a good life." She paused, then looked into my eyes. "Sometimes you have to make choices in life," she said. "Do I love David? Yes, I love him."

"That's all I want to know. If you're happy, I'm happy for you." I paused, then looked into her eyes. "Did we have something special, Elizabeth?"

"Yes we did," she said, smiling. "I hope you find someone who can give you the love you need. You're a very sensitive and wonderful person, Todd. You deserve the best."

"Thank you, Elizabeth." I said, still holding her hand. "You have no idea how much this has meant to me."

We talked about Bald Head and Southport, the old haunts, and old friends. We laughed and told stories, then she said she had to go. I followed her to the door, where I kissed her good-bye.

I DROVE TO NORTH MYRTLE to see Mitch a few weeks later. We met for dinner at the Marina Oyster Bar, overlooking the water where the *Carolina* was docked.

"That is one beautiful boat, Mitch. I know you're proud of her," I said, after Mitch and I ordered drinks.

"Thanks. It takes a lot of money and work to keep it up, but I'm happy with my business so far," Mitch said, taking a bourbon and water from the waiter. The two of us ordered an oyster roast, which was delivered in a steaming hot kettle. We were each given an oyster knife, cocktail sauce, melted butter, a roll of paper towels, and a trash can to put the shells in after we shucked the oysters.

"These look almost as good as the oysters you and I used to gather at Bald Head," Mitch said, opening one with an oyster knife. "I think these come from Louisiana."

The only oysters available out of season were from the Gulf.

"I saw Elizabeth in Southport," I said, opening an oyster.

"No shit. What did she look like?"

"She's gained a little weight, but she looks good. She's married and has a little girl. She was visiting Lucretia and her husband at their new place on Bald Head."

"Do you still have that old flame for her?" Mitch asked, struggling with an oyster.

"No, but I'm glad I saw her, and had a chance to talk."

"Did she have wrinkles, warts, and gray hair?"

"No, dumb ass," I said, laughing.

"We talked about things I wondered about all these years, and she told me she's happy."

"You know, no matter how hard you want something, you can't do it until you're ready. I'd be willing to bet you'll find a woman and fall in love in less than a year. You weren't ready until now. You had to let go of Elizabeth first."

"I didn't think of that, but you're probably right. We'll see what happens," I said, picking an oyster from its shell, smiling to myself.

MY BUSINESS DID BETTER. I began to see repeat customers, and I managed to save some money. I decided it was time to find my own place. I found a three-room house on At-

lantic Avenue for rent. It was partially furnished, with ap-
pliances, a bed, and an old sofa. I bought a television set,
some chairs, and a table.

"I'm going to miss you, Todd," Martha Jackson said.

"I'm not going anywhere," I said, packing my things in
boxes for the move.

"I know, but it won't be the same. I won't hear you
coming in late at night, worrying about whether you've
been drinking or not. You know, just being a general
mother hen," Martha said, laughing.

I stood and put my arms around her. "I love you,
Martha. You put up with me through my ups and downs
and didn't throw me out. I wouldn't have made it without
you." I kissed her on the cheek. She was crying. "Don't
cry," I said. "I'm just moving a few blocks away. I'll still
expect to get some of your good home cooking from time
to time."

"You've been like a son to us, Todd. No matter what
happens, you'll always have a home here. Remember
that."

"I know that, Martha."

OCTOBER CAME, AND with it, the end of the season. Captain
Jackson and I put out fish pots near the artificial reefs. I
took my boat one morning to check on them. Victor Slade
went with me. I had taught Victor how to read the Loran
and had taught him about navigating the Cape Fear. I
told Victor the coordinates of my favorite fishing places,
the artificial reefs, the wrecks, the deep holes, just as Captain Jackson had done with me. Victor was bright and
caught on easily. I liked him. He reminded me of myself
when I was that age—eager to learn, young, and strong. I
wanted to tell Victor what I'd learned since I'd moved to

Southport, but I realized that Victor would have to learn for himself. All I could do was be there when he needed me to answer questions, tell him the stories, and relate my experiences. I knew that I couldn't force knowledge on anyone. It was just like Mitch said—when you're ready, you're ready and no amount of effort is going to get you there before then.

The sea rolled dark and turbulent. Clouds filled the sky, but here and there, the sun shone through with brilliant rays of light. The clouds above us parted. The sun was glorious and warmed us, though the air was cold as it blew from the northeast. How many times had I ridden through these waters, I thought, and not once was it ever the same. The only thing that remained the same was Bald Head to the north and Oak Island to the south. Even they had changed, but more slowly. The sea changed constantly, as did the sky. But I knew if the land didn't appear to change, it was only an illusion.

SIXTEEN

I WALKED ALONE AT NIGHT sometimes, when I couldn't sleep. One cool night in November, close to midnight, I walked down West Street, which led downtown from my house. The street split into two narrow lanes that wound through a dense grove of oak trees. The oaks were twisted and gnarled, covered with green lichen, and laced with Spanish moss. A stiff breeze blew through the evergreen leaves above me, making a brittle sound. The limbs of the trees creaked, sounding like a wooden sailing ship at sea. I looked through the branches and saw clouds passing quickly overhead. The blue street lights gave the street the feel of an empty movie set after a shooting at night. I was lonely. I hadn't dated anyone in a couple of years because I had been so busy. I needed someone.

When I didn't eat with Martha and Captain Jackson, I ate out. I could have fixed food at home, but it was a way of getting out of the house and socializing. So I made the rounds of the restaurants in town. One night I was eating at Garrison's Restaurant near the marina and noticed a waitress I hadn't seen before.

"Are you new in town?" I asked, after I ordered a tossed salad and a plate of fried shrimp.

"No," she answered, looking down and smiling. "I grew up here."

"I haven't seen you before. I thought I knew everybody in Southport. What's your name?"

She was shy but attractive. Her dark brown hair was pulled back in a short ponytail. She was slim and pretty, with high cheekbones, big brown eyes, and a sweet smile. She looked two or three years younger than me. I was twenty-six.

"Hannah Garrison. What's your name?"

"Todd Field. Are you related to Jesse Garrison?" Jesse owned the restaurant.

"He's my father."

"I didn't know Jesse had a daughter."

"My mother and I moved to Wilmington when they divorced, so I've been away for a long time."

"Oh," I said, taking the iced tea she handed me.

I ASKED CAPTAIN JACKSON about Hannah Garrison the next day while we were putting out pots for black sea bass and lines for grouper and snapper, which would be shipped north.

"I haven't heard about her in a long time." Captain Jackson said, pausing. "Yeah, Garrison's had a real sad life. After his youngest daughter drowned, his marriage fell apart. His wife left him and took Hannah with her. His son, Gus, stayed with Jesse and helped him at the restaurant. Hannah was about twelve when she left Southport. I wonder what brought her back?"

"I don't know, but I'd like to get to know her better."

"The Garrisons are good people. Jesse was just dealt some bad cards in life. Got plenty of money, though. That can't hurt."

"That's not what I'm interested in," I said, defensively.

"Just kidding," Captain Jackson said, popping me on the shoulder with his fist.

Instead of going to a different restaurant every night, I began to eat at Garrison's more often.

"You're getting to be a regular here," Hannah said, taking my order. "It would be cheaper if you ate at home, you know. Don't you have anybody to fix dinner for you?"

"Nope, I live alone."

"I bet you got girlfriends galore," she said.

"Nope, just work hard, go home, go to sleep, get up, and work hard again."

"Sounds boring to me."

"Not really. It's a living. How about you? Do you have a boyfriend?"

"Yes," she said. "He is a marine at Camp Lejeune." She wiped the table, and put clean silverware down on fresh paper placemats. "He goes overseas a lot. I don't see him much."

"Would you like to go to a movie one night?" I asked.

"I don't know," she said, hesitating. "I'll have to think about that."

"Take your time. I'm in no rush."

THE NEXT TIME I WAS in the restaurant, I asked her out again.

"Have you thought about it anymore?" I asked.

"Yeah."

"What's your answer."

"What've you got in mind?"

"I don't know. They just opened a new movie theater in Shallote. Let's check it out."

"What's playing?"

"What do you want to see?"

"Anything is fine with me as long as it isn't violent or about kickboxing."

"Sounds good to me."

We saw *Romancing The Stone.* After the movie we drove to the waterfront and walked out onto the city pier. It was in the small park at the end of Howe Street, overlooking the Cape Fear River. The beacon from the lighthouse at Oak Island shone across the water, and the lights of a ship coming in from the ocean passed by slowly in the distance. A cool breeze blew over the water. Hannah wore a windbreaker, and I had on a light jacket.

"Why did you move back here?"

"To be with my father and brother. Dad told me he needed me at the restaurant. Mom didn't let me see them much when I was growing up. I wanted to get to know them better."

"Are you glad you moved back?"

"Yeah. I like it here. I like living in a small town. Wilmington is too big for me, but Southport is just right."

"I like it here, too."

"You didn't grow up here," she said, looking out at the water, then turning to look at me. "What brought you to Southport?"

"I grew up on a tobacco farm in Duplin County. I always wanted to live on the coast, so I moved here after high school. I've been here ever since. Once you get the sea in your blood, it's hard to get it out."

"I know," Hannah said, looking at the river.

"It's getting cold," I said, putting my arm around her. She snuggled up to me. "Are you in love with that marine?"

"Why do you ask?"

"I don't know, just curious."

She laughed softly to herself. "Whenever anything goes wrong, it is my fault. He told me he can't stand North Carolina, he wants to move back up north and live in a big city. I told him I want to live in a small town. He laughed at me, said I was backward. I don't know, I try to make him happy, but I never seem to be able to please him. I don't know what he wants."

"Why do you stay with him?"

"He's somebody to go out with and he's good-looking. I can't say I really miss him when he's gone. Let's talk about something else. I need to get home, anyway. My dad's going to be looking for me."

"Okay."

I didn't want to press too hard about her boyfriend, but the more I heard, the more I disliked him. The thought of some marine treating Hannah like dirt really made me mad.

"Good night," I said, at the front door of her father's house, a block away from the waterfront. I bent over to kiss her. She resisted at first, but then gave in. I kissed her long and hard. When I held her I didn't want to let go. She was special. The more I was with her, the more I wanted to be with her, and the more I knew I couldn't be without her.

"I HEAR YOU AND THE Garrison girl are an item," Martha Jackson said one night when I ate with them.

"I'm going out with her, if that's what you mean. She has a boyfriend who's a marine and he's gone a lot. She's probably just bored."

"I don't think so," Martha said, smiling.

"What do you mean?"

"A girl doesn't go out with someone unless she wants to. You're an attractive young man, Todd. Don't underestimate yourself."

"Yeah, but I don't have anything. Her father owns a restaurant. What would she want with me?"

"A lot."

WE PLANNED TO GO out one Friday night in January. She called the last minute to cancel.

"What's wrong? You've never done this before."

"I can't talk about it. I just can't see you tonight, okay?" she said, trying to get me off the phone.

"What about tomorrow night?"

"No, I can't do that, either."

"When can I see you then?"

"I don't know."

I TRIED TO FIGURE out what was wrong. Why didn't she want to see me all of a sudden?

We hadn't had a fight. We never fought. The next weekend I found out why.

STEDMAN MARSH, HER BOYFRIEND, had arrived unannounced at her father's house.

"Why didn't you tell me on the phone?" I asked her on Thursday night, when I saw her at the restaurant.

"I couldn't. He was in the room with me."

"Oh."

"I was miserable—he wouldn't leave. He came to tell me he was going on a secret mission in the Middle East, but he couldn't tell me where. I told him I was dating you and I didn't want to see him anymore. He got real mad and hit the dashboard of my car with his fist, breaking it. I told him I didn't love him anymore. He asked about you, what you did. I told him a little. He said you sounded like a bum. He said every fisherman he ever knew was a drunk. He doesn't drink. When I told him you drank, he said, 'See I told you so.' I told him he was all wrong about you. That you were a good person and I liked you." She looked down with tears forming in her eyes.

"Is that true?" I asked. "Do you like me?"

"Yes," she said, looking down, then into my eyes.

"I like you, too." I paused. "You aren't going to see him anymore, are you?"

"No, I'm not. I don't know why I stayed with him as long as I did. When he hit the dashboard like that, it scared me. He is so violent. I expected him to hit me next. He's a son of a bitch."

"I didn't know if I had done something wrong and made you mad or what," I said.

"It wasn't you."

WE SAW EACH OTHER almost every night after that. One day I drove Hannah to the end of Long Beach where we parked the car and walked out to the water. The day was clear and bright. A cool breeze blew in from the ocean, which swept through Hannah's hair, blowing it behind her like streamers. The sky was cobalt blue.

"Captain Jackson told me that your sister died when she was really young. What happened?" I asked, as we sat on the beach looking out at the ocean. Hannah had never talked to me about it.

"I was eleven years old, she was six. She was the most beautiful baby I have ever seen. She could do no wrong. My parents worshipped her. I felt like the ugly duckling beside her, being the middle child and not as pretty." She looked away from me, brushing her hair out of her face. "Her name was Angela, but we called her Angel. We were at Long Beach for a picnic, playing on the beach, and swimming. I remember Gus and I were building a sand castle. Mom was laying face down on a blanket getting some sun, and Dad walked to the car to get a beach umbrella. It was a beautiful, sunny day. Dad came back and said, 'where's Angela?' Mom jumped up, and we looked around and couldn't see her. Gus said he saw her playing in a tidal pool near the water. My dad and the lifeguard went into the waves where Gus said he last saw her. Two hours later they found her body."

She paused. "Mom never got over it. She blamed herself. Dad tried to keep their marriage together, but he couldn't. Finally Mom left, moved to Wilmington, and took me with her." Hannah turned and looked at me, her hair blowing in her face again. "The whole time I lived with my mother I never saw her go out with another man. She works in the women's department at Belk's Department Store. She never visited Dad. The only time I saw him was when he came to see us."

"How did you feel when all that happened?" I asked.

"We used to always go to church as a family. After that, Mom and Dad stopped going. I remember Mom saying one time, 'I can't believe in a God that would take my little Angela from me like that.'"

"Do you feel that way, too?" I asked, looking into Hannah's eyes.

"Yes," she said, turning to look at the ocean. "How could a loving God let little Angela die? An innocent six-year-old? I don't understand. It's not fair."

I put my arms around Hannah and hugged her. Her eyes were filled with tears. "Let's take a walk," I said.

"Okay."

After we walked for a while, Hannah said. "Todd, have you ever been in love?"

"Yes," I said, hesitantly. "With a girl named Elizabeth, from Raleigh."

"What happened?"

"Her father didn't want us to get married, so he shipped her off to a school in Virginia."

"If you loved each other, how could she let her father split you up?"

"I don't know. She had a different background than I did. She let her father push her around. All I know is that it ended and it hurt for a very long time. It's only been recently that I've been able to get over it."

She took my hand and leaned her head against my shoulder as we walked along the beach.

"I've done a lot of things that I'm not too proud of," I said. "I hated myself after Elizabeth left. All I wanted to do was hurt myself and be left alone." I looked out at the ocean, thinking about Tramps, Key West, Jennifer, the drugs, alcohol, Mark, and the gun. "I don't want to hide anything from you, Hannah."

"I know. I've done a lot of things I'm not proud of, either. But you don't have to tell me everything. I know what I want to know about you already."

"I love you, Hannah," I said. Then I kissed her.

"I love you too, Todd," she said after we kissed.

ONE NIGHT EARLY THAT spring I asked her if she wanted to go to North Myrtle Beach? This friend of mine has a boat that takes cruises at night in the ocean and serves a good seafood dinner."

"You mean Mitch Etheridge? I know Mitch."

"You do?"

"Yeah, we grew up together. That would be fun."

"If it gets too late to drive back, I'm sure we could stay at Mitch's." I was excited. "I'll find out and get in touch with you tomorrow."

"Okay."

I CALLED MITCH, WHO invited us to stay at his condominium after the cruise. He had plenty of room. Mitch knew Hannah. His mother knew Hannah's father very well. After Mitch's father died, Mr. Garrison went out with Mitch's mother every once in a while.

The night was cool, and the moon made a perfect cres-cent in the sky, which was filled with stars. There were only a handful of couples on the boat, and lobster was served by candlelight. Mitch made sure that the best of everything was served to Hannah and me. We drank wine and danced after dinner. We weren't aware of the other diners. We walked out on the deck at the back of the boat after dancing.

The moon made a path across the water, broken by the wake of the large, steel-hulled boat.

"Isn't it beautiful?" Hannah asked.

"Yeah. I love the sea at night. When I was in the Gulf of Mexico shrimping, I used to love to stay up after we hauled in the catch, to watch the sky and the sea. It's like you are in a big room all by yourself, with the sky for the ceiling and walls, and the sea spread out before you like a rich, dark carpet."

"All alone and no one to share it with?"

"No one to share it with." I said, looking at Hannah.

"You can share it with me," she said, reaching over to take my hand.

"The first time I met you I knew I loved you, Hannah," I said.

"When I first saw you, there was something there, like magic." She paused. "I knew I loved you too, but I was afraid to admit it."

I put my arm around her and kissed her.

BECAUSE IT WAS LATE when we got in from the cruise, we spent the night at Mitch's condominium. Mitch stayed with a friend in another unit in the complex. He gave us the key. Hannah slept in one bedroom, and I slept in another. I lay in bed with the lights out, thinking about the night. I couldn't sleep. I heard something outside my door, looked up, and saw Hannah standing in the doorway.

"Hannah," I said, sitting up.

"I don't want to give you the wrong impression," she said hesitantly. "But I was lonely. I want to be in bed with you."

"I couldn't sleep knowing you were in the other room by yourself," I said. "Come on in."

"I don't want to do anything, mind you. I'm not taking off my night gown."

"Don't worry. I have on my boxer shorts."

She got in the bed with me, and I put my arms around her. We kissed, then fell asleep in each other's arms.

SEVENTEEN

One Friday night in April, a few weeks after we ate on Mitch's boat, Hannah and I were walking in the park along the waterfront in Southport after Hannah got off from work. I decided I was going to ask her to marry me, but I was looking for the right opportunity. I chickened out several times but decided I would ask her that night. We walked to the end of the city pier and looked across the river at the Oak Island lighthouse and the lights of Fort Caswell.

"I don't own a restaurant or anything," I began, "and all I have is my boat. I'm just getting started in business, and it's a struggle." I hesitated. "If it's a rich man you want, you better look somewhere else."

"I'm not looking for a rich man, Todd. I like you just the way you are."

"Do you mean that?"

"I don't have any reason to lie, do I?"

We talked a little more, then Hannah asked, "Todd, have you ever thought about having children?"

"Yeah," I said, looking across the river. "I really want to have kids. I didn't have much of a childhood myself. I want to do all the things with my kids that my dad didn't do with me."

"I've always wanted to have children."

"You'd think as wild as I was when I was young that kids would be the last thing I'd want. But it's not true. I'm just as ordinary as the next guy when it comes to wanting to get married and raise a family."

"Maybe you got all the wildness out of your system and you're ready to settle down."

"Yeah. I'm sick of going to bars and picking up women. It's so lonely. Funny being lonely in a crowd, but it's true. I'm ready to settle down." I paused and looked at Hannah. "I'd like to settle down with you. Hannah, will you marry me?"

"Yes," she answered, then she put her arms around me and kissed me.

"Are you serious?" I asked, still surprised by what I'd asked and by her answer.

"Yes."

"You don't mind that I don't have any money?"

"No."

"Or that I'm a fisherman?"

"No."

"Or that I want to live in Southport?"

"Honey, those are some of the very reasons I love you."

I reached down and kissed her. "I can't believe it. I didn't think I would ever get up enough nerve to ask you."

"I'm not going to bite your head off."

"I know," I said, laughing. "I just thought you'd say no."

"I love you," she said, pulling me close. We stood at the end of the pier, hugging and kissing and going back and forth between "Do you really love me?" and "You do really love me," until reality slowly sank in.

The next day I woke up in a cold sweat. "What have I done?" I said to myself. A million thoughts flooded my head—I can't get married, I don't have enough money; I'm just getting started in my business; I can't afford a wife and children; Her family will hate me; What if she changes her mind? I thought of all the reasons I shouldn't get married. Then I walked to the restaurant for breakfast.

"I think we need some time to think about this," I said to Hannah after ordering breakfast.

"You're right. I don't know if I'm ready to get married. We've only known each other for a few months," she said, writing down my order, looking at the table.

"Let's not tell anyone for four weeks, okay?"

"Okay."

THE NEXT TUESDAY I picked up Hannah after work and we walked along the waterfront.

"I've got to tell Mitch, then Mama. She said she wanted to know if I was going to get married. And of course I have to tell Captain Jackson and Martha."

"I thought we were going to wait to tell people."

"We don't need to wait, do we?"

"Not if you don't want to. But before you tell anyone I want you to come home with me and ask my dad."

"Do I need to ask for your hand in marriage?"

"I know it's old-fashioned," she said, looking down, embarrassed.

"I want to do it right. If you think I need to ask his permission, then I will. I don't want to get off on the wrong foot with your family."

"My dad loves you."

"I don't know about that."

"When do you want to do it?"

"How about right now?"

"Now?!" she asked, looking nervous. "Gee, I don't know. It's so late."

"It's only ten-thirty. Isn't he still up?"

"Probably."

WE WALKED THE SHORT distance to her father's house on Bay Street. It was a two-story Victorian with a wrap-around porch, and it faced the waterfront.

"How are you doing, Todd?" Mr. Garrison asked as he opened the front door to let us in. Hannah and I sat down on a Victorian love seat in the parlor. I put my hand in Hannah's lap.

"Mr. Garrison, I need to, um, ask you something." I paused.

"Yes?" Mr. Garrison said.

"Well, Mr. Garrison, Hannah and I love each other very much." I cleared my throat. "And we want to get married."

"Is that right, Hannah?" Mr. Garrison asked her, smiling.

"Yes, sir," Hannah said, looking straight into her father's eyes.

"How do you plan to provide for my daughter, young man?"

"I have a boat. I work hard to make a living. It's a struggle, but my business is growing."

"I still plan to work, Dad," Hannah added. "I'm sure we can make out just fine."

Mr. Garrison walked over to us, arms held out. We stood and he hugged us. He was crying.

"Seems like you came here only yesterday, Hannah, and now you're leaving me again."

"I won't be far away, Daddy. We want to live in Southport. Todd said he doesn't ever want to leave here. I don't either. This is home."

"I give you my blessing. It would take a blind man not to see that you love each other. In the end that is all that matters. The rest will work itself out." He paused. "You are a fine young man, Todd. I've been watching you ever since I first saw you work with Captain Jackson. I would be proud to have you for a son-in-law."

I couldn't believe it was so easy. I wasn't afraid of Mr. Garrison. I had always liked him and felt the feeling was mutual. It seemed so natural, so right. But I couldn't believe how it all fell into place. We decided to get married the first Saturday in June at her church, Southport Baptist Church.

TIME PASSED VERY QUICKLY. I contacted Mama, Sally, and June Bug, who said they would come. Andrew Mason found out and called me. He had been elected to the city council in Clinton as its only black member. Mitch planned a stag party at the White Horse, a strip joint in Myrtle Beach, for the Wednesday before the wedding.

That Wednesday night we gathered at Mitch's condominium—Andrew, Mitch, June Bug, Victor Slade, Captain Jackson, and a few of Mitch's friends from Myrtle Beach. Hannah's dad wanted to join us but he had to go out of town. We had even asked Hannah's brother, Gus, but he said he couldn't come—too busy at the restaurant. I wasn't sure that was really it, though. I had a feeling Gus didn't like me as much as Hannah's father did.

At the White Horse, I sat in front, right at the edge of the stage. The stripper had been given her instructions, and she did her job expertly. The bar was packed with men, whistling and yelling to get her attention. But she didn't take her eyes off me.

When she got down to her G-string, she bent down and said, "You're too good-looking to get married. Why don't you stay with me tonight?"

I just laughed and put a dollar bill in her G-string. The others overheard her and started to tease me.

"Damn, Todd, I think she likes you a little too much," Mitch said.

Captain Jackson laughed and said, "Remember who's waiting for you back home."

"Well I'd sure like to take her home with me," June Bug said, smiling, as we got up to leave.

FROM THERE, WE ALL piled into Mitch's convertible, except for Captain Jackson who had driven his own car. Even though June Bug didn't know his way around, he drove because he was the only one who'd not been drinking. As we headed back to Mitch's condo, a blue light appeared in the rear view mirror.

"Oh, shit," Andrew said, sliding down on the floor of the back seat. "I can see it if this gets in the newspaper back home—City Councilman Thrown in Jail at Myrtle Beach!"

June Bug pulled over to the side of the road. "Yes, officer?" he said, very politely.

"One of your rear lights is out, sir," the policeman said. "I'm going to have to write you a ticket."

The officer, a pleasant man in his early thirties, looked at all of us crowded in the back seat of the car. "Have you boys been drinking?"

"Well . . . they have," June Bug said slowly. "That's why I'm driving. We had a party for my brother. He's getting married."

The officer looked carefully at each one of us. When he got to Mitch, his face lit up. "Say, aren't you Mitch Etheridge who owns the *Carolina*?"

"Yes, I am," Mitch said, sounding as dignified as he could.

"Great place you got there. We had dinner there the other night."

The officer hesitated for a minute, then turned back to June Bug. "Look. I can see you haven't been drinking. Drive your friends home and park this car until he gets the light fixed. I'll let this be a warning, okay?"

June Bug nodded.

"Thank you, officer," Mitch said, politely from the back seat. "You have a good night."

The rest of us just heaved a sigh of relief, grateful we'd had the sense to let June Bug drive.

A few years ago, I would have laughed about something like this. Now all I could do was shudder at the thought of having to explain a night in jail to Hannah and her dad. Life sure does change.

FRIDAY NIGHT BEFORE THE wedding, Mr. Garrison held a party at his restaurant for both families. It was the first time I'd seen Hannah's mother. Mary Garrison was very shy and reserved, but attractive for her age. She looked uncomfortable with the festivities. I saw Mr. Garrison walk to his wife's table, where she sat, alone. He spoke to her, walked away, then came back with a drink. She smiled at him for the first time that night. She took the drink, then Mr. Garrison left to sit at his own table with Gus.

Gus didn't have much to say to Hannah or me. After the dinner he walked up to Hannah, kissed her on the cheek, and said congratulations. He said nothing to me.

June Bug, Sally, her husband, and my mother sat at another table. Sally had gained weight, and my mother looked older. June Bug looked great. His complexion was ruddy and he was full of laughs and fun. He and Mitch had become fast friends at the stag party and were now making plans to decorate my car.

Several final toasts were made, then everyone left. Hannah told me she was tired and was heading home. I felt the same and went to bed as soon as I got home.

The next day, we were married. It was a simple ceremony. The Baptist preacher presided in the red brick church on Howe Street. Sun streamed in through the bright, stained-glass windows. The reception was held in the educational building in back. It too was simple—no alcohol, and only punch and sweets.

Mitch and June Bug had decorated my car with toilet paper and shaving cream, and tied cans to the bumper. Someone put a fish on the manifold. The waitresses from the restaurant put rice and toilet paper in Hannah's suitcase.

Making our escape, we drove to the marina, where I left my car. Then we cruised down the inland waterway in my boat, headed for Charleston. We spent the first night in Georgetown, South Carolina.

I'D BROUGHT ALONG A bottle of champagne. After we ate dinner at a restaurant near the waterfront, we headed back to the boat. I brought out the champagne and we drank a glass. Then Hannah started to undress.

I'd never seen her completely naked before. When we spent the night together at Mitch's condominium, she wore her nightgown. I couldn't take my eyes off her as she slowly revealed her plump, white breasts. Her tiny waist accented her hips, which were rich and inviting. As I took my clothes off she looked at me with obvious pleasure. I became aroused.

"You are more beautiful than I ever imagined," I said, kissing her.

"And you are more handsome."

I kissed her, then let my tongue run lightly over her neck, while slipping my hands over her breasts. She ran her fingers lightly over my body, covering my skin with goosebumps. We made love for a long time, then lay beside each other, not moving. We just basked in the feelings.

"That was perfect," she said, looking up at the ceiling, which glowed red from the setting sun. "It's like we were meant for each other from the very beginning. Isn't it funny? You go out with all kinds of people, but it never quite feels right. Then you fall in love and it all fits. It all makes sense."

"I know," I said, pulling up on my elbow and stroking her hair as it lay in wet tendrils on her forehead, which was flush and red. The sun was setting, but still lit the berth with a reddish light.

"I feel like I have known you all my life," she said.

"I feel the same way."

We were silent for a while, finished the champagne, then fell asleep. The next day when I woke up, I looked at Hannah, who was still sleeping, and realized that I would wake up beside her like this every day for the rest of my life. It scared me a little at first, but then the more I thought about it, the more I liked it. I leaned over and kissed her. Her eyes opened and she smiled at me.

"Good morning," she said.

"Good morning."

EIGHTEEN

Hᴀɴɴᴀʜ ᴀɴᴅ I ᴡᴀɴᴛᴇᴅ ᴛᴏ ʜᴀᴠᴇ children right away. She was
as fertile as the black soil of eastern North Carolina. In
September, Hannah began to tire easily. She had missed
a period.

"Todd, I think I'm pregnant," she told me one night
before going to bed.

"Really?!" I was so happy I could barely contain myself. I wanted to tell Martha, Captain Jackson, June Bug,
Sally, Mama, Mr. Garrison, everyone.

"Before you go tell everybody, let me go to the doctor
to make sure."

It took a few days before she could get a doctor's ap-
pointment. I was impatient. But I didn't say a word to
anyone until she found out for sure. She came back from
the doctor's office beaming.

"I'm pregnant. It must have happened in August. I'm
due in late April or early May. Can you believe it?"

I called everyone I knew. Mr. Garrison was excited
about his first grandchild. Mama was more cautious.

"Todd, it's mighty early to be announcing it to the
world. A lot can happen between now and then. I think

you should wait a few months before you go telling everybody."

But I couldn't help myself.

ONE DAY, SOON AFTER we heard, Hannah and I took my Boston Whaler to Bald Head Island for a picnic. In September it is beautiful on the island. We walked to the beach,
spread out a blanket near the water, and stretched out,
looking up at the clear, blue sky.

"If it's a boy, I want to name him after my Uncle Warren, who died in Vietnam."

"Isn't that morbid, naming him for someone who's
dead? What if something happened to him? Then how
would you feel?" Hannah asked, propping herself up on
one elbow.

"I want to name him Warren. My uncle was a great
guy. He's my guardian angel. He was the kindest man
I've ever known. It wasn't his fault he got killed in Vietnam."

"Okay, if you insist," she said. "What if it's a girl?"

"Then we'll name her Hannah."

"No. What about naming her after your mother?"

"No, we should name her Hannah. You're bringing
this child into the world, aren't you?"

"Yes."

"Then Hannah will be her name."

"We don't even know the baby will be born. I don't
know why we are worrying so much about what to name it."

"This baby will be born and be healthy and wonderful. Mark my word. We'll have to find a bigger house. Then
all the baby things. Maybe even buy a station wagon."

"Now how are we going to afford all that?"

"We can. I just need to work harder."

"I'll need to work hard, too."

"I wish you wouldn't," I said, looking over at her. "I wish I could make enough money for both of us to live on, so you could stay at home with the baby."

"You know we can't afford that."

"I know," I said, looking up at the clouds. "If I could just get my business going better. Now that I have responsibilities." I paused. "Let's walk to the cape," I said suddenly, jumping up and offering her my hand.

"I'm tired. I don't know if I can walk that far."

"Sure you can," I said, pulling her up.

We walked along the beach toward the cape. I looked out over the water, remembering all the times I'd spent on the island. Looking over the shoals, I thought about the fishing trips I had taken, about my boat, Captain Jackson, Mitch, and Victor Slade.

"You know the baby will slow us down a lot," Hannah said, brushing her hair away as the wind blew it in her face. "No night life. No eating out. A lot of staying home and baby-sitting. They say the first few months a baby doesn't sleep at night. That means somebody's going to have to get up every few hours to feed it. Are you ready for that?"

"As ready as I'll ever be. I don't need to go out at night when I have you. We have another life to look after now. There's no going back." I put my hand on her stomach. "I'm ready, are you?"

"I suppose so."

We walked to the cape and stood at the point where the ocean comes together on two sides, looked at the white caps over Frying Pan Shoals.

"Isn't it beautiful?" I said, holding Hannah from behind as the wind whipped around us. "Whenever I feel

low, I know I can come out here and stand on the cape
and feel right again." I looked over the ocean. "It's like
we are standing on an island in the middle of the waves.
It's a wonderful feeling."

"I like it out here, too, but I'm tired. Can we head
back now?"

"Do you want me to carry you?" I asked, picking her up
before she could answer. She giggled and didn't seem to
mind. I carried her down the beach halfway to where our
blanket was on the sand. Then I put her down.

"I won't be able to carry you, the picnic basket, and
the blanket, too," I said. When we got to our stuff we
walked across the deep sand of the dunes to the boat.

HANNAH WAS TIRED A LOT for the next few months, but she
continued to work until April. We took Lamaze classes at
the hospital, so I could be with her when she had the baby.
Her mood swings took some getting used to.

"I am so ugly," she said, looking in the mirror at her
bulging stomach in February.

"I think you're beautiful."

"No, you don't. How could you? I'm fat, bloated, and
ugly. I'm ashamed to go out in public."

I put my arm around her and looked at our reflection
in the mirror.

"I think you are the most beautiful woman in the
world." Then I kissed her.

She began to cry. "I'm tired of being pregnant. I want
to get control of my body again. I feel like something else
is in control, and I hate it."

One night we went to see a movie, *Beverly Hills Cop*, a
fast-paced action film. In the middle of the movie Hannah
jumped and said in a loud whisper, "It moved!"

"What?"

"It moved, I mean it **really** moved! I think it did a somersault."

She took my hand and held it to her stomach. I could feel the baby as it settled into a different position.

"See? It turned around completely."

At night as we were going to bed, I would put my ear to Hannah's stomach to see if I could hear the baby. I felt it push out with its tiny feet and hands. I also talked to it. We both called the baby Scooter, because it was so active in her womb.

"Scooter, honey, it's your daddy. Your mommy and I love you and want to see you soon."

"You're crazy," Hannah said, running her hands through my hair, as my head lay on her stomach.

"I want Scooter to know my voice and know we love him, even now."

"How do you know it's not a girl?"

"I don't. I just think it's going to be a boy, that's all."

She smiled and lay back on her pillow.

"I love you, you silly goof."

We continued to make love, though less often the closer it got to her due date.

After the first week in May, her due date passed. Hannah was ready to have the baby. We ate at her father's restaurant and went to see a movie. When we got home and went to bed, she put her arms around me and kissed me.

"I want to make love," she said. "The doctor told me if we make love, we might be able to induce labor. I am so tired of waiting for this baby I'm willing to try anything."

"If you say so," I said, looking at her belly sticking out from her body. It was the size of a ripe watermelon. It wasn't easy, but we made love. Then we fell asleep.

"Todd," she said, sitting up in bed. "I think my water broke!" It was two hours past midnight.

"Oh, shit!" I said, jumping out of bed and pulling my jeans on, forgetting my underwear. We had rehearsed this so many times, and she had a bag packed beside the bed, but suddenly I couldn't find anything.

She stood up, and clear liquid gushed from between her legs. I helped her to the bathroom, then put down towels on the floor of the hall to sop it up.

She put on some clothes and found her bag. I pulled on a T-shirt and tennis shoes, walked her to the car, and drove to the hospital.

The baby was slow. After we settled into her room, the doctor suggested we both rest. Her contractions were widely spaced at first. I dozed off between contractions, stretched out in a blue vinyl recliner beside her bed.

After dawn the contractions came more quickly. I helped her control her breathing and massaged her back to relieve the pain. I couldn't understand why the nurses weren't concerned when she cried out in pain during the contractions. She asked for drugs, and they did finally give her something for pain. But mostly they encouraged her to use the breathing techniques. By noon she was acting strange.

"Get the nurse. I need drugs! This hurts!" she shouted at me.

Another time she grabbed my T-shirt and twisted it up in her hand as the pain of the contraction came. "You did this to me!" she said with the look of a frightened animal.

The doctor told me not to worry, that it was natural for her to act this way and to just ignore it. The doctor helped massage her back and relieve her pain with his skilled hands. Then he motioned for me to follow him into a back room to change into green scrubs. After we changed we followed Hannah as she was rolled into the delivery room.

I held Hannah's hand as the baby was being delivered. I couldn't remember much of the screaming, the pain, the directions to push. It all seemed like a blur to me, or a dream. Then the baby emerged, glistening, wet, and bloody. Resting in the doctor's hands, it changed colors from gray to pink before my eyes, like a chameleon. It was a boy! The doctor shoved a pair of scissors into my hands. "Here, you cut the cord."

I didn't know what to do, but dutifully cut the gray mucous umbilical cord. When I cut it, it changed color instantly, turning dark and dead-looking. The doctor tied off the cord at the baby's belly button and began to re-move the afterbirth.

They wrapped the baby in a towel, put a little cap on his head, and rested him on his mother's stomach. Hannah was covered with sweat, and her hair stuck to her forehead. But she smiled a wide smile as she took the baby into her arms. The screams of pain during the birth changed to whimpers of joy. I looked at my son's eyes as they quietly surveyed the room. The baby was quiet and curious as he took in everything around him.

"Warren, I'm your daddy," I said, letting the baby clasp my big, callused finger with his delicate little hand.

When they wheeled Hannah out of the delivery room to a regular hospital room, they passed the lobby where Hannah's father, her brother Gus, Captain Jackson, and Martha were waiting. When I saw the Jacksons I started to cry. I couldn't help it.

"What's the matter?" Captain Jackson asked, putting his arm around me.

"I'm so happy," I said.

After Elizabeth, the abortion, and all I'd gone through, I thought I would never know what it was like to be a father. I felt God had given me a second chance. I was so happy and grateful. I held Hannah's hand as they wheeled her down the hall into her room. I didn't want to leave her side. But the doctor told me to go home and rest and let Hannah rest, too. When I got home, I fell asleep as soon as I hit the bed.

JUST AS HANNAH HAD said, for the first few months we got very little sleep. She got up at night to breast-feed the baby, and I got up to help with Warren, too. But I also had to get up early to go fishing, and I found myself dozing off at work from time to time.

Hannah stayed home for the first six months, then she decided to go back to work. I didn't want her to.

"I have to get out of here," she said, standing in the kitchen one day when I came home early from work. "I'm going crazy. All I do is talk baby talk. I'm climbing the walls."

"I wish you could stay home a little longer. Who is going to watch Warren?"

"I don't know. We'll figure something out."

I sighed. "Okay, but I don't like it."

I looked after Warren when I was home, but when we were both gone, we hired a black woman in her sixties, Helen Mize, to stay with him. We didn't make love for three months after having Warren—we were both tired, and Hannah was sore from breast-feeding Warren.

One night I pulled back the blanket and put my head on her breast. "Can I have some?" I said, in baby talk.

"What?"

"Can I taste your milk?"

"Sure, why not," she laughed.

I put my mouth to her breast and drew out the sweet milk. It did not taste fatty like cow's milk. It tasted like nectar—sweet and rich.

"That tastes good," I said, smiling.

"You're sick," she said, giggling.

"Can I have some more?" I asked, nudging up to her breast.

"Sure, that felt good."

I took some more milk, then began to kiss her neck and mouth. Soon we were making love.

IN NOVEMBER, I WAS working long hours with Captain Jackson and Victor Slade, fishing commercially. When I came home, I was exhausted. I said very little, ate quickly, and collapsed on the sofa after I ate.

"You come in from work, don't say anything to me, then flop on the sofa," Hannah said one night. "It's like we're two strangers living in the same house. I'm not sure what I'm doing here except to cook, wash clothes, clean house, and take care of the baby. Sometimes I think I don't know you any more."

"I'm sorry," I said. "I'm just so tired. When I come in, all I want to do is forget about the day."

"I feel like you don't love me anymore," she said, beginning to cry.

I stood up and wrapped my arms around her. "Honey, you know I love you. It's not that I don't care about you and Warren. I love you both more than anything in the world, but I'm tired after work. I'm sorry."

"I work, too, you know. Don't you think I'm tired when I come home? I can't forget everything and lie down when I come in like you do. I need some help, Todd."

"Okay, I'll try to help out more with the house."

I began to help more with Warren. Changing his diapers, giving him his bottle, watching him, bathing him, playing with him. I also began to help Hannah more. I couldn't cook, but I helped to clean the house.

By March of 1987, Hannah was pregnant again. I decided to look for a bigger house. I found one on Brunswick Street, near Captain Jackson's. It needed a lot of work.

It was a one-story, white frame house, with a picket fence and a bay window. It didn't have much of a yard, but it did have three bedrooms. And even though it looked small, it had enough room for a growing family. We borrowed the money to buy it.

Hannah and I worked day and night scraping paint, glazing windows, cleaning floors, and scraping up old linoleum. Hannah kept Warren in a Snugli close to her stomach, as she worked on the house while he slept. When he was awake, we kept him in a playpen or a wind-up swing. Victor Slade and I replumbed the house, hung sheet rock, fixed a few rotten sills, and built new cabinets in the kitchen. I hired an electrician to do the wiring. We worked all that spring, summer, and fall, on the house.

"That electrician charged twice what he said he would," Hannah said one night, going over bills with me.

"He said he couldn't use any of the old wiring," I said. "He said he had to completely rewire."

"That isn't what he told us to begin with."

"I know. But it needed to be done. I don't want to live in a house with unsafe wiring."

"What about the plumbing bill, and the lumber bill, and the sheet rock? Todd, how are we going to pay these bills and have enough money left over to finish the house?"

"I don't know. We can't stop now. We've got to finish it. We've gone too far. If we sell it now we'll lose money and still not have a house. If we keep it, we've got to at least make it livable."

Hannah decided to borrow some money from her father. She didn't want to. I was ashamed that she had to do it.

"I hate to ask my father to bail us out," Hannah said one night, sitting at the table after finishing supper. "Dammit, we should have known how much it would cost in the first place."

"It's still a lot cheaper than if we had bought a new house."

"We should have stayed where we were. We can't afford to own a house. It's that simple."

"But we need a bigger place with the new baby and all. I'd much rather make a mortgage payment and feel we are building something up than pay rent. That's like throwing money down a rat hole." I looked at her. "I thought you loved this house?"

"I did until it started costing so much."

"And we had to borrow money from your father?"

"Yes."

Costs continued to mount, then we had to buy furniture and curtains and paint. I borrowed more money, using the equity in the house for collateral.

"How are we going to make these monthly payments?" Hannah asked after we signed the new loan papers.

"I'll just have to work harder and get more business, that's all."

"I don't know about this, Todd. I don't like having all this debt."

"Then borrow some more from your father?"

"No way."

"Then stop complaining. We own this house and we've got to finish it. It's too late to change our mind. We've got to see it through."

"I know, but I don't like it."

I STARTED DROPPING BY the marina bar to have a beer before coming home after work. One led to two, and then three. Hannah began to complain about me coming home late.

One night in November, close to Hannah's due date, I was at the marina bar drinking my third drink, when the bartender, a large bearded man, handed me the phone.

"For you," he said gruffly.

It was Hannah.

"Todd, my water just broke. You need to come home. I'm afraid the baby's coming quickly this time."

I rushed home, packed Hannah's bags, and walked her to the car.

"You've been drinking, haven't you," she said on the way to the hospital.

"Yes. I didn't know the baby would come this early. I thought you were due in two weeks."

"You never know about these things. The doctor said it could come anytime now."

"I'm sorry, honey. If I'd known, I would have been at home with you."

Hannah didn't respond.

In the hospital, I sat in a recliner next to Hannah's bed, while we waited for the doctor to examine her. I was worried because we didn't take Lamaze this time. Hannah didn't like Lamaze, and I'd been drinking. I couldn't re-member anything about Lamaze and the breathing tech-

niques. I was afraid I would screw up. The doctor, a balding man in his forties, came in and began to examine
Hannah.

"The baby's breech," he said, calling in a nurse. "Prepare Mrs. Field for surgery. We're going to have to take it."
He explored some more.

"Does that mean a C-section?" I asked.

"Yes," the doctor said.

I was almost relieved. At least this way it would be quick,
and we wouldn't have to go through the hours of labor.
And I wouldn't have to try and remember my Lamaze
lessons.

"Can I please get something for the pain?"

"You sure can," the doctor said, smiling. "We'll give
you an epidural, and you won't feel a thing. You can watch
if you want."

"No, thanks," she said.

As they prepared Hannah for surgery, they told me I
could come in, dressed in scrubs and a sterile mask. Since
Hannah said she did not want to watch the birth, they put
up a screen between her head and the surgery. I thought
I wanted to watch, until they touched the scalpel to her
flesh. I decided to sit behind the screen and hold
Hannah's hand, instead. I did watch as they held the baby
up for both of us to see. She was a plump, healthy, baby
girl and cried a healthy cry. I once again cut the umbilical
cord and watched as they washed the baby, weighed her,
and laid her in a Plexiglas crib. Her eyes were wide and
full of wonder as they looked up at me, surveying her
strange new world.

We named her Mildred Garrison Field after Hannah's
father's mother. Hannah said having two Hannahs in the

house would be confusing. After Millie was born, I stopped going to the bar. Hannah needed me at home.

Work was not picking up. Fishing became more difficult. We had to go out farther and farther to get the good game fish. Some people said it was the pollution from the Cape Fear River. Some said it came from over-fishing. I don't know what it was. All I know was that the fish weren't there anymore. The recent recession and changes in the tax laws made some of my business customers cut back on entertainment. Instead of business picking up, as I had expected, it dropped off. I had to borrow more money just to keep up with the payments on the debt I had accumulated so far, and to meet my monthly expenses. I didn't tell Hannah everything. I told her I thought business was going to pick up, but it didn't.

"How much money do we owe, Todd?" she asked me one night after putting the children to bed.

"Twenty-five thousand dollars, not including the mortgage on the house."

"What?!" She was shocked. "How did that happen?"

"It's been hard, Hannah. I know business is bound to pick up, but for now I'm having to borrow money just to meet expenses. Then I get deeper and deeper in debt. I don't know what to do."

"Well, for starters, we're not borrowing any more money. If we have to sell this house, we'll sell it. We can always rent."

"I'd hate to do that. Can you go to your dad again?"

"If I do, you will have to promise me one thing—let me take over the finances and no more debt without telling me. No more spending either, agreed?"

"Agreed."

Hannah asked her father for another loan. He gave it to her. But my business was making less and less money. Her father's loan got us through the year. But after that we were in almost the same shape again.

WARREN HELD MY FINGERS as he walked across the kitchen floor. I smiled, and said, "Good boy. Hannah, did you see that? Warren can almost walk by himself."

Hannah breast-fed Millie while she sat at the kitchen table. She smiled as she watched Warren and me. I loved my children so much. I tried to be a good father and a good husband. I did my best, but somehow my best wasn't good enough. We both felt helpless as we sank deeper and deeper in debt. Hannah suggested I find another job.

"What can I do? Fishing is all I know."

"I don't know, honey. I just don't know," she said, hugging me.

NINETEEN

Victor and I filled the coolers with ice, beer, and soft drinks for the trip. It was June 1988, and we were preparing to take a party of five from Cone Mills for a trip to the Gulf Stream. The sky was pink and peach at the horizon. The air felt fresh and cool. Occasionally the early morning silence was broken by the sound of a gull, an egret, or a crane. I loved this time of day. I felt excitement and anticipation over what the day had in store for me. Gradually, the silence of the morning was filled with the noise of people and boats, and the cool morning air turned hot and muggy.

After Victor and I washed the boat down one last time, a car drove up. Our customers got out, holding cold Budweisers and talking loudly.

"Todd, how are you doing?" Jack Thomas called out. He was a balding man in his mid-forties, wearing khaki shorts and a flowered shirt. I stood over one of the coolers, helping Victor fill it with ice. Before I could answer, Mr. Thomas turned to his two companions and said, "I'd like for you all to meet Todd Field, one of the best charter captains in Southport." He slapped me on the back.

"How are you all doing?" I asked, with a wide grin.

"This is Jim Wallace and Billy Snipes. These gentle-men are trying to decide whether they should buy from Orton Chemicals. It's our job to convince them that they need to, isn't that right, Todd?" Mr. Thomas said with a laugh, slapping me on the back again.

"Let me tell you all something," I began. "If you haven't been entertained by Jack Thomas before, you'd better hold onto the seat of your pants, because you're in for the time of your life. I suppose I've taken Jack out a dozen times, and he is one of the hell-raisingest guys I've ever known. One thing is for sure. His customers are al-ways satisfied."

"Why do you think we're down here?" Mr. Wallace said. He was a tall, thin man and wore dark glasses. "But we don't want him to get too confident about our business." He winked at me. "We want him to work hard for it."

Mr. Snipes smiled.

"Always giving ole Jack a hard time. It gets harder to make an honest dollar every day, isn't that right, Todd?" Mr. Thomas said.

At thirty I was still strong and lean. I had gained a little weight since I'd gotten married, but the extra weight did me good. I wasn't so skinny anymore. I had a few wrinkles around my eyes, and the sun had leathered my skin somewhat, but not as bad as some.

"Who's this young fella?" Mr. Thomas asked, putting his hand on Victor's shoulder. Victor was twenty-four. Tall and wiry, with broad shoulders and long legs, there wasn't an ounce of fat on his body. Victor had a good tan, a flat stomach, dark eyes, and long, blonde hair that hung to his shoulders. I had long since cut my hair to a more conservative cut. He wore dark glasses, an orange nylon bathing suit, and no shirt.

"Victor Slade. He's been working for me for a few years now. He works with Captain Jackson, too."

"Fine-looking young man," Mr. Thomas said, squeezing Victor's firm shoulder. "You gonna skipper a boat someday?" Mr. Thomas asked Victor.

"Don't have enough money to afford a boat," Victor said, in a deep, baritone voice, with the accent of the Outer Banks.

"Victor will have his own boat someday. He's a hard worker," I said, looking at my friend.

As the men boarded the boat, Victor and I finished icing down the beer and soft drinks. Then I started the engines, and we made our way down the Cape Fear River into the Atlantic Ocean.

A sleek white, fiberglass, thirty-six-footer, my boat had a bridge, a head, a small galley, a V-berth in the bow, and a sofa that slept two. It was fully equipped with Loran, radio, radar, antennas, and outriggers, which kept the lines from tangling. When I first bought the boat, I named it the *Martha Frances,* but after I married I renamed it *The Hannah G.*

IT TOOK ABOUT FOUR hours to get to the deep blue waters of the Gulf Stream. Once there, we fished for marlin, without success. Then I asked Victor to put spoons on the lines. On the way out I saw several Spanish mackerel chasing schools of bait fish. I figured if we couldn't catch big game fish, we may as well fill the ice chest with mackerel. I headed back to Southport.

Two of the men were asleep, resting in the front of the boat. After a few hours of fishing unsuccessfully, they were slightly sick from drinking beer. They woke up when Mr. Thomas told them to take the rods, which were spinning with mackerel on the lines. About halfway back to Southport, I ran into a large school of Spanish mackerel. We trolled the area, steadily circling around, and crossing back and forth. As soon as one fish was taken off the line and the line thrown back in, we pulled in another.

Victor stayed busy taking fish off the lines, untangling lines, and throwing lines back into the water.

"I got one," Mr. Wallace yelled. Victor told him to hook it and reel it in. When it came to the side of the boat, Victor netted it and hooked it with a gaff, pulling it on board.

We lost a few fish because the men didn't properly hook them. Sometimes when they brought them to the side of the boat, they let the line drag in the water instead of pulling it up high, so the fish got away. Before long, we had caught fifty Spanish mackerel, filling the ice chests.

Victor's hands, legs, and stomach were splattered with fish blood. Delighted with the catch so far, the men started to drink more beer. They forgot about being sleepy and sick as the excitement of catching so many fish brought them back to life.

"HAD ENOUGH?" I called down from the bridge.

"Yeah," Mr. Wallace said, opening a can of beer.

Mr. Thomas climbed up to the bridge and sat down beside me. "Todd, this has been great. It couldn't have been better if we'd caught a white marlin. But I was wondering. Since we caught so many fish, could you take us sharking, like we did when I brought those guys out from Fieldcrest Cannon two years ago?"

I hesitated. Though the sharks are small, you have to be careful. I'd seen a shark bite a chunk out of a thick wooden chair on Captain Jackson's boat. I knew how dangerous they could be, even with experienced fishermen. "Okay, but your customers need to know this isn't child's play. I'll do it, but I'll let Victor take the bridge, and I'll handle the lines myself."

I asked Victor to join me on the bridge. "I want you to take the wheel," I said.

"Where to?" Victor asked.

"Go to the artificial reef, south 180 degrees."

The artificial reef, made of sunken liberty boats from World War II, was due west of the shoals, at the mouth of the Cape Fear River. After thirty minutes at full throttle, we came to a buoy that marked the artificial reef.

"This is it. Slow down and circle the area, keeping in sight of the buoy," I said to Victor.

"Okay," Victor said, putting on his T-shirt.

The canvas top covering the bridge kept the sun out, and with the constant breeze from the ocean, it was cool in the shade. I took several mackerel out of the ice chest, gutted them, and filled a bucket with their bloody guts. I hid several large hooks in the fish, using the entire fish for bait. They were between twenty and twenty-four inches long.

When I finished, I threw the contents of the pail overboard, chumming the water with blood and guts to attract the sharks. Then I cast the lines—two at a time, not four like when we caught the mackerel. I took one of the lines and gave the other to Mr. Wallace.

"Like I told Jack on the bridge, sharking is serious business, fellas. When I say jump, jump, okay? These will probably be sand sharks, but they can still do a lot of damage."

The men nodded in agreement, looking a bit frightened at the prospect. "What do we do if we catch one?" Mr. Snipes asked.

"We bring it into the boat and let it thrash around until it dies. It doesn't take long for a shark to die out of the water, but until then, they fight like hell. So watch out."

"Don't worry," Mr. Wallace said.

Soon sharks began to appear in the clear blue water, attracted to the fish guts. Mr. Wallace's line began to spin.

"I got one," he said. The line spun faster as the shark swam with the bait, far from the boat.

"Let it go until it wears itself out and the boat drags it a little. Then start reeling in," I said.

Then a shark hit the other line. It looked like the rod, wedged in a cup in the front of the wooden chair, would jump out of the boat and be carried away by the shark, but it held. I gave it to Mr. Snipes. Gradually Mr. Wallace and Mr. Snipes began to reel in their catches. It was tough going—as soon as they reeled in a little, the lines spun and the sharks swam away.

"Let me bring in Mr. Wallace's first," I said. "Bill, you take it easy. Don't lose yours, but don't be in a hurry to bring it in, either. The boat will drag him for a while and wear him out."

Victor continued to steer the boat in a wide circle at low speed. He never brought it to a complete halt.

"This thing is wearing me out," Mr. Wallace said, looking at me.

"Jack, you take it for a while," I said. Mr. Thomas took Mr. Wallace's place and began to reel in. Soon beads of sweat covered his forehead, and his arms strained as he tried to reel in the shark. As soon as he reeled in a bit, the line would spin and take off, the shark carrying it farther away from the boat.

"I don't seem to be making much progress," Mr. Thomas said.

"We need to wear it out first. The line is set so the shark can take it out after you reel in. If it is locked when you reel in, the shark will break the line. This will wear him down. Just stay with it."

Soon Mr. Thomas gave the rod back to Mr. Wallace, who after a while gave it back to Mr. Thomas.

"Looks like the shark's wearing us out, not the other way around," Mr. Wallace told me. Mr. Snipes, who was a more experienced fisherman than the others, kept his line taut but was in no rush to bring his in.

After a long struggle, we finally brought a fighting-mad, six-foot sand shark to the side of the boat. I gaffed it and lifted it into the boat with the help of Mr. Thomas, who had given the rod to Mr. Wallace. The fish thrashed around wildly on the deck.

The men jumped up onto the ladder leading to the bridge and moved back into the cabin. Mr. Snipes jumped out of his seat, leaving his rod. I stabbed the shark a few times with the gaff and stepped on the shark's head, try-ing to control it.

"It won't be long now," I said.

Sure enough, after baring its teeth and staring at the men with bone-chilling eyes, the shark stopped moving. I hauled it to the side of the boat, where I tied it securely. We then began to work on pulling the other one in.

During the excitement, I noticed a bank of clouds on the horizon. By the time I was free and could call up to the bridge, the clouds became black and ominous and were moving toward us. I was well aware of how fast storms come up at sea. I'd been out many times when a storm overtook me, transforming a calm, sunny day into a nightmare of fifteen- to twenty-foot waves, blowing rain, and lightning. I was afraid the storm would overtake us. We were about an hour from the mouth of the Cape Fear River.

Victor was worried too. When I joined him on the bridge, he said, "The wind is blowing the storm towards us."

"We'll bring the other shark in and call it a day," I said. "Head up the coast toward the river, and as soon as we get the shark settled down, give it full throttle."

"Look at that one, would you?" I heard Mr. Thomas say below. "It must be eight feet long."

I looked down at the back of the boat and saw Mr. Snipes bringing in a large, gray shark, which thrashed around violently in the water like a bull in a ring.

"Hold on! I'm coming!" I said, climbing down the ladder quickly to the deck below.

Mr. Snipes reeled the shark to the side of the boat, where it slapped the water fiercely with its tail. Mr. Wallace helped Mr. Snipes with the line while I gaffed the fish. Then Mr. Thomas helped me pull it into the boat.

Just as it hit the deck, the boat lurched to one side, pushed by a wave. The shark slid unexpectedly toward me. Before I knew it, the shark had clamped its jaws down on my left leg just below the knee. Blood was everywhere. Mr. Wallace began to scream as the shark slid across the deck toward him, away from me. I doubled over in pain. I could feel the shark's teeth rip through the flesh and grind against the bone in my leg. I knew it was bad.

Victor saw what happened and jumped down from the bridge, leaving the boat without a pilot. The boat washed back and forth by the waves, but Victor and Mr. Thomas managed to gaff the shark and keep it from careening across the deck again. Victor found a fishing knife and stabbed the shark several times as Mr. Thomas held his foot on its head and the gaff in its side. Finally the shark stopped moving, and Victor tied it to the side of the boat. Once they got control of the shark, Mr. Wallace, Mr. Snipes, and Mr. Thomas pulled me into the cabin. Victor followed.

"Victor, take control of the boat! We are going to be swamped if you're not careful," I told him through gritted teeth. I was in extreme pain.

I looked at my leg. The flesh and muscle of the right calf below the knee was in shreds. Victor ripped my pants leg off and told Mr. Thomas to shred the mattress ticking from the V-berth below, so he could make a pressure dressing by tightly wrapping the wound. They wrapped me in blankets. I was beginning to shiver with chills. I was afraid I was going into shock.

"You better get us to Southport quick, Victor," Mr. Thomas said.

Victor took the controls in the cabin and pushed it full throttle. Then he radioed to Southport to make sure they would have an ambulance waiting. When he told the marine operator where we were, they told him a bad storm was headed our way.

"You'd better go up to the bridge where you can see better, son," Mr. Thomas said to Victor. "We'll take care of Todd down here."

I was sweating and fought to stay conscious.

Victor left the cabin and climbed the ladder to the bridge. The storm soon overtook us. The waves got bigger and bigger, and the rain came down in sheets. Normally we would stay put in a storm like this and circle until it passed. But we had to get to port as soon as possible, so Victor pushed on through the storm. The sea changed from a calm, blue, glassy lake into a treacherous series of valleys and peaks. Ten- and fifteen-foot waves, capped with white foam, surged at the boat. Any one of them could capsize us if it hit broadside.

Victor scaled the huge ridges of the violent sea, at forty-five-degree angles. Each wave took great effort and concentration. He gingerly guided the boat up the wildly surging water, then tumbled down the other side with the white caps pushing from behind, threatening to wash into the boat if Victor didn't go fast enough to outrun them. As he conquered one, hundreds more were waiting. I was well aware of how many times I'd faced the same thing.

The mouth of the Cape Fear River, with Bald Head Island on the right, and Oak Island on the left, was the most dangerous part. The inlet was wide and normally little trouble. But since the storm pushed the waves against us broadside as we headed in, they threatened to capsize the boat. Even the wide inlet didn't allow a lot of room to zigzag and avoid the broadsides of the waves. I felt helpless, but I knew we were in good hands with Victor at the helm.

Soon the buoys marking the channel appeared. As the channel narrowed, it became more difficult to avoid the broadsides. Several times it seemed we were going to be swamped as the boat bobbed in the water like a cork, but when he made it past the lighthouse on Oak Island, the water became calmer. We were no longer in open sea. Southport was at the other end of the inlet.

At the marina, the rescue van waited with its red lights flashing. The dock was crowded with people. The wind was still blowing hard, and the rain made it difficult to see, but Victor skillfully made his way to the dock, reversing one engine, then forwarding the other, until he guided the boat to the side of the dock. Then the wind blew us into it with a crash. The men on the dock secured the boat quickly, and two men stepped on board with a stretcher.

I was still conscious as the rescue squad wrapped me in blankets and put me in the back of the van. The pain was so bad that my body acted like it wasn't there. God is good to us when something like that happens. I don't think I really knew what was going on. Hannah was there and knelt beside me, crying. She was so upset she couldn't talk. Victor climbed into the van and put his arm around Hannah.

"You saved my life," I said to Victor. Then I closed my eyes. Everything after that was a blank.

I LOST MY LEFT leg below the knee. My doctor told me I wouldn't be able to skipper a charter boat for some time, until I got used to my artificial leg. I didn't know what I was going to do. My boat was my livelihood. The debts we had were piling up, bills were unpaid, and now hospital bills were pouring in. It was more than I could cope with. I didn't know where to turn. I was sick with worry.

"I want you to come work for me, Todd," Hannah's father said at the house a few weeks after I got out of the hospital.

"I can't do that. I don't know anything about the restaurant business."

"There's nothing to it. I can teach you. Listen, you need to work to keep those grand-babies of mine in diapers. You might even like it."

I DECIDED TO SELL the *Hannah G.* Victor wanted to buy it, but he couldn't afford it. A group of doctors from Greensboro bought it for a tax shelter. They paid Victor to run it for them. They didn't want to make money, they wanted to lose money. Victor didn't mind the paycheck, though. He continued to work for Captain Jackson, too. I used the money from the sale to pay off all my debts except the house mortgage.

I was so busy settling my affairs that I didn't have time to get depressed. I went to physical therapy and learned how to use my artificial leg. I had more time to spend with Hannah and the children than I'd ever had before.

THE FIRST DAY ON the job at the restaurant, Gus, Hannah's brother, walked up to me and handed me a mop.

"Just because you only have one good leg doesn't mean you get charity around here. Garrisons always work for a living. Don't expect to get any special favors from me, Captain. Maybe my dad thinks you're the greatest. I know better. I remember you from your party days."

"Well, those days have been over for a while. And I'm not looking for favors, Gus," I said, taking the mop.

"What are you doing with a mop, Todd?" Jesse Garrison asked, walking up to Gus and me.

"Gus told me I start at the bottom," I said.

"No, no, Todd, you need to learn about management."

"If Gus says I need to start with a mop, then that's where I'll start," I said, staring at Gus. "I don't want any sympathy, and I don't want any special favors. If I am going to work here, I plan to work hard just like everybody else."

TWENTY

I worked at the restaurant for the next year, doing whatever needed to be done. I mopped the floors, bussed the tables, washed the dishes, worked the cash register, put out the salad bar, and waited tables. I even helped the cook a few times, but since I couldn't cook worth a damn, I'm not sure how much help that was. Hannah worked as a waitress. Many days we kept the kids with us at the restaurant.

I knew that my days on the water were over, and this was a great opportunity. So I worked my tail off. After a while even Gus started acting a little nicer to me. Jesse was always good to me. I still went fishing with Captain Jackson a little during the week, when the restaurant was closed, and I took the Boston Whaler out in the marshes to Bald Head with Hannah and the children. But working on the boat was no longer my livelihood. Now the restaurant was. After we paid off our debts, I had enough income so that we weren't always in trouble. Hannah was even able to save a little.

In September 1989, we heard about a terrible storm that had started in the Caribbean—Hurricane Hugo. It did

major damage in the Virgin Islands and Puerto Rico and
was now heading straight for the North and South Carolina coasts. It was one of the biggest storms of the century,
with winds higher than any except for Hurricane Hazel
back in 1954.

We didn't know where it would hit. The six o'clock
news said the eye would pass over Myrtle Beach. That
meant the storm would be strongest between North Myrtle
and Cape Fear, as hurricanes spin counterclockwise and
the worst damage is always to the north of the eye. This
did not sound good for Southport.

I LOADED THE BOSTON WHALER on the trailer and took it inland, leaving it at Victor Slade's house near Shalotte. Then
I boarded up the windows of our house on Brunswick Street
and helped Jesse tape and board the windows at the restaurant. All day the town prepared for the worst. It could
hit anywhere from Charleston to Baldhead, but no one
knew where.

We decided to stay at the restaurant. Our house was
surrounded by big old oaks and was close to the water. The
restaurant was on high ground and built of brick with a
strong reinforced concrete frame. Jesse wanted to stay
there. He was afraid of looters. Gus, Hannah, and I
couldn't talk him into staying further inland at the high
school, where the authorities were evacuating the town to.
So we decided to stay with Jesse. Jesse kept his shotgun
with him.

"I'll be damned if I'm going to spend the night in a
high school gym," Jesse said.

"But that's where we're supposed to go," Hannah said.

"I don't care. I have all the food and drink I need
right here, and a good generator to boot. Somebody's got

to stay here to protect the place," Jesse said as he watched Gus and me finish nailing sheets of plywood over the plate glass windows in front of the restaurant.

"My restaurant is built as well as any damn gym. It's got a reinforced concrete frame, brick walls, and there aren't any trees nearby to blow into it. We'll be just as safe here, if not safer."

After we saw there was no talking him out of it, and knowing that he was probably right about being safe in the restaurant, Gus and I agreed to bring our families to the restaurant. Jesse offered the same to all his employees. Several of them lived in Shalotte and Holden Beach and wanted to stay home. But two of the men who worked in the kitchen, and one of the waitresses took him up on the offer and brought their families to the restaurant.

IT WAS HARD TO SLEEP that night as the winds rose outside. Gus and I peeked outside a few times to see the wind whipping the tops of trees like toys, and the sign in front of the restaurant singing and twisting in the wind and rain. The rain blew almost horizontally, and the traffic lights bobbed and swung out of control on the overhead wires. At about ten o'clock the electricity went out and Jesse went out back to start the generator.

"Daddy, are we going to die?" Warren asked, looking up at me. He was wrapped in a pastel blanket decorated with bears and drums. Warren was three.

"No, son. We're safe in Granddaddy's restaurant."

Warren placed his head in my lap, and I stroked his short, blonde hair.

Hannah held Millie, who was almost two, in her lap. She was already asleep. The wind whistled outside. We could hear the sign in the parking lot creak, groan, and sing with a high-pitched sound. We'd already lost the plastic panels with the name of the restaurant on them.

The cablevision was out, so we pulled up the rabbit ears on the portable television set. We still couldn't find news on the progress of the storm, so we listened to the radio. About nine o'clock the radio said the storm was headed toward Charleston. At midnight, when it should have hit Myrtle Beach, the radio said the eye of the storm was beginning to pass over Charleston. It then quickly made its way across South Carolina, toward Charlotte and the mountains.

WHEN WE GOT UP the next day the electricity was working, and the day was one of the clearest and most beautiful I have ever seen. The sky was cobalt blue and lightly feathered with white clouds very high up. The streets were littered with limbs, a few trees were uprooted, and the plastic was out of the restaurant sign, but other than that, there was little damage.

I jumped in my jeep and drove to our house. A live oak tree had fallen in the side yard, just missing the house. It had crushed the picket fence that ran along the side of the property, but other than a few branches, sticks, and leaves on the roof, there wasn't much damage to the house. We heard the damage to Charleston was terrible. Even Charlotte, as far inland as it was, was without electricity for weeks. But our stretch of the coast had been spared. It was the worst storm in a hundred years. There were a number of deaths in the Caribbean and in the Carolinas, but we were okay.

IN THE SPRING of the next year, Jesse called me into his office.

"Todd, it's been almost two years since you started working at the restaurant. Frankly, I wasn't sure how it would work out when I first hired you, but you've done a great job. You weren't too proud to do the grunt work, and you've worked hard. You earned the respect of Gus and everyone who works here. I think you've learned a hell of a lot about the restaurant business in the process."

"I've enjoyed working for you, Mr. Garrison. I appreciate your taking a chance on me," I said, taking a seat in front of Jesse's desk.

"It has been a pleasure, son." Mr. Garrison reached into the top drawer of his desk and took out a document. "This is an option on a piece of property in Holden Beach that I signed last week. I want to build another restaurant. I've been thinking about this for a long time. Holden Beach is where a lot of tourists go and it's a good market."

"I didn't know you wanted to build another restaurant."

"I hadn't told anyone, not even Gus, until last week. I told him not to say anything to you about it."

"What does he think?"

"He thinks it's a good idea." Jesse paused, then looked at me. "I want you to run it."

"What?" I felt the color go out of my face. I was shocked. "What about Gus?"

"He agreed with me. After it's up and running, I want to give that one to you and Hannah and give this one to Gus."

Tears came to my eyes. "I'm sorry, sir." I was embarrassed. "I just don't know what to say. Thank you. I can't believe it."

"It isn't built yet, and I'll expect you to oversee the project from the ground up."

"Yes, sir. I'll need lots of help from you."

"Todd, you could do it blindfolded. You can do anything you put your mind to with no help from anybody.

But, of course, I'll be there to help you. As far as I'm concerned, the restaurant will belong to you and Hannah as soon as it's built. I'll put that in my will in case anything happens to me and give it to you all as fast as my accountant will let me."

"Does Hannah know?"

"Yes. I told her yesterday. I swore her to secrecy."

WHEN I GOT HOME Hannah had a bouquet of roses and a bottle of champagne on the kitchen table. She hugged me when I opened the screen door to the kitchen.

"You didn't tell me!"

"Daddy said he would kill me if I said anything. He said he wanted to tell you himself."

"You two are something else."

"No, Todd, you are something else. You deserve it. For almost two years you've worked like a slave in that restaurant. I thought my brother was going to kill you the first week you went to work. He was madder than a hornet. But now you all are best friends. He is happy because he gets the old restaurant. We still have our work cut out for us, building from scratch."

"But just the name, Garrison's, will mean so much. Anyone who knows us in Southport will know the new one will be just as good," I said.

"I hope so." She hugged me. "I love you."

"I love you, too." I said, resting my head on her shoulder. "Where are the kids?"

"They're with Gus and Sandra. Gus thought we should have a romantic night together to celebrate."

"Well, isn't that nice of that ole son of a bitch," I said with a wide grin.

After we ate by candlelight, Hannah led me to the bedroom, where we made love until we fell asleep in each other's arms.

The next morning I walked through the living room in my white boxer shorts and looked at the bay window. The windows were open and the breeze caught the white sheer curtains, making them billow out. It was bright and sunny, and the light filled the room. I had never forgotten the dream I had while Mitch and I were drifting on the cork hatch in the Gulf of Mexico. It was the dream of supreme happiness in a room just like this one, filled with light and the curtains billowing out. I realized this was it. This was where the dream had led me.

CAREFULLY, I GUIDED the boat through the winding creek of the marshes behind Baldhead Island. Warren, who was eight, and Millie, who was six, sat in the back wearing big, orange life preservers. Warren's hair was so blonde it was almost white, sticking up short and straight in a crew cut. Millie's hair was dark brown and tied in a ponytail that hung down her back.

I slowed the boat as we approached the sand spit at the end of the creek, leading to the beach. I got out of the boat, pulled it up on the sand, and tied it to a large piece of driftwood. The marshes were public land and anyone could use them. The developed part of the island was filled with high-priced houses and condominiums. There was a restaurant, shops, a club-house, and a marina. Where the children and I walked over the dunes to the beach, it was still as wild and free as when I first saw it. It was protected now.

"Daddy, tell us about Blackbeard and the pirate gold," Warren said, as we walked across the dunes to the beach. Warren carried a fishing rod and a white plastic bucket.

"Yeah, Daddy, tell us about the buried treasure," Millie said, carrying her fishing rod.

I told them about Blackbeard and Stede Bonnet, about when the Spaniards occupied the island and burned Brunswick Town, and about the pirate gold that is supposedly buried on the island.

"Can we dig for gold?" Warren asked. His bathing suit hung loosely around his slender, tanned waist.

"Maybe later. Right now I'm going to teach you all how to catch fish in the surf. Tomorrow we're coming back to drag a net in the creek for shrimp, and maybe gather some oysters and clams. After we go fishing today, if we have time, we'll go crabbing." I was tanned and tried to stay in good shape. My waist was a little thicker, and the lines on my face were deeper, but Hannah told me when I smiled I still looked like an eighteen-year-old.

"Daddy, can you bait my hook?" Millie asked, trying to slide a piece of raw shrimp on her hook after we climbed the dunes out to the beach and stood at the edge of the water. The ocean was calm and the waves rolled in, smooth, and shimmering like glass. The sound of the surf was everywhere, loud but soothing. It was a hot, sunny day in September, but the breeze from the ocean made it cool on the beach.

"Sure, honey," I said, taking the piece of shrimp and slipping it on the hook.

"Me, too," Warren said, holding his fishing rod out to me.

I took the lines and cast them into the waves. Soon Warren had a fish.

"Reel in fast. Don't lose it," I told him.

Warren reeled in haltingly as he struggled with the reel. He had a six-inch spot on the line. Warren's face beamed with pride.

"That's great, son," I said, taking the fish off the line. I started to throw the fish back into the water because of its size.

"Can we keep it?" Warren asked, looking hurt.

I stopped myself, filled the pail with water, and put the fish in it. Warren and Millie watched the fish swim around in the bottom of the pail.

"Can I keep him and put him in my fish tank?" Millie asked.

"He's about the right size for a fish tank," I said with a smile. "Sure we can keep him, as long as he lives. They don't live very long out of the salt water."

I then baited and cast Warren's line back into the waves. I cast Millie's line too.

"You got one," I said, watching Millie's line tighten. I helped Millie reel in the fish. It was another spot, a little larger, but not large enough to keep if we were really fishing. But I took it off the line and put it in the pail.

We caught several more spots and one blowfish. The children enjoyed watching it swell up, bristling its sharp spines. We then walked back over the dunes to the creek. I tied some day-old fried chicken from the restaurant, to strings with lead weights attached, then pitched them into the creek and gave Warren and Millie each a string.

"Be real quiet now," I said, putting my finger over my mouth. "If you talk much you'll scare them away."

"I got one," Warren yelled excitedly as he saw a blue crab sidle toward the chicken under the water, nibbling the loose skin.

"Pull it in real slow," I whispered. "You don't want it to let go. When it gets close enough to the bank, I'll catch it with the net."

Warren was excited but did as I told him, slowly pulling in the line. When it was close enough to the bank, I scooped up the crab and the chicken in the net. I then shook it out into a white pail. I wasn't as nimble as I used to be, but I had gotten used to the artificial leg and could get around now almost as well as I did before the accident.

I crouched down on my good leg and looked out over the marsh, watching the wind lay the saw grass down, making it shimmer with sunlight, then wave in the wind. I heard the birds and insects all around us and smelled the salt air and fishy smell of the marsh. The children crouched down beside me. They asked questions about the island, the birds, and the crabs.

The restaurant in Holden Beach was doing well. I smiled as I thought about the restaurant, Hannah, and the children, and I wondered what I had done to deserve so much.

June bug was engaged to be married. Andrew was going to run for Congress in the new Black congressional district created in eastern North Carolina. If he was elected he would be the first Black congressman from North Carolina in a hundred years. Mama and Sallie were still in Clinton and doing well, as were Captain Jackson and Martha, though she was trying to get him to retire. Mitch had gotten married, then divorced, then spent some time chasing women in Myrtle Beach. Finally, after realizing he still felt guilty about his father's death, he saw a counselor. He got married again just recently, and this time, he seems to be at peace.

God had given me another chance and I wasn't going to waste it. I was determined to break the old patterns set by my daddy and his daddy before him. My family was the most important thing to me now. I would be there for them and protect them when they needed protection. And I'd help them when they needed help, like others had done for me—Jesse Garrison, the Jacksons, Uncle Warren, Mitch's dad. And, yes, I would stand aside when the time came and let them go their own way. But that was in the future. For now I must be there for my children as I was that day with Warren and Millie.

"Daddy, the crab's going to get me," Millie said, dropping her string and running away from the water.

"It's all right Millie, honey. The crab won't hurt you. I'll catch it with the net." I held Millie in my lap as she cried. "Don't be afraid. Daddy's here to protect you. As long as I'm here, I promise I won't ever let anything hurt you. Do you understand?"

"Uh huh," Millie said, nodding her head up and down with tears streaming down her face.

End

©Patricia Rendleman

About the author

Edward P. Norvell is a North Carolina writer whose work
has appeared in numerous magazines and newspapers,
including *The Student, The Mosaic, Bad Apple, The Higginsville
Reader, North Carolina Homes Magazine,* and *the Salisbury Post.*

He received a law degree from Wake Forest School
of Law and served as the Rowan County Clerk of Court.
In addition to to his writing and private law practice, he
teaches business communications at Catawba College.
Southport is his first novel.